"I—well, I found this baby on my back porch."

"What?" Allison jerked to full attention. "Have you contacted the police? If someone abandoned a baby on your porch, the police need to know. The baby must belong to someone."

Jamie paused. "I think—actually, she belongs to me. I mean, if you count backward nine months..." He let out a long breath. "I just...I don't know what I'm supposed to do."

"How old is the baby?"

"I would guess about two weeks."

Sheesh. "Here's what you need to do, Mr. McCoy. Call your health care provider and have the baby examined. Then go to the police and see if they can help you track down the mother. Child abandonment is a crime."

"She didn't abandon the child," he retorted. "She gave the child to me. I just need to know what temperature the formula's supposed to be."

Allison gave him directions. Could this loser last until evening? Could his baby? "I teach a course in child care for new fathers, Mr. McCoy. I call it the Daddy School. Be there tonight."

Dear Reader,

I remember the first time I left my husband alone with our first child. The baby was one week old, and an order I'd placed at the maternity shop had finally arrived. I asked my husband if he could handle our precious newborn by himself during the half hour it would take for me to drive to the store and back. "Of course I can," my husband boasted. "He's my son. I'm his daddy."

So off I went—and came home to quite a scene: my husband and the baby on the dining-room floor, surrounded by diapers, wet-wipes, wadded-up tissues, waterproof pads, cotton balls and a damp undershirt or two. My husband was out of breath and glistening with perspiration, but he'd never looked more proud of himself. Drowsy and content, the baby was nestled in his lap. "I had to change his diaper *five* times while you were gone," my husband told me. "By the third diaper I knew what I was doing. I'm his dad, after all."

My husband has always been my hero, but that afternoon fourteen years ago, when he valiantly changed five diapers in thirty minutes, his hero rating rose about a hundred points. To me, fathers—devoted, loving fathers—are the greatest heroes of all.

Father Found is dedicated to my husband and all the heroic fathers in the world.

Judith Arnold

FATHER FOUND
Judith Arnold

Harlequin Books

TORONTO • NEW YORK • LONDON
AMSTERDAM • PARIS • SYDNEY • HAMBURG
STOCKHOLM • ATHENS • TOKYO • MILAN
MADRID • WARSAW • BUDAPEST • AUCKLAND

ISBN 0-373-70763-0

FATHER FOUND

FATHER FOUND

CHAPTER ONE

GUY STUFF by James McCoy—

Women love to whine about their biological clocks. They think they're the only ones under pressure to do certain things before they lose the chance. Don't they realize that men measure their lives by the biological clock, too? Come on, guys: it's our turn to whine.

Granted, we don't have our alarms set for babies. But we do have to race the clock trying to get certain stuff accomplished before we're no longer able. This, in case you were wondering, is why men are so resistant to the concept of growing up.

Take, for instance, basketball. When men hit the big three-oh, they lose their jump shot. Oh, they might be able to score a layup here and there, just as women in their middle years still manage to get pregnant. But by and large, attempting a jump shot past the age of thirty isn't safe. The percentages aren't with us. That's why you see so many guys in their late twenties elbowing their way toward hoops in gyms, schoolyards and driveways across the land. We've got to get as many jump shots in as we can before the clock strikes thirty.

Or beer. Until a man blows out thirty candles on a cake, he can drink all the beer he wants without having to pay the price. He might find himself emptying his bladder in inappropriate places and saying things he'll regret once he regains full consciousness, but his gut will remain a thing of beauty...until the dreaded biological timepiece declares otherwise. The minute a man crosses the thirty-year mark, abs abruptly turn into flabs, steel into jelly—and the prime culprit is beer. This is why you see so many twenty-something fellows chugging brewskie after brewskie. They know Father Time is gaining on them. Gotta drink now, while "six-pack stomach" still refers to said organ's shape and not its contents.

Women like to whimper about how if they don't get preggers by their thirtieth birthday, a horrific time bomb is going to explode. Their priorities are pretty skewed if you ask me. Sure, I'd like to have a baby someday, maybe, if I ever choose to make an acquaintance with maturity. But right now, folks, I'm recovering from my thirtieth birthday. And I'm in mourning for that beautiful, smooth-as-silk layup I used to have. I guess I'll just drown my sorrows in a glass of mineral water. Beer? Not hardly. *Tick tock, tick tock.*

AS IT WAS, Jamie McCoy was drinking coffee—a double-size mug of java, black and strong. Leaning back in his hinged chair, he skimmed the text on his computer monitor and sighed. He needed four hundred more words for the column, but he wasn't going to come up with even four more until he drugged himself with a bit more caffeine.

It was only 10:00 a.m., a bit early for him to be awake and at his desk. Maybe he was feeling his age, after all. Maybe the fact that he was at work before noon meant that, at long last, he was ready to behave like a responsible adult.

He'd spent the weekend celebrating his thirtieth birthday at his buddy Steve's cabin on Lake Waramaug in the northwest corner of Connecticut. They'd rowed around the lake in Steve's dinghy, pretending to fish but catching nothing and not really caring. They'd dined on charred red meat off the grill, washed down with a bottle of vintage Bordeaux. They'd lounged on the porch into the wee hours, reminiscing about their Dartmouth days and arguing over which one of them had the lower grade-point average, which one of them had the prettier girlfriends and which one scored more goals in lacrosse. In all cases, it was Jamie, but Steve didn't want to admit the truth.

Jamie was admitting the truth now: his glorious male-bonding weekend was over and he was going to have to squeeze out a thousand words for his weekly column if he wanted to continue living in the style to which he'd grown accustomed. He lifted his mug to his lips, realized it was empty, and shoved away from the desk.

His office occupied a wing off the kitchen. Both rooms shared a glorious view of the woods behind his house. He'd planned it that way. On those rare occasions he actually ate at his kitchen table, as opposed to at his desk, or on the screened porch attached to the rear of the house, or in front of the jumbo TV in his den, he liked to gaze out at the untamed forest that extended north of the sprawling ranch house he and an architect had created by tacking rooms and extensions onto the ugly little cottage he'd bought five years ago, before he'd gone into national syndication and gotten rich.

There wasn't much logic to the layout of Jamie's house, but that was fine. There wasn't much logic to the layout of Jamie's life, either. And despite that lack of logic—or maybe because of it—he was having a blast. Things happened to him serendipitously, jumbled, unplanned but usually welcome and always manageable. He rolled with the punches, and so far, the punches had sent him staggering in the right direction.

He pushed himself to his feet, stretched and glanced at the Monday morning *Arlington Gazette,* which lay open on the desk beside his computer. Somewhere within its pages might lie inspiration. Frequently when he was stuck for a column idea, he found fodder in the pages of the local daily newspaper. There were always weird occurrences, silly to-do's, items of greater interest than Jamie's thirtieth birthday.

He'd already read the sports pages, but he would need more coffee in his bloodstream before he tackled the other sections of the paper. He carried his mug down the short hall to the kitchen, moving directly to the coffeemaker, which stood on one of the clean white counters rimming the room. People entering the stainless-steel-and-tile kitchen would probably get the mistaken impression that Jamie was neat and serious about cooking. In truth, he was neither.

His kitchen was always neat because he never cooked.

He filled his mug, inhaled the aromatic steam rising from the hot brew and heard the mew of a kitten. Frowning, he glanced around the room, searching for the source of the sound. He didn't own a kitten. Pets were nice, but they required care. Jamie was still too new at being thirty to want to take on that kind of responsibility. And if he suddenly became softheaded enough to get a pet, he'd get a dog. Cats were so girlish.

He heard the mewing again. Somewhere in the immediate vicinity, a small animal was whimpering. Perhaps the critter had gotten lost in the woods and emerged into his yard. If it belonged to someone, it should be wearing a tag and Jamie would be able to return it.

Tracing the sound to the rear of the house, he surveyed the screened porch through the glass door before opening it. If there happened to be a sickly animal on the porch, he didn't want to let it indoors. It could be a bat or a rabid raccoon. Did bats and raccoons mew?

Other than his deck furniture—cushioned chairs, a glass-topped table and a lounge chair—he saw nothing. Cautiously, he pushed open the door and stepped onto the porch. The screened walls let in the scent of an early summer morning, dewy grass and flowers from the late-blooming rhododendrons bordering the house.

The cries sounded louder, filtering through the screens. He padded barefoot across the porch to the door that opened onto an unscreened deck and the backyard.

An animal was definitely out there—only it wasn't a cat or a bat or a raccoon. He heard a feeble wail, thread-thin yet anguished. His frown deepening, he shoved open the door and stepped outside.

There, on his deck, was a baby.

He stared for a long, stupefied minute. A *baby*. On his deck. Crying.

It was tucked into a boat-shaped plastic seat framed with hefty metal struts and lined with padded plastic cushioning in a pastel yellow pattern. The seat cradled the baby, who was strapped in with a belt and covered with a downy yellow blanket. Without stripping the baby naked, Jamie couldn't say whether it was a girl or boy.

What he could say was that it was tiny. It must be incredibly young. Golden hair lay in gossamer wisps on its head, its nose was a shapeless little button of flesh, its lips were puckered and its skin was ruddy. Its hands, smaller than the top joint of Jamie's thumb, clenched and splayed, clenched and splayed.

"Hey," Jamie murmured, hunkering down next to the baby. Its eyes were so glassy with tears, he couldn't tell what color they were. On the far side of the seat stood a large suitcase and a shopping bag filled with packages of disposable diapers.

As if Jamie McCoy knew how to put a diaper on a baby.

"Who left you here?" he asked, feeling like an idiot. The baby wasn't going to answer his question.

He was afraid to pick up the baby. If he touched it, it might bond with him or something. Or he might leave fingerprints all over it. Or hurt it. He had no idea how to hold an infant.

Scowling, he circled the plastic seat to the suitcase,

hoping to find a luggage tag fastened to the handle. No tag, but he discovered a sealed white envelope taped to the side of the suitcase. Jamie had to resist the urge to tear the envelope apart. It could be evidence. He would have to open it carefully.

He did, peeling the flap back along its edge, managing to avoid ripping it. A folded, lined sheet of stationery fell out. "Dear Jamie," it said, "Remember Eleuthera? Well, guess what. Her name is Samantha and she's yours."

Jamie sank onto the step next to the baby. Eleuthera. He'd gone there for a wild vacation week last September. The Bahamian resort had been hopping with hot-to-trot studs and studettes. One studette, a breathtakingly gorgeous New Yorker named Luanne Hackett, had found her way into Jamie's hotel room. They'd spent nearly the entire week trying out a generous number of *Kama Sutra* positions.

Jamie had liked Luanne. More than lust had been involved, for him at least. He'd asked for Luanne's phone number back in the real world, and she'd given it to him. A few days after he'd returned to Connecticut, he'd dialed the number and wound up having a bizarre conversation with a confused woman with a Spanish accent. She'd told him that he'd dialed correctly but that no one named Luanne Hackett had ever lived there.

Jamie had been ticked off. If Luanne hadn't wanted to hear from him once their vacation had ended, she should have said so. Jamie wouldn't have had anything to do with her in Eleuthera if he hadn't thought she was worth his time back home, too. Much as he loved sex, he didn't make a habit of getting involved with women he didn't like.

But so much for that. She'd been a pleasant memory until he'd found out she'd given him a bogus phone number, whereupon she'd become a somewhat less pleasant memory. And then he'd pretty much forgotten about her.

Until this Monday morning in late June, nine months and two weeks later.

Could this little baby be two weeks old?

Wait a minute! He'd used precautions with Luanne. Even though he'd been a mere child of twenty-nine last September, he had been responsible enough to protect himself and Luanne. If memory served, they'd burned through quite a few boxes of condoms. Condoms were supposed to be, what, ninety-nine percent effective?

Damn. He'd never really thought about that other one percent. Not until now.

He stared at the baby on his porch, fussing and squirming and swatting the air with her miniature hands. "Samantha," he said aloud, and then terror seized him, tightening his throat and making him feel as if he were going to throw up. Fortunately, all he'd consumed so far that morning was coffee—not enough to fuel his brain at maximum function, but at least it didn't make him nauseous.

Samantha did.

No, not Samantha. The situation. The realization that Luanne Hackett, a woman who hadn't even had the courtesy to give him her real phone number, had somehow found Jamie and dumped this baby on him.

Oh, God. Oh-God-oh-God-oh-God. He was in major deep trouble.

"ALLISON? It's for you."

Allison Winslow looked up from the inventory list

she'd entered on her clipboard. As usual, supplies were running low. The reigning bureaucrats of Arlington Memorial believed that new supplies should never be reordered until the shelves were nearly bare. It was a stupid way to run a hospital, but there wasn't much Allison could do about it. She was only a nurse on one of the lowest rungs of the ladder. The higher-ups weren't eager for her opinion regarding supplies.

She didn't care about her place in the hospital's hierarchy, though. She would rather be a nurse than a paper pusher or a number cruncher—and she would rather work in neonatal pediatrics than in any other specialty. Except for her daily battle to get more cotton swabs, more antiseptic soap, more sterile receiving blankets, diapers and ointment into the supply closet—not to mention more money into the department for programs to prepare new parents for the challenges that would face them once they left the maternity floor with their precious babies—she really couldn't complain.

Smiling at Margaret, the senior nurse who'd summoned her to the station, she reached across the counter and lifted the receiver. "Allison Winslow," she identified herself.

"Um...hello?" The voice on the other end of the line belonged to a man. A tense, even panic-stricken man, judging by the way his husky baritone caught in his throat and wavered as it rose in a question.

A rookie father, no doubt. He was probably frantic because he'd just spent a half hour attempting to burp his baby but failed. Or perhaps he was minutes from summoning paramedics to his house because his child had developed a heat rash under its chin. If new mothers were riddled with anxiety, new fathers were a thousand times worse. Anything that didn't go by the book threw them into a tizzy. Being informed that there *was* no book threw them into an even bigger tizzy.

Allison was the hospital's expert on new fathers. She had a genuine talent for untizzying them. "Hi," she said gently. "This is Allison Winslow. What can I do for you?"

"Um..." He sucked in a shaky breath. "I have this baby?" he half asked.

"Yes," she encouraged him, trying not to laugh out loud at his earnest apprehension.

"See, I don't—I don't know any pediatricians. I mean, I haven't got any idea how to find one, and—"

"You have a baby and you haven't got a pediatrician?" She always advised patients to line up a pediatrician before the baby was born. Nowadays, most health-maintenance organizations had a pediatrics staff to choose from. Maybe this man was new in town and needed a recommendation.

"I was hoping you might help me. I called the hospital and they told me you were the lady to talk to."

"Yes." She kept her tone calm and reassuring.

"You see, I— Well, I found the baby on my back porch."

"What?" She jerked to full attention, her amusement dissolving in the blue-white glare of the fluorescent overhead lights. "What do you mean, you *found* a baby?" Hearing her end of the call, Margaret perked up, too, her eyebrows quirking with surprise.

"I was just going to get some coffee, and I heard

this sound, and I thought it was a sick animal. Only it turned out to be a baby.''

"On your back porch?''

"She was just left there in this seat...I don't know, I think maybe it's a car seat. And there was a suitcase full of stuff next to her, packed with little clothes and...cripes, it's the tiniest clothing I've ever seen, all these snaps and stuff.''

Leaning over the counter, Allison groped for a pencil and paper. "Tiny clothes?''

"And bottles and cans of formula. And diapers. Lots of diapers. Hundreds of them.''

"Hundreds of diapers.'' She jotted "one hundred diapers'' on her scrap paper, then wondered why she'd bothered.

"I mean, I don't know what I'm supposed to do.''

"With the diapers?''

"With anything. Like, am I supposed to heat the formula?''

He'd found an abandoned infant on his porch and he was worrying about formula? "Have you contacted the police?'' she inquired. "If someone abandoned a baby on your porch, the police need to know. The baby must belong to someone.''

"I think, actually, she belongs to me.''

Allison took a deep breath and collected her wits. Nothing the man had said made much sense. But she didn't want to scare him away. If she mentioned the police again, he might pack up his baby and his bottles of formula and disappear. And then the baby would have no chance at all.

"What is your name?'' she asked as calmly as possible.

"Jamie McCoy.''

"Mr. McCoy—" she scribbled his name onto the paper "—are you saying an infant was abandoned on your porch and it's yours?"

"Well, I…I mean, sperm-wise…yes. It's mine."

"Where is the mother?" *Ovum-wise,* she added silently.

"Who the hell knows?"

Oh, great. This was one of *those* guys, the kind who spread their seed around so carelessly they lost track of the fertile fields they'd sown. Allison had some teenage fathers in her fathering-skills class for teenagers scheduled at the YMCA that evening. Jamie McCoy would fit right in. He was undoubtedly a swaggering adolescent whose girlfriend had dumped his mistake in his lap and walked away. Allison wasn't sure she blamed the girl.

"*Who* is the mother?" she asked.

"Her name is Luanne Hackett. I think."

"You think?" McCoy dropped another few notches in Allison's esteem.

"The thing is, the woman lied. She told me she was from New York City, but the phone company has no listing for her. She gave me her phone number, but it turned out not to be hers. For all I know, she could have given me a false name."

"But she gave you her baby."

"Hers and mine. I mean, it must be mine. If you count backward nine months…" He let out a long breath, punctuated by a curse.

"All right." Allison cut him off. "Do you have health insurance? Are you included in your parents' policy?"

"My parents?" He snorted. "I've been on my own a long time."

"Medicaid, then," she guessed. If he was on his own, he was probably on some kind of public assistance.

"I'm insured," he said, sounding almost impatient.

"Well, then, why don't you call your health care provider and get a recommendation for a pediatrician."

He cursed again under his breath. "I guess that's what I'll have to do."

"Is it a problem?"

"Look, I just found out I've got this kid. It's not like I want to go fill out a bunch of forms and try to explain this thing to my doctor. I just...I mean..." He sighed once more, then added tentatively, helplessly, "I don't know what to do."

She nibbled her lower lip and gazed at the scrawl of her handwriting across the sheet of paper. "One hundred diapers. Jamie McCoy. Insured. Mother?"

"How old is the baby?"

"I would guess about two weeks old."

Sheesh. Two weeks old, the mother was gone and the father didn't even know how to prepare formula. Allison shuddered to think of the child's prospects. "Here's what you need to do, Mr. McCoy. Call your health care provider and get a pediatrician. Have the baby examined. Then go to the police and see if they can help you track down the mother. Child abandonment is a crime."

"She didn't abandon the child," he retorted. "She gave the child to me."

"She left the child on your back porch. I hardly consider that the proper way to work out custody arrangements."

"Look, the mother isn't the issue, okay? I need to know what temperature the formula is supposed to be."

She cautioned herself not to push too hard. If she did, she might lose him, and if she lost him, she would lose his baby. Tracking down the mother could wait until Allison was certain the baby was safe. "A pediatrician can advise you about formula. For now, you can fill a bottle with it, then set the bottle in a pot of hot tap water. Not boiling, hot. You don't want to burn the baby's mouth."

"Hot, not boiling," he repeated slowly. She imagined that he was writing down her instructions.

"Test a drop on the inside of your wrist. It should be lukewarm. If it feels hot on your wrist, it's too hot for the baby."

"Inside of my wrist. Okay."

"Check her diaper frequently. New babies urinate and move their bowels on no set schedule, and if she wears a soiled diaper for any length of time, she'll develop skin irritations. Wash her bottom carefully with warm water whenever you change her. Wet cotton or a wet washcloth will do it. No alcohol. No powder. Make sure she's completely dry before you put a new diaper on."

"Completely dry," he recited.

"Is there an experienced woman you can call on? Your mother, maybe?"

"I'd just as soon not involve my mother in this right now," he muttered.

"All right, then." Shoving back a stray curl that had unraveled from her barrette, Allison glanced at the wall clock above the nurses' station. Nearly noon. Could this loser last until evening? Could his baby?

"I teach a course in child care skills for new fathers, Mr. McCoy. It's a program I call the Daddy School."

"The what?"

"The Daddy School. I have a class scheduled for tonight at six o'clock at the downtown YMCA. It's an eight-week program. You missed the first class, but if you stay afterward, I can get you up to speed. The other students are fathers-to-be—unless someone's baby has been born in the past week. But the information I teach is useful even if your baby has already been born. I cover all the basics of child care. Like how to change diapers and warm formula."

"Great. That's what I need to know. Meanwhile, I guess I'd better change a diaper and warm some formula." He sighed. "There's got to be an easier way to feed a baby."

"There is. It's called breast-feeding."

"Yeah, well, that's not really an option here."

His words sounded weary yet underlined with laughter. For a frenzied new dad caught in a strange predicament, he hadn't lost his sense of humor. He was definitely different from her other teenage students, who still squirmed and snickered like kindergartners whenever she broached such subjects as women's anatomy.

She wondered what McCoy looked like. She wondered how he'd gotten into such a fix and how he was going to get out of it. She wondered whether he was salvageable as a father.

She wondered what kind of woman he'd hooked up with if that woman could lie about her identity, dump a newborn infant on his porch and vanish.

She wondered why his name had a familiar ring to it.

As a matter of fact, she was just a bit too curious about Jamie McCoy.

"What time did you say this class was?" he asked.

"Six o'clock. Do you know where the YMCA is?"

"Center Street, right?"

"On the corner of Center Street and Dudley Avenue. We meet in one of the community rooms on the first floor."

"I'll find it. What does it cost?"

"There's no charge," she told him. For its first trial run, she'd gotten the hospital to cover the costs. Which was a good thing, since most of her younger students wouldn't have come if they'd had to pay.

"I'll be there." She heard a click, and Jamie McCoy was gone.

"What was that all about?" Margaret asked as Allison hung up the phone.

Another errant lock of hair curled against her cheek. She tucked it behind her ear and frowned. "A guy who just got custody of a baby he didn't even know he'd fathered," she said. "It sounds like a disaster."

"Men," Margaret snorted, then turned back to her work. In her midfifties, Margaret had never married and didn't even seem to like children that much. Allison still hadn't figured out how the woman had risen to the position of head nurse on the maternity floor, where she had to deal with babies and daddies, as well as mommies, every day.

Well, Allison loved babies. She respected and admired mommies, and she believed men could usually be redeemed.

She wasn't so sure about Jamie McCoy, though.

Something didn't seem right about him. He'd started the conversation sounding as frenetic as most unprepared fathers, but by the end of the call she was convinced he wasn't like the rest. He had money, he didn't depend on his parents...and he'd cracked a joke about breast-feeding. Who was he?

A jerk, she reminded herself. Someone alarmingly indifferent about the woman who had given birth to his child, a woman even more unconcerned about the child than McCoy was. Allison was probably going to hate him.

Her personal opinion of him was irrelevant, though. She would teach him what she knew about babies and paternity. Every child born into the world deserved a capable, loving father. And it was Allison's job to make sure babies got what they needed. That was why she'd become a pediatrics nurse and why she'd started the Daddy School.

She picked up her inventory list and headed down the hall to the supply closet. But her mind was no longer on the department's lack of cotton swabs and bed pads. It was on Jamie McCoy—and on his baby.

CHAPTER TWO

SHE WAS the only woman in the room.

It wasn't as if they were all alone, of course. Nine other guys were seated on folding metal chairs in a semicircle. Two of them looked old enough to be fathers. The rest were barely out of puberty. One of them looked years away from sprouting facial hair.

They were a motley group. The young guys were dressed in oversize jeans, T-shirts that could have doubled as highway billboards, advertising all manner of brand-name junk, and expensive, enormous sneakers. One had a silver ring through his nose; another had a tiger tattooed onto his forearm; yet another had a cigarette tucked behind one ear.

The older guys looked like antiques in comparison. One had a bald spot as round as a bagel poking through his hair. The other had a golf look about him; he wore a collared polo shirt the color of fermented raspberries. It hurt Jamie's eyes.

He was the only one in the room with an actual baby. He'd brought Samantha with him because the prospect of hiring a qualified baby-sitter boggled his mind.

Samantha was quiet at the moment, but he wasn't sure how long that would last. He'd learned, after a long and generally abysmal day, that at regular intervals she liked to do an uncanny impersonation of an air-raid siren. At least she was dry—although he wasn't sure how long that would last, either. He had exhausted more than a dozen diapers on her, as well as a large percentage of the itty-bitty clothing in the suitcase. When she wasn't leaking from one end, she was leaking from the other, spewing white fluids from her mouth whenever she belched, as if she were auditioning for a remake of *The Exorcist.* The receptionist who'd made an appointment for him at his HMO's pediatrics office for tomorrow had assured him that it was perfectly normal for babies to spit up half of everything they ate.

Normal, perhaps, but disgusting. He'd thought diapers were bad. The barfing was arguably worse. Maybe it was an early warning sign of alcoholism: Samantha would chugalug an entire bottle at one sitting, and then she'd hurl and pass out.

He'd tried to catch a few winks while she was sleeping off her formula jags on the makeshift bed he'd prepared for her—a mat of folded sheets spread across the thick carpet in his bedroom. But he'd been too worried to rest. What if she rolled over and banged herself on the dresser? What if she choked? What if she started howling again, or mewling? What if, what if, what if.

How did people survive parenthood, anyway?

More than once during the day, he'd considered telephoning his mother down at her no-kids-allowed retirement community in Arizona. She'd survived the great challenge of parenting him, so she must know the secret. Yet how could he phone her and his father, two nice, decent, middle-class retirees, and say, "Hi, folks—guess what? You're grandparents! I don't know where the mother is—I'm not even sure *who* the mother is—but this baby showed up on my back porch, and by the way, can two-week-old infants roll over yet?''

If he called them with that sort of news, they'd probably have heart attacks on the spot. Bad enough he had an out-of-wedlock baby on his conscience. He didn't want to have the deaths of his parents on his conscience, too.

Before he resorted to shocking his parents into coronary crisis, he decided to give the Daddy School a try. The nurse he'd spoken to at Arlington Memorial, Allison Winslow, had to know what she was doing. Maybe she could give him some pointers on how to stop Samantha's heaving fits. If not, maybe Nurse Winslow could offer some laundry tips.

He arrived at the class ten minutes late. It had taken him that long just to figure out how to strap the baby seat into the passenger side of his sporty Miata coupe. He'd had to park in the far corner of the lot behind the YMCA building; the only empty spaces near the door had been marked Handicapped Only. As he lugged the squirming baby in her car seat and a backpack stuffed with several tons of infant paraphernalia across the lot and into the building, it occurred to him that having a newborn ought to qualify a person as handicapped.

He found the room easily enough, swung in through the open doorway to find seven tattooed and body-pierced adolescents laughing about something and two genuine adult males who looked serious enough to be *his* father. Then he noticed the woman at the far end of the room, standing beside a blackboard. When her gaze met his, he nearly dropped the baby.

Allison Winslow was gorgeous.

Well, technically, she wasn't. She was a bit too tall, a touch too thin and way too pale. Her hair was a tumble of auburn curls that she'd attempted to tame with a barrette, but rippling tendrils had escaped from the clasp to frame her cheeks and drizzle down her back. She wore a pair of pleated white slacks, a white pocket T-shirt and clean white sneakers.

Nurse's clothes, he reminded himself, although all that white made him think of angels. Allison Winslow could pass as an underweight Botticelli angel with that absurdly lush copper-tinged hair and her wide, round green eyes and her pursed cherry red lips.

Her expression was quizzical as she looked him up and down, her brows arched and her chin raised. Without speaking a word, she was issuing a demand.

"Is this the class for new fathers?" he asked.

Before she could answer, one of the youths hollered, "Dude, looks like you got here a little too late."

"It's only ten past six," he said.

"I think he means," the woman explained, "that you already have your baby. These fellows haven't become fathers yet." She no longer seemed to be questioning him with her gaze, but she still looked bemused. "You must be Mr. McCoy."

"Yes."

"Come in. You've found the right place." She gestured toward an empty seat in the semicircle of folding metal chairs at the center of the room.

Jamie lugged the car seat over, set it carefully on the floor and then lowered himself into the chair. Not surprisingly, the baby began to whimper. He'd learned from painful experience that it didn't take much to get her going. Merely putting down her seat was enough.

"That baby is *small,*" observed the bald guy, who sat to the right of Jamie.

He nodded, thinking, "Small but lethal." His gaze arced across the room to the nurse. She was staring at him, making him feel as if he'd done something wrong. He supposed he had, misusing a condom and accidentally fathering a child. He supposed he was the world's worst screwup—except that at least some of the tattooed kids in the room had to be screwups, too. Why didn't the pretty nurse stare at them, instead?

"I'm Allison Winslow," she informed him. "We've been discussing some of the changes a baby causes in both fathers' and mothers' lives. Some of this may not be pertinent to you, but you may as well listen."

"Man, that thing is *tiny,*" said the kid seated on Jamie's left. "How old is it, anyway?"

"It's not an it," Jamie snapped. The kid had a silver skull-and-crossbones dangling from his ear-lobe. "It's a girl, and she's two weeks old."

"That's a girl?" a boy across the room asked, rising from his chair and peering into the car seat. "How can you tell?"

"The usual way, stupid," one of the other boys teased him.

"What, she's got PMS?"

"Sure sounds like it, the way she's whining."

"Guys, settle down," Allison said firmly. She ruminated for a minute, then shrugged and tossed the stick of chalk she'd been holding onto the tray under the blackboard. "You know, it's very special having a newborn in class with us. Maybe Mr. McCoy could show us how to hold her."

"Hold her?" Jamie shot Allison a frantic glance. Whenever he picked Samantha up, he was afraid of dropping her or hurting her. She *was* tiny, and his hands were big, and he was positive that if he held her the wrong way, he would break all her bones without even realizing it.

"Sure. Babies love to be held." Allison strode across the room to the car seat, gesturing for the others to gather around. "I can't emphasize how important it is for you to hold your babies. There's a condition called 'failure to thrive...'" She deftly worked the straps holding Samantha in the seat, straps that had stymied Jamie for longer than he'd like to admit. The buckle popped open and the baby began to fidget. Allison slid one arm under Samantha, cupped her hand around the baby's head and lifted her up, easily wrapping the blanket around her as she did.

The baby made a soft sound, half a sigh and half a gurgle, as Allison straightened up and tucked her into the curve of her arm. "Hello, there," she murmured, gazing directly into the baby's face, sliding her index finger against Samantha's palm and smiling as Samantha's hand curled into a fist. "Hello, sweetie. What's your name?"

"She ain't gonna answer you," one of the boys volunteered.

Ignoring him, Jamie said, "Samantha. Her name is Samantha."

"What a lovely name! Hi, Samantha," Allison

cooed. "You're a sweetheart, yes, you are. What a wonderful little girl you are!"

Jamie's vision seemed to blur as he watched Allison cradling the baby in her arms. He wasn't thinking about angels anymore. Madonnas, maybe. He sensed a connection between Allison and Samantha, something so pure and intimate it went beyond arousing him. Allison looked as if her arms hadn't been complete until the moment they'd shaped themselves around Samantha. She looked as if the baby were a part of her, fulfilling her.

Why didn't he feel fulfilled when he held his daughter? For one thing, the whole idea that he *had* a daughter still freaked him out. She was a person, a real, live human being, and she owed half her genes to him. He, Jamie McCoy, had a *daughter*.

It was just too weird.

But if Samantha was a stranger to him, she was even more a stranger to the nurse holding her. So why did Allison look as if she'd been designed for no other purpose than to hold Jamie's baby? Was it something they taught in nursing school or did she possess some deep well of maternalism that men could never begin to understand?

Allison lifted her face and studied the males surrounding her. Jamie had expected to see rapture that matched what he was feeling when he watched her. But she was clear-eyed and poised. "See how I'm talking to her?" she lectured the class. "You should always talk to your babies—and use a soft, gentle voice so you don't frighten them. Let your baby become familiar with your voice. Let the baby hear words. This is the baby's introduction to language—listening to its parents."

She moved to the center of the semicircle so they could all see her. "Always hold the baby's head when you carry it. Babies' necks aren't strong enough to support their heads, so you have to support the head with your hand or your arm. By talking to a baby and cuddling it, you actually help it to thrive. 'Failure to thrive' is a syndrome in which babies stop eating, stop responding to their environment, stop growing. And one thing that contributes to this problem is if you don't talk to your baby and hold it and make it feel secure and loved." She met Jamie's gaze and smiled. "Show us how you cuddle your baby."

He swallowed, conscious of the class's attention on him—and more important, Nurse Winslow's attention. Picking up his daughter in front of witnesses, one of whom was a slender, statuesque woman with eyes the color of birch leaves in the spring, made his palms go slick with perspiration. If he blew this, if he failed to support Samantha's head adequately or dropped the blanket or any of a number of mistakes... It was a test, and his chances of passing weren't good.

He stood as Allison carried Samantha to him, and positioned his arms in front of his chest. Allison arranged the baby in his embrace, smoothing the blanket around her and nudging her head into the crook of his elbow. "There you go. That's one way to hold a baby. You can also hold a baby on your shoulder, but you can't make eye contact if you do that. This way, you can look right into her face and let her get to know you."

Jamie wanted to look into Allison's face, but he didn't dare. If he let his concentration drift the slightest bit from Samantha, something ghastly would happen. He kept his gaze fixed on her pink, round visage, on that wispy pale hair, on her thin purple eyelids, the hints of two arched shadows where her eyebrows were supposed to be, the delicate notch in her upper lip.

"Talk to her," Allison reminded him.

Talk to her? What was he supposed to say? "Hi," he began, feeling like a first-class idiot.

Samantha clearly had no intention of holding up her end of the conversation. Instead, she moved her hands around, poking at her chin and groping upward until she managed to get a few fingers into her mouth.

"So, Sam, how about those Red Sox, huh?" If she wasn't going to indicate what subjects interested her, she could darned well listen to *his* subjects. "Think they've got a prayer of winning the pennant this year? You're right. They don't. It's the curse of the Bambino."

"Hey, they got a chance," the kid with the nose ring interjected. "You see the way they're batting?"

"Forget it," the guy in the golf shirt retorted. "Yankees all the way."

"Okay, fellows, we're not going to turn this into a baseball argument. We're going to discuss the demands having a baby makes on both you and your baby's mother. Perhaps Mr. McCoy can start things off by telling us some of the changes he's experienced since Samantha entered his life." Her smile as she turned to Jamie was cool and expectant—but her eyes sparkled with laughter, as if she enjoyed putting him on the spot.

He was not amused. The biggest change he'd experienced since Samantha arrived was to learn in the most abrupt way possible that he was a father—but he wasn't going to admit to his classmates that someone had left his daughter on his porch with a note and a bag of diapers.

Allison Winslow was waiting for him to speak. So was everyone else, he realized as he scanned the room. He cleared his throat, discreetly flexed his fingers so his hand wouldn't go numb under Samantha's head and said, "One thing that's changed is, I'm tired. She keeps me hopping constantly. Every time I put her down, she wails."

Allison nodded and wrote *fatigue* on the blackboard. Evidently, this was a good answer. He might just graduate from Daddy School, after all.

She turned back to her students. "You will discover that spending time with an infant is very tiring. Jamie is right—may I call you Jamie?"

"Sure."

She resumed talking. "Not only will you be tired, but the baby's mother will be even more tired. Even if she has a normal delivery, giving birth to a baby is a physically exhausting thing to go through. If she has to undergo a C-section—remember, we discussed C-sections last week?"

The students nodded.

"If she has one of those, it's major surgery. It will take her *weeks* to get her strength back. And it's up to you as the father to help her out. You're going to be tired, too. Even if the mother is breast-feeding so you don't have to do the night feedings, the baby will wake you up at night. During the day, you have to feed the baby, carry the baby with you, clean up after the baby, change the baby's diapers—"

"I ain't doin' that!" one of the boys shouted out.

"You certainly are," Allison declared with finality. "And it's going to tire both you and the mother. And what happens when everyone is tired?"

"You go to sleep," one joker muttered.

"You get into bad moods," Allison said. "You argue. You bicker over trivia. You yell at each other." She wrote *bad mood* on the blackboard. "The mother is likely to be even more tired and moody than you. She might have sudden bouts of crying. This is called postpartum depression." She added that term to the blackboard list.

One of the boys groaned. "Great, man. She's on the rag, she's depressed. She gets pregnant, she's no longer on the rag—and she's depressed. She has a baby and she's depressed. *I'm* getting depressed just thinking about it."

"That's not surprising," Allison said smoothly. "It can be depressing to realize you can't just hang out with your friends at night. You can't go to a movie on a whim, or go to a club. You have responsibilities now. You've got to spend time with your baby. How do we deal with this depression?"

"Drugs!" someone hollered.

Allison smiled indulgently. "You find the joy of having a baby," she suggested. "You look at the world through your baby's eyes, and you see what a wondrous place it is. You realize that you're one of the two most important people in that child's life, and you make the most of it. You do *not* ignore the baby or run out on your responsibilities or dump all your anger and frustration on your wife or girlfriend. Instead, you revel in what's good about being a dad. You've created a new life, and that baby loves you and depends on you more than on anyone else. That's a very exciting, powerful position to be in.''

Jamie glanced down at Samantha. She had practically stuffed her entire hand into her mouth. Her eyes were closed, and she made muted snuffling noises, like a wild boar rooting around for truffles. He contemplated the position he was in—his arms growing numb, less from her weight than from his anxiety about dropping her—and decided that, while it was powerful in a way, it really wasn't all that exciting.

"Why don't we go around the room, now, and talk about some of your fears?"

"I thought we were going to learn how to give bottles," the bald one said.

"We'll discuss basic child care in our next class. Tonight we're talking about emotions. I'm sure some of you are a little worried about what life is going to be like once you have a baby. Jamie, do you want to get us started?"

"No," he said quickly. He had so many fears, he couldn't begin to name them. Every time he contemplated the word *daughter* his blood pressure soared and his throat closed up. Jamie McCoy, Mr. Nonchalant himself, wasn't used to feeling so inadequate, so overwhelmed. He certainly wasn't going to reveal his soul-deep dread to a roomful of men.

She held his gaze for a prolonged second, then looked at her next victim. "All right, Ray, why don't we start with you? Are you worried about how you're going to feed your baby? I don't mean just fixing bottles. I mean being able to pay for food."

The younger guys scuffed their toes against the linoleum floor, stared at the pale green walls, nudged each other in the ribs and smirked. The older men became obsessively fascinated with their cuticles. But slowly, carefully, Allison Winslow extracted their fears from them. The kids were afraid of being chronically broke and having to spend what little money they had on their babies instead of on themselves. A couple of them were worried about finishing school. The bald guy was worried about getting ridiculed because he and his wife had decided that he would take a paternity leave while she returned to work. The golf shirt was worried about whether he and his wife were going to be able to sail to Bermuda with their baby in August. All of them were worried about getting sex on a regular basis.

Jamie relaxed in his chair, letting Samantha rest in his lap, although his arms remained snugly around her. His problems were nothing like those of his classmates. He didn't have to worry about money. His weekly column earned him a tidy sum. The only school he had to worry about for the time being was the Daddy School—although heaven knew what college was going to cost by the time Samantha was eighteen. Sailing to Bermuda wasn't high on his list of things to do. As far as getting sex on a regular basis...

His gaze swung back to Allison.

For God's sake, he shouldn't be thinking of her in that context. She was a nurse, a teacher, a lady dressed in white wearing disturbingly clean sneakers. She was a woman who worked in a hospital during the day and taught classes at night and who made him feel like a fool because she'd had to teach him how to hold his own child. She was a tall woman with hair so thick and curly a person could lose small objects within the waves. She was a slender woman with a few golden freckles dancing across the bridge of her nose, with small, high breasts and a waist so narrow he couldn't imagine her ever becoming pregnant.

He wondered if she was married or involved with someone. He wondered if she ever dated her students. He wondered why on earth he was thinking about her when he had an innocent little baby in his lap, blinking her big dark eyes and sucking on her knuckles and reminding him with her mere presence that he wasn't going to be able to go on a date until he figured out how to hire a baby-sitter.

"Okay, class. That's it for tonight," Allison announced, compelling him to tear his gaze from the baby on his knees. "Next week I'm going to bring some life-size dolls with me, and we're going to do some hands-on practice with diapers and bottles. If you have any questions during the week, or anything you want to talk about privately, you all have my phone number at the hospital."

The students stood slowly, stretching their limbs, a few of the teenagers punching each other in a typical male tribal custom. One of them hovered over Jamie and peered down at the baby. "Sixteen years from now," he warned with an enigmatic smile, "you better make sure you keep her away from guys like me."

Jamie cursed under his breath. He could scarcely contemplate surviving the next twenty-four hours as a father. How in God's name was he going to survive Samantha's adolescence? Was it too soon to have her fitted with a chastity belt? Or would it be easier to castrate any male who came within ten feet of her?

He felt overwhelmed by the enormity of his responsibility. He simply couldn't deal with it. Yet who was going to defend his daughter's honor if not his daughter's father? His daughter's mother? A woman who had abandoned her own child on a porch and fled, not even bothering to make sure someone was home?

Still pondering such weighty questions, he wasn't aware of the departure of his classmates until the room's silence distracted him. Looking up from his dozing daughter, he realized he and Samantha were alone in the room—except for Allison Winslow.

She leaned her hip against the desk at the front of the room, her legs crossed at the ankle and her arms folded across her chest. "You're older than I expected," she said.

"I think I've aged ten years since this morning."

She laughed. Her laughter sounded like well-tuned wind chimes, light and lilting.

"You'll get the hang of fatherhood," she assured him. "Very few people are born knowing how to be a parent. They learn, either from their own parents or from a class like this or from hands-on experience. Sooner or later, you'll be a whiz at it."

"I can't imagine I'll ever be a whiz at fatherhood," Jamie predicted glumly. "In fact, I can't imagine putting the baby back in her seat without making her cry."

Allison laughed again, pushed away from the desk and ambled over to his chair. He allowed himself a glimmer of hope that she would take the baby from him, but she dashed that hope by lifting the car seat instead. "Just put her in," she ordered him. "Gently."

"I'm telling you, she's going to cry."

"So she'll cry. And then she'll stop crying. Babies don't have many ways to express themselves. They cry because they don't know how to say, 'Stop it!' or 'I want it!' or 'That seat isn't as comfortable as your arms.'"

"Thanks," he grumbled. He didn't believe his arms were that comfortable, at least not for a baby. But the instant he released Samantha in the seat, she burst into tears.

"You ought to get a stroller," Allison suggested. "It's a lot more convenient than hauling the car seat around. They make strollers that can fold flat and fit in a trunk. The back can be positioned so the baby can lie down and sleep or sit up and view the world."

"Stroller," he repeated, committing the word to memory. "I have a feeling I've got to get lots of stuff. I just don't know what. I was hoping I'd learn in this class."

"We'll be covering the subject of baby gear," Allison confirmed, "but probably not until the fourth or fifth class. You're a bit ahead of the rest of the students."

"Isn't that just like me? Way ahead of the class. Maybe you could send me to the library while the rest of them finish the math work sheet."

She laughed again. "No extra credit for you, Mr. McCoy. You may be ahead of the class, but I have yet to see any A-plus work."

"Okay. I'll buy an A-plus stroller. And all the other stuff I need, if only I knew what stuff to get. Maybe we could brainstorm a shopping list for me," he suggested, smiling. "Have you got a minute?"

She glanced at her watch. "Sure."

"How about let's go get some coffee?" Asking
Allison to have a cup of coffee with him wasn't a
date. It was the act of a desperate man. He knew he
was going to have to put some heavy-duty mileage
on his credit card for Samantha, but he didn't know
where or how to begin. Crib or cradle? Playpen or
cage? Hundreds of disposable diapers or thousands?

Allison scrutinized him as if she, too, wanted to
ascertain that this wasn't a date. She must have read
the near hysteria in his expression, because she relaxed and nodded. "There's a place across the
street," she told him. "I'd kill for a cup of coffee."

"They'll probably give us coffee if we give them
money. No bloodshed necessary," he said, flashing
her a quick, nervous grin. She responded with a cool
smile that informed him she didn't think much of
him.

Ordinarily he didn't worry about how a woman
viewed him. Most women thought he was a cute
scamp or a sexy devil or fun to be with, or at the
very least wealthy enough to be worthy of their interest. If the chemistry fizzled, he shrugged it off—
but frequently things went well. He'd had his share
of romantic disappointments, but he'd had more than
his share of triumphs.

Allison was seeing an entirely new side of
him, however. She was seeing the inept side,
the out-of-his-depth side, the slept-with-a-woman-he-
shouldn't-have side. The father side.

Whatever kind of impression he was making on
her, it wasn't stellar. If luck was with him, he would
emerge from their time together with a not-too-

tattered ego and a comprehensive shopping list of items for Samantha. Hoping for anything more would be a waste of time.

CHAPTER THREE

THE ARLINGTON YM-YWCA was located in the heart of the city's old downtown district. A great deal of the commercial traffic had detoured to strip malls on the outskirts of town, but Arlington's downtown hadn't quite died yet. Across the street from the YM-YWCA stood the editorial offices of the *Arlington Gazette.* Down the block to the east, the Connecticut Bank and Trust Company occupied a six-story office building—a veritable skyscraper by Arlington standards—and down the block to the west reigned the city library, a grand domed building with a remarkably ugly modern wing tacked on.

Nestled into the northwest corner of Connecticut, Arlington was close enough to New York City to attract weekend yuppies with money to spend on vacation homes. It also boasted a sizable native population, a mishmash of rich and poor and in-between. Allison had lived her entire life in Arlington, and she loved the city the way a mother loved a child, in spite of its flaws. She'd visited bigger cities, newer cities, cleaner, hipper cities, but none of them had ever made her long to pull up her roots and settle elsewhere.

She wasn't sure which whether Jamie McCoy was rich or working class, whether he was a local or a yuppie invader. She wasn't sure why his name sounded vaguely familiar. It had nagged at her ever since she'd gotten his call at the hospital that morning. Was there a not-so-famous actor named Jamie McCoy? Someone from a now defunct TV show, perhaps?

When the streetlight turned green, she crossed the road, Jamie dragging behind her with that unwieldy car seat and his backpack. She'd offered to take the pack for him, or even the baby, but he'd insisted he could manage. He would have managed much better if he'd left the car seat in his car and carried Samantha in his arms. But like so many men, he seemed skittish about holding his baby.

The coffee shop she entered was, like the neighborhood surrounding it, a bit shabby but hanging on. Allison frequently dropped in for a snack after swimming laps at the Y, and she knew the place stayed open late into the evening to accommodate the night staff at the newspaper. At seven-thirty, she and Jamie had their choice of booths. The dining room was nearly empty.

Allison tossed her canvas tote onto one of the empty seats, then slid in after it. She tried not to laugh as Jamie wrestled with his assorted gear, wedging the bulky car seat onto the narrow banquette, shrugging out of his backpack, searching for a place to stash it and finally shoving it under the table. He sat, then eyed the baby apprehensively, as if certain she would awaken at any moment.

If she did, Allison wouldn't be surprised. Babies had an instinct for sensing the most inconvenient times to fuss.

A waitress dropped two laminated menus onto the

table and eyed the baby. "Wow, that's a young one," she said in a loud, nasal voice.

Jamie cringed and shot the baby another anxious look. She continued to sleep, her face angelic, her lips puckering as if she were dreaming of food.

The waitress eyed Allison, sighed and shook her head. "Jeez. Took me a year to lose all the weight, and look at you. Less than a month and you've got the figure of a teenager. Some gals have all the luck. We've got some specials tonight—a roast half chicken with bread pudding, linguine with clam sauce, and moussaka."

"Thanks." Allison smiled at the garrulous waitress, not bothering to correct her about Samantha's parentage. "Could you bring us some coffee while we look at the menu?" She realized she was starving, not having eaten anything since a salad and a granola bar at noon. She doubted Jamie would mind if she ordered a sandwich, too. If he didn't want to keep her company while she ate, he could leave.

She hoped he wouldn't want to, though. She assured herself she wanted him to stay only because she was curious about him. Her curiosity had nothing to do with his incredible eyes, gray and blue and green and amber all mixed up together, his strong, hard chin and his athletic build, tall and solid without an ounce of excess bulk. He had the sort of body that filled clothes well, and he held himself proudly, almost defiantly, shoulders squared and jaw angled. He struck her as the sort of man who was comfortable inside his skin.

But it wasn't his physique or his glittering eyes or his quirky smile that intrigued her. It was the combination of him and his baby. He wasn't like the other Daddy School students. She'd been completely wrong to assume, when he'd telephoned her at the hospital that morning, that he was an irresponsible kid.

He was an irresponsible adult, a man who shouldn't be in the predicament he was in. He was old enough to know better. Allison would be wise to remind herself of that whenever she found herself becoming enchanted by his beautiful eyes. She didn't need a man in her life—and she definitely didn't need an unwed father with a confoundedly familiar name.

"I'm going to order a hamburger," she told him. "I hope you don't mind, but I'm hungry."

"So am I," he said, skimming the menu. "Are the hamburgers good here?"

"They're hot and greasy and way too big."

He lowered the menu and grinned. "That's the way I like them." When the waitress returned with two cups of coffee and a pitcher of cream, he ordered hamburger platters for both of them.

Allison studied him warily. She wondered if his ordering for her meant he intended to pay. She supposed that if he did, it was only his way of thanking her for her time. Given what she was paid to impart knowledge on child raising to her students in the Daddy School, she wasn't averse to being treated to a hamburger.

She felt his gaze on her as she added some cream to her coffee and stirred. He'd better not give her a lecture on cholesterol consumption. She got enough ragging at the hospital when she chose cream over skim milk in her coffee or ordered a burger instead of a cup of nonfat yogurt. She knew everything there was to know about proper nutrition, but sometimes a person simply needed to add a dose of fat to her diet.

He said nothing, only watched her stir in the cream and take a sip. When she lowered the mug, he was smiling enigmatically. His eyes dazzled her with their multitude of colors.

His constant gaze made her...well, not quite uncomfortable, but a little uneasy. Just because he was her own age, give or take a couple of years, shouldn't shift the balance of power so much. She was the teacher, after all, the wise woman, the guru. He was the ignorant turkey with the unplanned baby. She shouldn't be daunted by his sex appeal.

She shouldn't even consider him in the context of sex appeal.

She decided to invent a new context, pronto. "All right, I give up," she said. "Who are you?"

His smile deepened as he perused her across the table. "Who am I? Jamie McCoy."

"I know I've heard your name before, but I can't recall where. It's been driving me crazy all day."

"James McCoy," he told her.

"James McCoy?" She blinked in shock. "The guy who writes that hilarious column in the newspaper about why men are so goofy?"

"That's me."

"You're kidding! No way!"

Laughing, he held up his hands in mock surrender. "You're too clever. I can't fool you. I'm actually the reincarnation of Napoleon."

"You can't be," she said, playing along. "You're much too tall."

"I took growth hormones between incarnations."

She chuckled and took another sip of coffee. "You're really James McCoy?"

"I really am."

"I read your column every Sunday in the *Gazette*. I've learned more about men from you than from anyone else."

"Is that so?" When he smiled, little creases fanned out from the corners of his eyes. "What have you learned?"

"That men are idiots."

He joined her laughter. "Ah, the power of the pen. I'm obviously getting my message across." He cocked his head slightly, the hint of a challenge coloring his smile. "I take it you haven't learned this great truth from experience?"

"My experience with men, you mean?" she asked, then shut her mouth and fought against a blush. Her words had come out all wrong. She wasn't going to discuss her experience with the opposite sex, either generally or specifically.

If Jamie was fishing for information about her personal life, she supposed she ought to be flattered. It happened that she had no time for a social life these days, particularly given that when a woman reached her late twenties, establishing connections with eligible men tended to get more complicated. Sometimes she and her best friend, Molly, would read the personals out loud for a laugh. Just last week, they'd found the perfect man in the back pages of the *Gazette:* "DWM, bald, paunchy, late forties, looking for kinky sex, no commitment." Apparently there was, indeed, an honest man on the planet.

Allison would like to find a man that honest for herself, one willing to give as much to the relationship as he took from it. But while the man seated across the Formica-topped table was obviously neither bald nor paunchy, the last thing she wanted was to encourage the interest of the father of a newborn conceived with a woman whose identity he wasn't even sure of. Just because Jamie McCoy was the author of a series of brilliantly funny newspaper essays about men and their foibles didn't mean she approved of him.

He was clearly awaiting a response from her. Once she'd felt her cheeks cool off, she said, "My experience with men has taught me how to be tolerant."

Her answer seemed to please him. "Thank God for that. If women weren't tolerant of men, the human race would become extinct." His smile faded as he glimpsed the next generation, slumbering in her car seat next to him. Whoever the baby's mother was, she must have tolerated Jamie at least once, nine months ago. When he lifted his gaze to Allison, his smile was gone.

She tried to convince herself that was good. He had a delicious smile, a naughty, subtly erotic smile. When he wasn't smiling, she could remind herself of what a goof this chronicler of goofy men really was.

He drank some coffee, his eyes never leaving her. "The class was interesting tonight," he said, and once more she reminded herself not to be flattered. "I was expecting you to teach things like how to heat formula."

"I taught you how to heat formula this morning on the phone."

"You know what I mean. Practical stuff. Nuts and bolts. I didn't know we were going to be talking about our fears."

"That's at least as important as the nuts and bolts. Men don't like to admit they can't handle anything. They refuse to ask for directions when they're driving, and they're just as afraid to ask for directions when it comes to child care. They see it as losing face if they have to admit they don't know everything about everything."

"Gee, maybe I should be taking notes," he muttered, his grin returning. "It sounds like a good idea for my next column. 'News Flash: Men Don't Know Everything About Everything!'"

She smiled. "I like to get expectant fathers to address their fears early on. Once they can admit they're scared, they won't worry about asking any question they want. The nuts and bolts are easy once all the defensiveness gets cleared away."

"Well, then, I'll try not to be too defensive." He drank some more coffee. "So, what do you think, Teach? Am I going to flunk the course?"

"No." She glanced at his tranquil baby, then back at him. "Have you made an appointment with a pediatrician?"

He nodded. "Tomorrow at nine-thirty."

"How about the police?"

He lowered his gaze to the steam rising from his mug. Her comments about male defensiveness, idiocy and tolerance hadn't ruffled him, but this question obviously did. A muscle ticked in his jaw; he stilled it by taking a long drink of coffee. "No," he finally said. "I haven't called the police."

"Why not?"

"They're going to ask a lot of questions I don't feel like answering. Some things are none of their business, you know?"

She searched his face, wondering how best to open his mind to all the options, all the odds...all the legalities. "I think it *is* their business when a baby is abandoned," she argued delicately.

"Samantha wasn't abandoned. She was left in the custody of her father—which happens to be me."

"She was left on a porch. What if you'd been out of town for a week? What if you'd moved and some other family was living in your house? What Samantha's mother did was a criminal act."

"All right, well, whatever. I *do* live there, and I *was* home and Samantha is fine."

"But the mother shouldn't have done what she did."

"Who am I to cast stones? Maybe I shouldn't have done what I did nine months ago. It's too late to worry about that now. It doesn't matter anymore."

"It could," she said, observing him closely, prepared to measure the impact of what she was about to suggest. Already he didn't look terribly happy. Shadows were gathering in his eyes, dulling their natural sparkle, and the muscle in his jaw started ticking again. But Allison was never one to shy from the truth. "Are you sure Samantha is yours?" she asked, softening the question with a sympathetic smile.

His reaction proved that he'd never considered any other possibility. His eyes opened wider and he fell back in his seat. He raked a hand impatiently through his hair. She could see the tension in his fingers, the harsh angles of his knuckles as he shoved back the thick waves. "Of course Samantha's mine," he declared uncertainly.

"How can you be sure?"

He opened his mouth and then shut it. His eyes narrowed. He glanced at Samantha, then shook his head and pressed his lips into a grim line. "I don't have to be sure. I mean, why would anyone leave a baby who *wasn't* mine on my porch with a note saying it *was?*"

"Why would anyone leave a baby on your porch, period? Whoever left Samantha obviously wasn't thinking clearly."

"Yeah, but...but the note said Eleuthera."

"Eleuthera?"

He sighed. "We met in Eleuthera, in the Bahamas, nine months and a couple of weeks ago—the woman who...the woman whom I *think* we're talking about. It was a resort. We hit it off. I thought I was being careful, but hell, even when you're careful something can go wrong."

"Yes, but how do you know Samantha is the product of that liaison?"

"Because the note *said*..." He drifted off, looking even more troubled. Allison had almost expected him to be relieved by the possibility that Samantha might not be his. He hadn't wanted this baby. He hadn't planned on it. He was a single man who'd had to be taught the proper way to hold an infant. Shouldn't he be thrilled by the chance that he could hand the child over to the authorities and be done with fatherhood until he was ready for it?

He shook his head again, dismissing her implications. "All right, look," he enunciated slowly, as if she were dim-witted and needed to be walked through the process. "I was with a woman, okay? I met her, I liked her, I had sex with her. I thought we would see each other again once we left Eleuthera,

because she told me she lived in Manhattan and I
told her I lived in Arlington. When I got home, it
turned out she didn't want to see me. So that was the
end of it. At least I thought that was the end of it,''
he added, eyeing Samantha cautiously.

"But how can you be sure that was the woman
who left the baby?"

"I just am. No one else would have done this to
me. And besides, the note... It said Eleuthera. Who
else would have left that note?"

"I see." He seemed awfully touchy, unwilling to
entertain any other theories, even when those theories, if proven true, could save his butt. "Assuming
that this woman you liked and exchanged numbers
with nine months ago is in fact the mother of Samantha, how do you know the woman wasn't involved with somebody else? Sure, she remembered
you from Eleuthera. But it's just possible—" again
she kept her gaze steady on him, gauging his reaction
"—that she could have become pregnant by someone else. How do you know for sure that this baby
is yours?"

If he'd been standing, she imagined he would have
had to sit. He looked weak, dazed, even more overwhelmed than before. He turned to observe the baby
in the seat next to him. His frown deepened. "She's
got to be mine. Look at her. She looks exactly like
me."

Allison rose and leaned across the table to study
the baby. Newborns' faces were undefined, their
bones still growing. For a very young infant, Samantha was certainly prettier than average. Other than
that, though... "I really can't see the resemblance."

"Look how blond she is! I was blond when I was a baby."

"Jamie." She smiled at his obstinacy. Surely once he thought about it he would realize that not being the father of a newborn, a virtually motherless refugee who'd appeared uninvited and unexplained on his doorstep, wasn't such a bad thing. "Lots of babies have blond hair. It doesn't mean you're blood relations."

He shifted in his seat. He stared at Allison, then past her, then at her again. "What would it take to find out?" he asked, his voice low and taut. "A blood test?"

"A simple blood test might prove it, especially if you have a rare blood type. If the blood test didn't rule out your paternity, you could have a DNA test done."

She saw the cartilage in his throat move as he swallowed. His gaze drifted back to the baby beside him. As if on cue, she issued a heartbreakingly sweet sigh.

"What would happen then?" he asked, his tone even more muted. "To her, I mean. What if I had this DNA test and it turned out she wasn't mine? What would happen to her?"

"She would enter the foster care system. Social services would take over. And of course the police would try to track down her mother, which they should be doing in any case."

"Foster care? Samantha would be placed with total strangers?"

"Well, Jamie, what are you? I mean, you're a total stranger to her, too."

"Maybe this morning I was." He fell silent as the

waitress arrived with their hamburger platters and a bottle of ketchup. Once she departed, he ignored his food and leaned forward, his elbows on the table and his face just inches from Allison's. "I've had this baby living with me all day. What would be the purpose of sending her to live with strangers? What could they do for her that I can't?"

"They'd have experience with young children," Allison explained. "They would be screened by social workers. They'd know all about heating formula."

"I can learn that. I've *already* learned it. I'm not a moron."

"The social workers would place her with a family that included a stay-at-home mom."

"I work in an office in my house. I'm a stay-at-home dad."

"Yes, but you do work. You'd have to hire someone to look after her while you worked."

"If I have to, I will. I'm just saying, Allison, I don't see the point in tearing her away from a man who's probably her father and passing her along to someone she isn't even related to. If she's going to stay anywhere, it may as well be with me."

"If you want to be a foster father, you could certainly ask for consideration from the caseworker assigned to her."

"There wouldn't be a caseworker assigned to her if she was really my daughter, right?"

He no longer sounded uncertain. He seemed to be questioning her more to learn the legal procedures than to figure out whether—and how—to unload the baby. In some strange way, he could be ready for fatherhood.

"There still might be a caseworker assigned to her," she told him. "Not to remove the baby from your home but to make sure the baby is safe. But it's possible social workers wouldn't have to be brought into it. Either way, the police still need to be notified. The mother committed a criminal act. They need to find her."

"But in the meantime..." He relaxed at last, settling back against the banquette and reaching for the ketchup. "In the meantime, I don't see any reason to stick Samantha with someone else. Foster parents wouldn't know the mother. I would. If the police have to find her, maybe I could help them track her down."

"I'm sure they'd welcome your help."

"And then what? If they found Luanne, they'd toss her in jail?"

Hearing the woman's name jolted Allison. She hadn't minded thinking of the mother in the abstract, but now that the woman had an actual name, Allison inched closer to believing that Samantha was the result of Jamie's brief acquaintance with the woman.

"If they found her, it would be up to them to work everything out. Up to them, and to you. I'm not a lawyer, Jamie, or a social worker. I'm a nurse. I can help you take care of Samantha. Beyond that, you'd have to speak to the police."

"All right." He concentrated on squeezing ketchup onto his burger instead of fathoming the intricacies of the foster care system. He seemed resigned to the prospect of taking care of a newborn, but she sensed a glimmer of excitement in him, too, as if he welcomed the challenge.

"Which brings us back to where we started. If

you're going to keep Samantha, even if only temporarily, you'll need to buy supplies.''

"Right." He pulled a napkin from the dispenser on the table and plucked a pen from his shirt pocket. "What should I get?"

She suppressed a grin. How could a man who used a napkin to write a shopping list actually think he could handle the titanic job of caring for a newborn? "Here, write on this," she said, removing a lined notepad from her tote. "You'll need a crib—a Porta-crib would work for now. It's small and flexible. Some sheets for the crib, and blankets."

"I've got a blanket," he said. "And anyway, it's summertime."

"Babies still need to be kept warm. Get a couple of spare blankets. If she wets one of them, you can use the other while you do the laundry."

"Oh, God, the laundry. I need more detergent." He scribbled a note to himself. "I've been washing clothes all day."

"Get some bibs. It'll help make her outfits last a little longer. You'll need lots of bottles. And of course the stroller."

He diligently recorded everything she listed in a broad, scrawling script. He might ace her course, after all. Any student who took such comprehensive notes—who cared so deeply about doing the right thing—was destined to graduate at the top of his class.

"What else?" he asked, awaiting further instructions.

She continued her list, rummaging through her memory, naming the necessities. She'd begun her day contemplating inventory, and it appeared that she was ending it the same way: reviewing supplies.

Telling Jamie McCoy what to get was more fun than battling the pencil pushers in the hospital's administrative offices. If budgeting was a problem for him, he didn't let on. He simply wrote whatever she said, earnestly and somberly, as if he believed that Allison was handing down gospel from on high.

After he'd covered the sheet with a list that ran from alphabet blocks to zinc oxide ointment, she added one final item, something he wouldn't find in any store. "A baby-sitter."

"I'll work on it," he said.

"I'm serious, Jamie. If you intend to keep writing your column, you're going to have to hire a nanny, or at least a part-time caregiver. Someone who can be on call while you're buried in your work."

"I'm sure I'll be able to get my work done."

"It won't be easy with Samantha around," Allison warned.

Jamie shot a quick look at the baby, then clicked his pen shut and gave Allison an unjustifiably confident grin. "Writing the column," he boasted, "will be a piece of cake."

CHAPTER FOUR

GUY STUFF by James McCoy—

If anyone ever decided to compile an encyclopedia on babies, the *P* volume would be the largest. Everything to do with babies seems to start with *P*...or should I say, pee.

Consider all the other P-words that go along with babies: Puke. Pat-a-cake. Pacifier. Pablum.

Who invented the term *pablum*, anyway? Granted, what babies eat is disgusting—which is probably where puke comes in. But pablum, the soft, icky stuff they devour—also known by the P-word *pap*—might strike us as more appetizing if it had a nicer name. "Potage of cereal with a soupçon of banana," for example. Potage starts with a *P*.

So does pizza, but babies need teeth to eat that. And how do babies get teeth? With yet another P-word: *pain*.

JAMIE READ what he'd written and wrinkled his nose. One thing he'd learned in the past couple of days was that humor didn't come easily when you were running on an average of two hours' sleep a night.

A certain little lady was driving him nuts. At the pediatrician's office, she'd barely tipped the scales at eight pounds, but as best Jamie could figure, seven and a half of those pounds were vocal cords. All she seemed to do was wail, eat, burp, puke, pee and wail again, with occasional lapses into slumber.

He had never before known such a demanding female.

When panic about his infant-size blond bombshell wasn't tearing him apart from the inside out, he was haunted by thoughts of another woman. A woman more mature, less fussy, more sensible but somehow just as demanding. Merely thinking about Allison Winslow kept him from falling asleep. Merely recalling the combination of sympathy and steel in her gaze as she insinuated that Samantha might not be his own genetic offspring made Jamie toss and turn at night. Merely reminiscing about the lush, dense tumble of her hair made him hard.

And that made him feel guilty. Jamie's attitude toward sex had always been supremely healthy. But now that he was a daddy, with a sweet, defenseless, howling banshee of a baby in his house, it seemed inappropriate for him to entertain erotic thoughts about a woman.

Spending a fortune on Samantha did nothing to assuage his guilt. Yesterday, armed with the shopping list Allison had dictated to him at the diner, he had journeyed with Samantha to the mall. He'd bought Samantha a crib—polished oak with a curving Deco-style shape. That hadn't seemed sufficient, so he'd also bought, to hang from the ceiling above the crib, a mobile constructed of little helicopters whose rotors spun when they picked up a current of air. He'd bought crib sheets and a blanket featuring a pattern of rainbows and stars, and a matching set

of what the saleswoman called bumpers, though they
certainly wouldn't have fit on any car he'd ever seen.
He'd bought every style of pacifier he could find and
a menagerie of stuffed animals that would put the
Bronx Zoo to shame. He'd bought a few more teeny-
tiny outfits—why they couldn't make baby clothing
with man-size snaps instead of fasteners the size of
dried lentils he didn't know—and a stroller sporting
a price tag that rivaled that of a Mercedes Benz.
"This stroller is imported," the saleswoman had explained while he'd kicked the tires and tested the
steering. "It's made in Denmark. All the well-
educated parents buy this model. You certainly
wouldn't want to put your daughter in a lesser product."

He certainly wouldn't. Hell, he'd graduated from
an Ivy League university with a gentleman's C. He'd
be damned if he put his daughter in anything less
than the Danish model.

But none of his expenditures quelled her chronic
fussing. He began to wonder whether she would calm
down if he presented her with a tennis bracelet or
maybe sprang for a weekend for two at Canyon
Ranch.

Not likely. She was obviously playing hard to get,
hoping to milk him for all he was worth. Yesterday
evening, he'd attempted to finish his column on turning thirty, but every few minutes he'd been interrupted by Her Royal Highness, Princess Snit. Desperate to fax out the column by deadline, he'd
arranged her in the crib with all the rainbow linens
and watched as she systematically shoved every single pacifier away and shrieked. Eventually she managed to stuff enough of her hand into her mouth to

silence herself. He'd raced back to his office, reread his column and decided it made no sense. Now that he'd spent a few days taking care of Samantha, he had even less understanding of why women were concerned with having babies before their biological clocks ticked their last tock. Such women ought to spend a few minutes with Samantha. It would cure them in a jiffy.

During rare moments of peace, when the kid actually shut up to suck a bottle or sleep one off, Jamie's thoughts drifted back to Allison Winslow. He wondered if she wanted kids of her own. She knew what she was doing when it came to managing infants. He couldn't help assuming that Samantha wouldn't be performing her air-raid-siren routine if Allison were around to keep her in line, to hold her and stare at her and talk to her.

Recalling her instructions, Jamie kept trying to talk to Samantha. But he felt like a bloody fool every time he did. "Hey, Sam, how's tricks?" he would say, and she would blink at him and pout. "Tell me, does this formula stuff taste better from a clear bottle or a pastel one? I've got pink, I've got yellow, I've got blue. What do you say?"

What she said was unprintable. She clearly thought he was a first-class imbecile. He didn't blame her.

Allison knew the secret, though. She knew how to relate to babies, how to make casual conversation with them, how to gaze into their faces in such a way that they didn't cross their eyes trying to gaze back.

Maybe it was a woman thing. Maybe all women were born knowing exactly what to say to newborns. It was probably some sort of sisterhood, a coven, a secret knowledge girls started sharing at pajama parties when they were twelve. It was what they whispered about in high school when they trooped en masse to the ladies' room. Jamie had always wondered why no teenage girl ever went to the bathroom alone. He used to think they traveled in a group so they could fix each other's hair and gossip about boys. But probably they were teaching each other the secret woman-baby communication code.

If Allison was with Samantha, would she tell the baby to pipe down so she could have a few uninterrupted minutes with Jamie? If she won those few uninterrupted minutes, would Allison be receptive to a romantic overture? Would she slap his cheek and gather up his baby and storm off to the police, believing that even if he was Samantha's father, he was unfit to raise her?

Well, she *would* go to the police. And Jamie knew he was going to have to do that, too. The pediatrician had pronounced Samantha strong and healthy, but he'd also asserted that Jamie was going to have to get her a social security number, and to do that he would need documentation—preferably a birth certificate. Luanne had left enough clothing, formula and diapers to last two days—Jamie had learned this as day two wound down—but neither the suitcase nor the shopping bag had contained Samantha's birth certificate.

Jamie had to find Luanne.

If he did, he damned well might tell her to take the kid back. Parenthood was too much for him to handle, really. If he were able to experience about seventy hours of continuous sleep, he might be willing to share custody. But whatever the ultimate custody arrangement was, he had to get hold of Samantha's birth certificate.

Gritting his teeth and praying for his editor to be too rushed to read the thirtieth-birthday column carefully, he faxed it to his syndication company. Then he turned from his computer and reached for the Arlington telephone directory, to look up the police department's nonemergency number.

The idea of baring his soul to a cop about the circumstances of Samantha's arrival on his doorstep didn't sit well with him. His past experiences with police officers hadn't been particularly pleasant: a speeding ticket; the time in high school when he was one of about twenty kids partying noisily at Sue Potter's house when her parents had gone out of town; the time he and Mike Rauer got caught trying to liberate a stop sign when they were eleven and the patrolman had driven them home in his cruiser—which had actually been pretty cool—and presented them to their long-suffering mothers with the prediction that they were destined for bad things.

Maybe he could avoid the police by working with a private investigator. Some up-to-date Sam Spade might be able to track down a hard-bitten dame like Luanne.

The yellow pages included half a column of private investigators. Jamie wasn't sure how to go about selecting one. It wasn't the sort of thing he could ask a neighbor about the way he might ask which lawn service or dentist they used. "Hi, Gloria? You and Stan wouldn't have a P.I. you could recommend, would you?"

At a loss, he ran his index finger down the list until he found an honest-sounding name. Tom Bland,

private investigator, answered his own phone, which
made Jamie think he might be a one-man operation.
But so was Sam Spade, wasn't he?

By the time he'd finished talking to Tom Bland,
Jamie realized that the detective's integrity was a serious flaw. Bland had told him that if a woman abandoned an infant it was a criminal matter, and Jamie
really was going to have to take his problem to the
police.

Pretty much what Allison had told him. Perhaps,
once the dust had cleared and Samantha had learned
how to sleep through the night, Jamie could introduce Allison to Tom Bland. They'd probably hit it
off.

He didn't want to introduce Allison to another
man, though. He wanted to transform Samantha so
that she was no longer a problem. And then he
wanted to make a play for the tall, stern nurse with
the elegant bone structure and the phenomenal hair,
the woman who knew how to hold Samantha and
talk to her and soothe her. The beautiful Daddy
School headmistress who had told him to go to the
police.

"YOU FOUND HER on your porch?"

Jamie tried not to squirm beneath the stark gaze
of Detective John Russo of the Arlington Police Department. Russo was a lean, angular guy not much
older than Jamie, with dark hair a few inches longer
than Jamie expected to see on an officer of the law.
He also had a framed photograph of a little dark-
haired boy on his desk. This Jamie interpreted as
proof that Russo was a family man who would no

doubt condemn Jamie for his failure to use a condom correctly while in the presence of a crackpot lady.

Jamie had been assigned to Russo by chance. He'd walked into the police station, interrupted the receptionist's exuberant burbling about how adorable his little baby was and said he needed to talk to a detective. Russo had been available, and now he was taking Jamie's statement, clacking the information on a typewriter, which seemed awfully anachronistic. Jamie had performed well on questions like, "What is your name?" and "What is your address?" In fact, Russo had displayed a glimmer of respect when he'd realized that Jamie was the author of "Guy Stuff," the weekly column run in the *Arlington Gazette* and sixty-seven other major city newspapers.

But now they'd dug a little deeper into the situation, and Russo suddenly didn't seem quite so respectful.

"All right, look," Jamie said, attempting the same ingratiating smile that used to work when he got sent to the principal's office. "I thought Luanne Hackett was a decent human being. She had me fooled. I admit it, I was a poor judge of character, to say nothing of a jerk—"

Russo held up his hand to silence him. "This isn't about your being a jerk," he said, implying that he agreed with Jamie's self-assessment and didn't think it warranted discussion. "You said you found the baby on your porch on Monday. Today is Thursday. Why didn't you report this sooner?"

Jamie groped for an explanation. It wasn't that he wanted to redeem himself—Russo probably considered him beyond redemption. It was that, frankly, Jamie wasn't sure why he hadn't gone to the police sooner. He recalled his reaction when Allison had first suggested that he involve the police—genuine ambivalence.

Russo's expression grew less critical, more quizzical. Jamie sighed. "I wish I could give you a nice, easy answer, but I can't. I don't know. I guess part of it was embarrassment. Maybe part of it was denial. I couldn't believe I got into such a scrape. I mean, I'm a Boy Scout, always prepared. In this day and age, you'd be insane not to protect yourself. I might have legal grounds for a suit against the manufacturer of the condoms I was using. What do you think? Could a criminal case be made?"

Russo smiled faintly. "Why didn't you report the baby on Monday?" he repeated, his fingers resting against the typewriter keys.

Samantha chose that moment to shriek. She'd been dozing in her state-of-the-art stroller, but something had apparently spooked her, and she instantaneously announced her new state of awareness with a top-decibel howl.

Maybe she'd wet herself, but Jamie wasn't going to change her diaper in the middle of the bustling squad room. Either she was going to have to learn to time her bladder functions better or she was going to have to live with a damp di-dee for a few more minutes.

He rummaged in his knapsack for the three different pacifiers he'd brought and attempted to stuff them into her mouth. She didn't shut up until she'd gotten her thumb and forefinger wedged between her lips.

Sighing again, this time from exhaustion, he straightened up to find Detective Russo watching him intently, almost sympathetically. "You've got a kid, too," Jamie said, gesturing toward the photograph on the desk.

Russo's gaze flickered toward the photo and he nodded. "Yeah."

"So you must have survived the horror of the first year, huh?"

Russo studied his son's picture for a moment longer, then snorted. "The first year isn't as bad as the second," he observed.

Great. Something to look forward to. "I think the reason I didn't report her to the police right away," Jamie confessed, "was—I don't know, call it hubris. I thought I could handle everything. I thought, hey, what's the big deal? I know how to change the oil in my car. I know how to repair a leaky faucet. I can handle a baby. Piece of cake, you know?"

"And then you discovered it wasn't so easy," Russo guessed.

"It's a bitch," Jamie concurred. "I'm taking this class in fathering skills, but the nurse who teaches it told me I had to talk to you guys about the manner in which I gained custody of Samantha. So, here I am. Allison had better appreciate it."

"Allison?"

"The nurse who teaches the class. Allison Winslow. She works in the maternity department at Arlington Memorial, and on the side she runs this program she calls the Daddy School to teach jerks like me how to deal with babies."

Russo jotted Allison's name onto a scrap of paper. Then he returned his attention to the triplicate form scrolled into his typewriter. "Tell me some more about the mother of this baby."

"I can tell you what she told me about herself," Jamie offered. "But I don't know how much of it is true." He recited Luanne's full name, the phony number she'd given him and a general description of her. Specifics eluded him. She had long ago become blurred in his memory, a sexy, attractive woman who had deceived him for no good reason. Had her hair been ash-blond or strawberry blond? In the age of Clairol and L'Oréal, did it really matter? Given the way she'd dropped off her baby and vanished, she might be a brunette named Katrinka Jones by now.

"Do you have any idea why she might want to avoid you?" Russo asked.

Jamie scowled. He didn't like the way Russo's left eyebrow rose, the way his smile quirked with irony. Was he implying that Jamie was less than wonderful, that after spending a week in his bed a woman would be inclined to enter the witness protection program? "I swear to God, what happened in Eleuthera was mutually pleasant," he said. "The only thing we argued about was politics. She's a militant capitalist. I'm a seat-of-the-pants anarchist. That was all theoretical, though. When we weren't debating philosophically, we were getting along all right."

"Obviously." Russo eyed Samantha, who had started to snore. "Are you sure the baby is yours?"

Jamie swore softly. He didn't like Russo sowing seeds of doubt so soon after Allison had asked the same question. He didn't like the vague temptation that doubt posed for him. If he underwent testing and learned that Samantha wasn't his, he would be done with the police, with Luanne and with the baby. He would be able to return to his carefree life, his columns, his ragtop Miata and his eight hours of beauty rest every night.

And what would happen to Samantha? She would get shuffled around by the bureaucracy. She would wind up being monitored by underpaid social workers and cared for by someone who didn't give a damn whether or not her stroller was the best money could buy.

He wouldn't wish such a fate on any child, let alone his daughter. *If* she was his daughter.

"Yes," he heard himself say. "She's mine."

Russo perused him thoughtfully, then broke away and began to type. Jamie sat in his chair, idly pushing the stroller back and forth in a lulling rhythm. Why was he so determined not to find out whether Samantha was his? Granted, ignorance had its advantages, but in this case he couldn't figure out what they might be.

The typewriter clicked and clattered. In the distance a phone rang. Two uniformed officers laughed over a joke. Russo kept typing, slow but steady—the same tranquil tempo Jamie used to rock the stroller.

He glanced at the framed photo on Russo's desk. The boy looked a lot like his dad: dark eyes, dark hair, a solemn, angular face. What would Samantha look like in a year, or two, or ten? If Jamie gave her up, he would never know.

"Okay," Russo said, lifting his hands from the keys. "You can go now."

"What's going to happen next?"

"We'll run Luanne Hackett's name through the computer and see what comes up. Maybe it's an alias. Maybe we'll get a social security number on her. Maybe she has a pattern of giving birth to babies and abandoning them on people's porches.''

The notion jolted Jamie. That Samantha could have half siblings was simply too weird. It didn't seem to matter that the little girl was destroying his life. He felt protective of her. He didn't want her to end up like Luanne's other abandoned babies.

"So...meanwhile, I'm just supposed to go home?"

"I'll be in touch," Russo said.

Jamie stood slowly, giving Russo a chance to tell him something more. Surely Russo ought to be bristling with energy and theories, listing the steps he would take, putting together a task force to track Samantha's mother down. Surely he should be calling a special meeting of the entire Arlington police force, introducing Jamie and Samantha and explaining why it was essential that the department use every resource at its command to find the heinous woman who'd abandoned Samantha, to bring her to justice.

But Russo only stood when Jamie did and shook his hand. "Good luck with the baby," he said. "Maybe you can write about her in your column."

"I can't use her in my column," Jamie argued. "She isn't funny enough."

Russo grinned. "That could change. I'll be in touch," he repeated, then pulled his report from the roller of his typewriter and walked away.

Great. Detective John Russo would be in touch. What was Jamie supposed to do while he was waiting?

Take her home. Feed her. Change her diaper. Burp her. Bathe her. Feed her again.

Talk to her. Make eye contact. Hold her. Be a daddy.

If only he knew how.

He could learn if he had to—and he *did* have to. Allison could teach him. He was already an expert on subjects he never would have imagined. He knew what no-tears shampoo was. He knew the pros and cons of Wet Wipes. He knew that a father could either save to send his child to college or he could buy a Danish stroller, but unless he was Bill Gates, he probably couldn't afford to do both.

But if Jamie knew so much, how come he still felt like an ignoramus? The next Daddy School class didn't meet until Monday. He didn't think he could wait that long.

He hoped Allison wouldn't mind if he dropped by the hospital for a quick tutorial, just to get him through the next few days. She was a nurse; it was her profession to help parents and their babies. Surely she would allow him a bit of remedial instruction—for Samantha's sake.

"THE MOST IMPORTANT thing," Allison lectured the five new mothers in the nursery, "is never to let go of your baby. Babies squirm, and just like the highway, they're slippery when wet. Always keep a firm hold on them."

She was teaching the techniques of bathing a newborn to the women. They were a typical group—bleary-eyed, bulky in their loose-fitting hospital gowns and bathrobes, their smiles giddy and anxious and brimming with love. As Allison demonstrated on one woman's baby, the other four stood beside their babies' isolettes, absorbing her every word.

"Always dry the baby off gently but quickly," she continued, swaddling her victim with a soft towel as she spoke. "Remember, their bodies' thermostats aren't fine-tuned yet. They get cold very easily. They're so used to being nice and warm inside your bodies."

The women nodded, looking awed by Allison's deftness with the fussing infant. Within a minute she had him diapered and snapped into pj's. She ran a comb through his sparse black hair, arranging it stylishly, then passed him to his mother. The women in the room applauded.

So, Allison realized, did the man in the doorway.

What was Jamie doing on the maternity floor of Arlington Memorial Hospital? Who had allowed him upstairs? Why was he watching her give Marilyn Glatz's baby a bath?

And why on earth did her heart do a silly little dance at the sight of him?

He wasn't the best-looking man she'd ever met. It was just those uncanny green-gray-gold eyes, and his adorable smile, half arrogant, half helpless, and his athlete's body. It was just that Allison was worried about his little girl.

Right now the little girl seemed quite content in a luxurious stroller. Evidently Jamie had done some shopping since he and Allison had shared an evening of burgers and talk after class on Monday. Maybe he'd stopped by to show his teacher what a diligent student he was.

"We're doing baths now," she told him.

"I can wait," he said, gesturing toward the corridor. He waved, then steered around and out the door.

The mothers in the nursery paid him little attention. They were too eager to try out the skills Allison had taught them. One by one, she led them to the plastic basin, had them fill it with tepid water and talked them through a bath. "Watch the umbilicus," she warned onc. "You don't want to rub there. The dead skin has to fall off on its own. If you tear it, it will take longer to heal...." The words flowed naturally from her, as if she had nothing on hcr mind except belly buttons.

But Jamie occupied a solid spot in her brain, just as he had ever since he'd entered the room at the YMCA ten minutes late for class Monday evening. Not once in the past few days had she ever completely erased him from her thoughts. At odd moments, she found herself worrying about the legalities of his situation, about the imposition his baby must place on him. She was concerned with his attitude, his unreasonable confidence and his genuine fear. She was troubled by the understanding that nine months ago he'd been with a woman whose behavior left a lot to be desired, and that said something about Jamie's lack of judgment.

Surrounded by spotless chrome, sterile towels, antiseptic soap and stacks of diapers in the nursery, she was still worrying about him.

She had more important things to focus on. Just that morning, Margaret had told her that her pilot Daddy School program, while an excellent idea, was a one-shot deal. The hospital didn't plan to fund a second class. If Allison wanted to continue teaching new fathers, she would have to find the funding elsewhere. If she didn't, struggling new fathers like Jamie would be left to fumble along without guidance.

She observed as the final mother took her turn at

the plastic basin. None of the women was as adept as she was, but she assured them all that in time they would be varsity bath-givers. "It's just a matter of practice," she said. "Don't be afraid. Stay calm, stay alert and you'll do fine."

She shooed them out of the nursery, sending them pushing their babies' isolettes down the hall to their rooms. Then she dried her hands, moisturized them with lotion and collected the damp towels for the hospital laundry. When the room was tidy, she left in search of Jamie.

He was seated in one of the small lounges near the nursing station looking uncomfortable. His daughter was tucked into his arms, and he was peering into her face, but he wasn't smiling as she flailed at him, reaching for his nose.

"Let her touch you," Allison urged.

He flinched and glanced up. "She's going to stick her fingers up my nostrils."

"She's trying to touch what she sees. That's great. It means she's experimenting with eye-hand coordination. Go ahead, get closer to her. She won't stick her fingers up your nostrils."

"Promise?" he asked dubiously.

Allison smiled.

Jamie bowed his head toward the baby. She smacked her little palm against the tip of his nose. "Ouch!" he grunted. She whimpered.

"Great moments in child rearing," Allison teased, approaching the sofa where he sat. Before she took a seat, she circled the expensive-looking stroller. "Nice wheels," she commented.

"It cost more than my car."

"I don't doubt it." She lowered herself onto the sofa and scrutinized him. His eyes were circled with shadows and his hair was mussed, but all in all he didn't look too terrible.

Then again, Jamie McCoy probably couldn't look terrible even if he tried.

"What can I do for you?" she asked.

"I don't know," he admitted. "I just... I wanted to see you." He leaned back as Samantha reached for his nose again. Her movements distracted him, denying him the chance to elaborate on his statement. His words hung in the air, implying a significance he couldn't possibly have intended.

Why did he want to see her? It couldn't be *her* he wanted to see. It had to be her expertise he had come for—advice, emotional support. She herself meant nothing to him.

"I went to the police," he told her. "I did what you said. I reported the whole thing. I..." He let out a long breath, then caught his baby's fidgeting hand with his thumb. The baby curled her fingers tightly around him and gave a little frog kick with her legs. "I don't know how to do any of this, Allison. I'm trying, but I feel way out of my depth."

"That's perfectly normal," she assured him, curiously touched by his earnest desire to do things right. "Most new parents feel the same way."

"You're so good at it," he complained with a smile.

"I'm a professional."

"Are you busy tonight?"

She blinked. Once again, his words must have conveyed more than he meant. "Busy? Meaning...?"

"Meaning," he said, gazing directly into her eyes, "I want to take you out."

CHAPTER FIVE

"SO, I AGREED to have dinner with him on Saturday," Allison said, tearing spinach greens into a salad bowl with near violence. "And I think it's a terrible mistake."

"Going out with him on Saturday is *not* a terrible mistake," Molly assured her. "If you'd agreed to go out with him tonight, it would have been a mistake. By putting him off till Saturday, you not only make him wait—you know, increase the anticipation and all that—but a Saturday date is more...I don't know. More meaningful? More romantic? More—"

"Expensive, probably," Allison muttered. She looked at the result of her destructive impulses—mangled shreds of green heaped high in the bowl—and sighed. "I don't know why I told him yes. It's been eons since I've gone out with someone new."

"Obviously. If you went out more often, you wouldn't be so tense about it now. Grammy? Come in here and tell Allison she did the right thing when she agreed to go out with that guy on Saturday night."

"Wait, Grammy—let me help you," Allison called over her shoulder. She dried her hands on a dish towel and moved to the arched doorway connecting the kitchen to the living room.

Her grandmother was moving more slowly these

days. Allison had taken her to see an orthopedist, who'd insisted that knee-replacement surgery would do wonders for her, but Grammy had argued that a knee replacement would last only twenty years. "I'm seventy-seven," she argued. "They do the replacement now, and what's going to happen when I'm ninety-seven? Do you think I'm going to want to go through surgery again at that age?"

Grammy was stubborn, but Allison adored her. So did Molly, who wasn't even related to her. Molly Saunders and Allison were such close friends, Grammy treated Molly like just another member of the family. She and Allison had met in kindergarten twenty-three years ago, and the chemistry between them had been right, even though Allison was lanky and quiet while Molly was bouncy and bubbly. Allison had admired Molly's garrulous personality; Molly had considered Allison brainy and classy. Their differences complemented each other, and for Allison—who'd had no siblings—Molly was almost a sister, someone with whom she could try out ideas, shop, share secrets and dreams.

In high school they'd been nicknamed the "Allie and Molly Show," and even when they'd headed off to different colleges—Allison to the University of Connecticut and Molly to Simmons College in Boston, they'd remained in constant touch, visiting each other at school and seeing each other when they returned to Arlington for the holidays. Over the years, Molly had spent countless afternoons in the Winslow home, where Allison's grandmother had run the household while Allison's mother had been at work.

Like Allison, her mother and her grandmother had both been nurses at Arlington Memorial. Grammy had been widowed before Allison was born, and Allison's mother had gotten a divorce when Allison was too young to remember much about it. Her father had made the mistake of hitting her mother once, and that had been enough to win him permanent exile from the family. Allison's mother had reclaimed her maiden name—Winslow—and changed Allison's name to Winslow, too.

Allison's mother remarried when Allison was in her teens, and five years ago her stepfather had been transferred to North Carolina. Allison's mother had offered to take Grammy with them, but Grammy wouldn't hear of it. Arlington was her home, and just because she had arthritis and couldn't get around so fast didn't mean she was the least bit inclined to move to some godforsaken place called the Research Triangle—which she insisted on calling the Bermuda Triangle. Grammy would stay right where she was, thank you. If Allison wanted to stay, fine. If she wanted to move on, that would also be fine. Grammy didn't need anyone taking care of her. She could manage on her own as long as she didn't have to climb stairs.

Allison had considered finding an apartment for herself once she'd completed her nursing degree, but she'd decided against it. She didn't like the idea of her grandmother living alone. And she was used to the modest, cozy Cape-Cod-style house where she'd grown up. She knew the home's quirks and charms. She knew exactly which dials to adjust when the furnace took too long to click on and where to hit the window frame in the first-floor bathroom when humidity caused the sash to swell and stick. She knew which floorboards squeaked, which stairs creaked.

She knew the idiosyncrasies of the garage door and the coolest corner in the cellar. She'd planted the daffodils along the front walk and climbed the crab apple tree in the backyard.

Besides, she adored Grammy, even if the old woman was headstrong and outspoken. And no one else would take as good care of her as Allison did—at least, not without letting her know she was being taken care of. And Grammy would never tolerate the knowledge that she was being taken care of.

Her grandmother was already halfway across the living room, the remote control in one hand and her cane in the other. Despite the limp caused by her arthritis, she was a vibrant, beautiful woman. Her hair, mostly silver, still held hints of auburn, and her eyes were so sharp she rarely needed the eyeglasses she wore on a silver chain around her neck. She was tall and slender, her cheeks so smooth she was often asked who did her face-lift. "Mother Nature," she would answer. "God was the attending nurse."

"I don't need help," she snapped at Allison now, though she happily relinquished the remote control en route to the kitchen. "Molly, tell her it's about time she went on a date."

"That's exactly what I did tell her," Molly assured Grammy. "I told her that just because her first date in eons—*your words*," she reminded Allison, "happens to be a guy who couldn't keep his pants zipped nine months ago doesn't mean he won't keep his pants zipped this weekend. Unless, of course, she doesn't want them zipped."

"Oh, please," Allison complained, placing the remote control on the table beside Grammy's favorite easy chair and returning to the kitchen. "People make mistakes. I'm trying not to hold anything against him."

"Good policy," Molly teased. "I wouldn't hold anything against him, either. Unless, of course, you want his pants unzipped."

"What are you talking about?" Grammy asked. "Did his trousers break?"

"He's one of Allison's Daddy School students," Molly explained. "He fathered an out-of-wedlock child."

"Well, at least he isn't shooting blanks," Grammy remarked phlegmatically. "Be careful, Allie. Make him marry you first."

Allison tried not to let their jokes rattle her. "Stop it, both of you," she demanded, unable to keep a straight face. "If you don't stop, I might have to poison you both."

"Poisoning is uncalled for," Grammy said, trudging to the counter and adding a splash of whisky to her iced tea. "I don't care if this fellow is an immoral, profligate swine. You don't have to fall in love with him. Just go out on Saturday night, order the most expensive dish on the menu and then the hell with him."

Molly roared with laughter as she carried the salad bowl and the cruet of dressing to the table. Try as she might to pretend indignation, Allison couldn't prevent herself from smiling as she pulled the tray of lasagna from the oven. While she cut and served the lasagna, Molly uncorked a bottle of wine for her and Allison.

"I'll tell you, Molly," Grammy confided, "if Allison doesn't start putting more effort into her social life, I'm going to run an ad for her in the personals.''

"Don't do me any favors, Gram," Allison muttered.

"I'll put one in for you, too, Molly. I don't understand it—the two most beautiful graduates of Arlington High School are still single in their late twenties."

"Everyone's still single in their late twenties these days," Molly explained, too cheerful to take offense at anything Grammy said. "The parents who send their kids to my school are all in their midthirties."

"They have to be in their midthirties to afford the tuition you charge," Grammy teased. "In the good old days, when parents worked, they sent their kids to a neighbor. Nowadays they pay, what, eight thousand dollars a year so their kids can be taken care of by strangers."

"My staff and I aren't strangers," Molly argued. "We're trained child care professionals."

"'Child care professionals,'" Grammy scoffed. "Fancy name for what we used to call a baby-sitter."

"Eat your dinner, Grammy," Allison suggested with a grin. "Stop picking on Molly."

"Would you rather I picked on you?" Grammy asked, then laughed at herself. "Tell us some more about this young man, other than the fact that he fathered an out-of-wedlock baby. What does he do for a living?"

"He writes a newspaper column."

"About what?"

"Men."

"Plenty of material to work with, there," Grammy observed.

"He's really funny," Molly chimed in. "I read his 'Guy Stuff' column every week."

"What have you learned from it?" asked Grammy.

Molly grinned. "For one thing, it's helped to clarify why the two most beautiful graduates of Arlington High School are still single in their late twenties. Most men our age haven't grown up yet."

"And he admits this in print? Well, he must be a fool, proclaiming the truth so bluntly." Grammy turned back to Allison. "What else do you know about him?"

"Not much," she confessed.

"You must know what he looks like."

Allison sighed. What Jamie McCoy looked like was a big problem. Feature for feature, he wasn't exactly movie star handsome. Yet he appealed to her in ways she wasn't used to. At the oddest times she found herself going dreamy at a memory of his eyes, glinting with color and laughter, or the sturdy breadth of his shoulders, or the awkward tenderness of his large, endearingly clumsy hands as he held his baby. They were hands that would not be clumsy with a woman. She wasn't sure how she knew that, but she knew.

"He's okay looking," she allowed, then felt her cheeks grow warm. Evidently she was blushing, because Molly and Grammy snorted in a chorus of disbelief. "All right. He's good-looking," she corrected herself. "But his looks don't matter. This isn't going to turn into a blazing love affair. Grammy had the right idea—I'll order something very expensive for dinner and then I'll never see him again."

"You'll see him on Monday in Daddy School," Molly reminded her.

"Which is another good reason I should never have said yes to a date with him. I'm his teacher."

"Meaning, what?" Molly asked. "If he doesn't put out, you'll give him an F?"

"Oh, stop!" Allison felt her cheeks burn even hotter. "The way things are going, we'll all be lucky if I can finish up this Daddy School program before Arlington Memorial pulls the plug. Margaret says the hospital doesn't want to fund me anymore."

Molly paused with her wineglass halfway to her mouth and scowled. "Fund you? What's the big deal? They're paying the YMCA some puny amount to rent the room."

"And they're paying me a small stipend," Allison said. "They gave me a paid week last month to put the curriculum together. And I've asked for supplies—some photocopied instruction sheets and some dolls, diapers and bottles for hands-on training. All in all, the hospital's kicked in a few thousand dollars."

"That much, huh." Molly scowled. "Gee, do you think they can spare it?"

"They don't have to give you any money," Grammy interjected. "Go to the pharmaceutical companies. Those folks pay for everything. At least they did in my day."

"They give the hospital freebies," Allison agreed. "But then it's up to the hospital whether or not to share the goodies with me. Arlington Memorial doesn't want to. They say the Daddy School isn't serving the hospital's target market. Daddies don't give birth, after all." She picked at her salad and sighed. Maybe, if she hadn't been so addled about the news that the hospital wanted to stop supporting the Daddy School, she would have had the presence of mind to say no when Jamie McCoy asked her out to dinner—and if she weren't so addled about her date, she might be able to think clearly about the funding problem. But for some reason, now that Jamie had landed on her mental scale, her equilibrium was way off. She couldn't seem to get her thoughts back into the proper balance.

"That's ridiculous. The hospital's being short-sighted," Molly fumed. "If fathers don't learn proper child care, babies are going to get sick."

"Which would mean more business for Arlington Memorial," Grammy added. "That's all they care about—making money. Forget all this nonsense about a revolution in health care. Bottom line—it's all about money."

"It would be such a shame if the program fell through," Allison lamented. A breeze tugged at the yellow gingham curtains framing the open window above the sink. She glanced at Grammy to make sure she wasn't getting a chill, then stabbed a chunk of lasagna with her fork. "Silly me. I had thoughts of expanding the Daddy School."

"If you're silly, I'm twice as silly. I had the same idea," Molly admitted.

Surprised, Allison frowned at her friend. "You did?"

"The other day, this father came in to pick up his two-year-old from the Young Toddlers group at the preschool. He told me his wife was in Michigan on family business and he was soloing with the kid. He didn't know what he was doing. He was totally lost.

I was helping him pack up Matthew's things and the father was saying, 'Look, he's got paint on his arm. Do I have to give him a bath? I don't know how to give him a bath. I've never given him one before.'"

"How could this father not know how to give a two-year-old a bath?" Allison shook her head.

"Obviously Matthew's mother has been supervising all the baths for two years. Just because babies grow into toddlers doesn't mean their dads are ready to take over." She took a sip of wine. "Anyway, after Matthew and his father left, I got to thinking that the Daddy School needs a class for fathers of older kids. It could be kind of a postgraduate program."

Allison lowered her fork and studied her friend on the far side of the circular pine table. Molly's heart-shaped face shone; her eyes radiated intelligence and enthusiasm. Of course there should be a class in the Daddy School designed for fathers like the one Molly had just described!

But it wasn't going to happen, not without adequate funding and support from the hospital. "What a lovely notion," she murmured glumly. "I'd love to set up a class for fathers of older kids—and you could teach it. All we need is for someone to die and leave us a ton of money."

"Don't look at me," Grammy said. "I have no intention of dying, not even for your school."

Allison smiled, but she wasn't happy. "It breaks my heart to think the program will end. I know my students are getting a lot from it."

"And one of those students may be getting more than he bargained for," Grammy added. "Where is he taking you for dinner, anyway? And what are you going to wear?"

There they were, back to Jamie McCoy. Allison had almost welcomed the opportunity to fret over the future of her new-father classes, since it distracted her from thoughts of her impending date.

But even if she, Molly and Grammy spent the rest of dinner talking about the Daddy School's looming funding crisis, Jamie McCoy would have occupied an implacable region of her mind, just as he had ever since he'd entered her classroom four days ago. No matter where she'd been or what she'd been doing, he'd always been there, like a shadow, following her, silent but real.

Why fight it? Her grandmother and her best friend seemed hell-bent on analyzing her wardrobe. "Her closet contains way too much white," Grammy carped, but after all, as a nurse, Allison tended to wear white a great deal of the time. She listened as they bandied about unsolicited suggestions: how to style her hair for the big date, which earrings to wear, whether her black sheath was too dressy, her green dress too short. Grammy advised her to wear flat shoes even if Jamie was sufficiently taller than her. "Men love to tower over their women," Grammy explained. "It deludes them into thinking they have some power in the relationship."

"I'm going to wear comfortable shoes," Allison declared. "And I was figuring on nice slacks and a cotton sweater. He didn't say we were going anywhere fancy."

"The man is a syndicated columnist. He's got to be rolling in dough." Molly snapped her fingers.

"Hey, maybe you could get him to underwrite the Daddy School."

"Oh, for God's sake! I haven't even gone out with him and you want me to hit him up for money?"

"He'll probably be hitting you up for something, too," Grammy predicted. "Be cagey, Allison. Make sure you get more than you give." And then she and Molly were off again, plotting, scheming. Should Allison play the femme fatale or the centered earth mother? They opined that either way would work as long as she didn't act like a nurse. She was used to taking care of everyone else, but on Saturday night, she was going to have to let him take care of her. She should forget about his performance in school and concentrate on his performance as an escort, a host, a man. This was going to be an adult outing. Allison had better make the most of it. And forget about wearing slacks. Either the black sheath or the green, they resolved.

She listened to their loving admonitions, filling in the blanks. Yes, she had a tendency to take care of everyone. Yes, Saturday night would be an adult outing.

And yes, Allison should make the most of it—because heaven knew, dates with men like Jamie McCoy didn't happen very often in her life. She wasn't going to forget what he'd been up to nine months ago—that would be impossible. But she might as well enjoy a night out on the town with a tall, attractive man with laughter and the devil in his eyes.

"WHAT DO YOU MEAN, you aren't coming?" Jamie raged into the telephone.

"I'm sorry, Mr. McCoy," Sara Doolan singsonged, sounding not the least bit sorry. "But, see, I broke curfew last night and my mom says I'm grounded tonight? Like, my boyfriend's car broke down and we couldn't get home? And now my mom's so PO'ed, and she's grounded me?"

Why did the girl phrase every statement to come out sounding like a question? Was he supposed to answer her? Was he supposed to express sympathy because she'd stayed out half the night with her boyfriend in his broken car?

"So, like, anyway, so I can't baby-sit for you, Mr. McCoy. Because I'm like grounded?"

He had spent countless hours and phone calls trying to round up a baby-sitter. He hadn't realized that baby-sitters had to be booked months in advance. It had been nothing short of a miracle that Sara Doolan, the friend of a niece of his accountant, had been available to watch Samantha while he and Allison went out for dinner.

Typical of miracles, this one evaporated in the harsh glare of reality. He was supposed to pick up Allison in twenty minutes, and Sara Doolan was grounded for the rest of her life. She ought to count her blessings. Right now, Jamie wanted to wring her neck.

But he couldn't drive all the way across town to the Doolan house for the meager pleasure of throttling Sara. He had to locate another baby-sitter, fast.

"Do you have any friends who might be available?" he asked, obviously desperate. Given what a ninny Sara was, he shouldn't be asking her for recommendations.

"I'm sorry, Mr. McCoy, but all my friends?

They're either already baby-sitting or, like, they've got boyfriends? Or they're grounded, too."

No surprise there. Why wouldn't Sara surround herself with friends as useless as she was?

Samantha belted out a five-alarm howl before Jamie could think of a tactful way to tell Sara exactly what he thought of her and all her grounded friends. "Thanks, anyway," he said, quickly disconnecting the call and racing through the house to get Samantha out of her crib.

She was soaking. She must have peed enough to fill the Great Lakes. Her clothing was wet, her sheet was wet, her blanket was wet and her hair was wet, although Jamie assumed that was due to sweating and crying. A boy might be able to contrive a way to pee on his own head, but girls would likely find such a feat anatomically impossible.

Cringing, he lowered the side rail of her crib and popped open the microscopic snaps on her outfit. He peeled the soggy fabric off her skin, then lifted her, holding her damp body as far as possible from himself so he wouldn't get her mess on his clean white shirt and khaki slacks. He hustled her across the hall to the bathroom, placed her in the plastic tub he'd bought after witnessing Allison's maternity ward seminar on bathing infants, and ran a damp wash cloth over Samantha while she squirmed and bawled.

"Ever hear the expression 'When it rains, it pours'?" he asked her, figuring he would win daddy points by talking to her. "Well, Sammy, you poured. We're talking monsoons, sweetie. Macrowhiz. I'll bet you cut about three pounds in fluids in the past five minutes. We could call it Samantha McCoy's Weight Loss Strategy."

Samantha responded to the sponge bath by turning down the decibel level. She did her mewing kitten impersonation, followed by an aria of gurgling, then pawed his sleeve with her wet hand, leaving a splotch of moisture on the cotton. At least it was only water. It wouldn't leave a stain.

A day ago, the process of getting her dried, diapered and dressed would have taken him a good ten minutes. But repeated practice at the 3-D routine had enabled him to shave a good four minutes off his time. He actually took pride in his diapering technique—all in the wrists, he'd learned—although he had to admit that deft diapering was a mighty peculiar thing for someone like him to be proud of.

While wrestling with the stupid little snaps of her clean pj's, he glimpsed his watch—6:18. The restaurant reservation was for seven. Talk about racing against the clock—no thirty-year-old childless woman had ever felt the pressure he was feeling right now.

He tucked Samantha under his arm like a football and hurtled down the hall to the kitchen, wondering why there was never a pro scout around when he was performing with the flair of a Dallas Cowboys running back. Shifting Samantha to his other arm, he flipped through the phone directory as if he had a prayer of finding anything listed under "baby-sitters." He had less luck this time than he'd had searching for private investigators in the Yellow Pages. "Baby-Sitters," it said, "See 'Child Care Providers, Day Care Services, Nannies, Nurses.'"

He'd love to see one particular nurse. He'd love to take her out for dinner and talk to her about anything but babies. But without a baby-sitter, that objective seemed unattainable.

He hoisted Samantha onto his shoulder and stalked back to the spare room he'd converted into a makeshift nursery. He'd left the window open, and a balmy breeze wafted through, spinning all the propellers in the helicopter mobile. For a moment he was dazzled by the spectacle. Samantha didn't even spare it a glance. She nestled against his shoulder, smelling like cool bath water and clean clothing.

He fell still, standing in the slanting evening sunlight, watching the brightly colored rotors whirl and feeling the soft weight of his daughter against his chest. For a moment he found himself unable to breathe. How could the tiny human in his arms be simultaneously the bane of his existence and the most awe-inspiring creature he'd ever encountered? How could this little girl be so sweet and peaceful and clean—and yet be destroying his chance for romance with Allison Winslow?

If it weren't for Samantha, Jamie wouldn't be racing around like a maniac, late for his date with Allison. He wouldn't be frantic for a baby-sitter. He wouldn't be standing in Samantha's room, his mood growing dismal as he lowered his gaze from the festive mobile to the sodden bed sheets in the crib below it.

On the other hand, if it weren't for Samantha, he would never have met Allison in the first place.

Propping the baby more securely against his shoulder, he used his free hand to swipe the sheet and blanket off the crib. He had thought the saleswoman had simply been trying to separate him from his money when she'd insisted that he buy two complete sets of bed linens for the crib, but now he was grateful that she'd persuaded him. He put Samantha on the floor for the minute it took him to make the crib with a fresh sheet, and by the end of that minute, she was revving up to scream. Once again he propped her in one arm and scooped up the sheets with the other. He carried them to the laundry room—a room he'd never given much thought to before last Monday—and then returned to the kitchen to consider his options, ghastly though they were.

He could call Allison and cancel their date. He could call and tell her he was going to be late, quite possibly extremely late, because it might take hours for him to dig up a baby-sitter.

Or he could bring Samantha with him.

She was cuddling into his neck again, her head snuggled into the hollow of his throat and her wispy hair tickling his chin. When she wasn't exuding body fluids and blaring vocal offensives, she was actually nice. If luck was with him—and damn, he'd already had enough bad luck—Samantha ought to fall asleep right about when he and Allison entered Reynaud, the elegant French restaurant where he was planning to take Allison in the hope of making a better impression on her than he had thus far.

He could lower the back of Samantha's stroller and cover her with a blanket, and she would sleep through dinner. Surely no one in the restaurant could complain, especially if they recognized the excellent quality of the stroller. It was either that or cancel the date.

He knew other women. He had an active social life, and one dinner date more or less wasn't going to matter much in the grand scheme of things...

except that Allison was special. She could save his butt, and he was close to worshiping hers. More important, he understood that if he didn't go on this date, Samantha would have won. He would have been defeated by fatherhood. He would have lost the life he'd been living, the life of a successful single guy.

"Okay, Sam," he murmured, reaching for his backpack and a box of diapers. "Let's see how badly you can screw things up for me tonight."

It took him another five minutes to pull Samantha's car seat from the Miata and install it in the back seat of his Range Rover. He hated driving the Rover in the summer, but the Miata was a two-seater. Unless he locked Samantha into the trunk, which was admittedly a tempting idea. He raced back into the house to retrieve the directions Allison had given him to her home, which was about two miles from the hospital. When he returned to the garage, he was lugging the stroller and the baby.

What a date—showing up at a woman's house with a stroller. He'd have to do better than that. He'd have to leave Samantha and the stroller in the Rover while he explained the situation to Allison: "Hi, Allison. I know how important fatherhood is, and to prove my commitment to my child, I brought her along for the evening." No.

"Hi, Allison. Samantha was in the mood for Reynaud's bouillabaisse, so I brought her along." Not quite.

"Hi, Allison. Once again, I'm doing everything wrong—but I mean well, so I'm hoping you'll cut me a little slack." That would be honest, at least.

Honest or not, it wasn't particularly romantic.

Flowers might help. A single rose would be appropriate. A single long-stemmed beauty, along with a sheepish smile and a plea for forgiveness.

Allison might consider a single rose a cliché, though. Maybe he ought to go for something playful—a bouquet of daisies to put her in a childlike mood. Or sultry—orchids, pansies, something like that. But then Allison might assume he was trying to send her an erotic message. Which, admittedly, he was.

He wound up spending ten minutes he didn't have at the flower shop. He wound up spending fifty dollars. "You really must have done something terrible," the florist teased as she wrapped the enormous bouquet in green cellophane paper. "Most men buy atonement for a lot less money."

"This woman is worth every penny," Jamie insisted, even though he had no way of knowing if that was true.

He arrived at Allison's home fifteen minutes late. She wasn't pacing the small brick front porch or standing in the window with a shotgun aimed at his privates. In fact, the modest gray-shingled house looked welcoming, its windows bright with light and the lamp above the front door glowing amber. The house was exactly the opposite of his: small but organized, no strange annexes, no architectural whimsies. The lawn was neatly mowed and edged, and daffodils lent their sunny yellow color to the front walk.

Samantha was sighing and blowing saliva bubbles as he rolled down a window and got out of the car. "Behave yourself," he warned her as he gathered the huge bouquet, which seemed to weigh more than

Samantha. He strode up the walk, trying to recall which justification for Samantha's presence sounded the least lame.

Maybe, just maybe, Allison wouldn't care about his having brought Samantha along. Maybe she would be so happy to see Jamie that nothing else would matter.

Sure. And maybe pigs could fly.

He climbed the steps to the front porch and rang the bell. After a moment it was opened by a tall, thin, elderly woman with startlingly clear green eyes and a scythe-sharp chin. Despite the cane she leaned on, she looked almost dangerously vigorous. Her hair was a thick, wavy mane of silver interlaced with reddish strands, and her apparel—a cardigan sweater, a blouse and summer-weight wool trousers—seemed youthful.

Jamie must have rung the wrong bell. He glanced over his shoulder at the roadside mailbox beside which he'd parked. The number on it was the number Allison had given him. This had to be her house.

So who was the elderly woman? Whoever she was, her eyes grew round as she studied the flowers. "For me?" she said. "You shouldn't have."

"I...uh..."

"Never mind. They're probably for Allie, aren't they."

Allie. He liked that nickname. It made Allison seem a little less daunting. *Allisons* knew everything a person needed to know about babies, whereas *Allies* got down on their hands and knees and played with babies.

"You're late," the elderly woman accused.

"I know." Was she going to invite him in, or was his punishment to be denied entry?

"If Allison were a weaker soul, your tardiness might have broken her heart." She pivoted to face the flight of stairs that rose behind her. "Allie? The fellow with the broken zipper is here, and he's brought enough flowers to decorate a funeral parlor."

Jamie shifted from one foot to the other. Even if the woman hadn't invited him in, even if he had no idea who she was, he decided he liked her. Her comment about his zipper puzzled him, though. He glanced down to make sure it was shut, then lifted his gaze just as the old woman stepped aside.

He instantly forgot all about her, about his zipper and about the disaster awaiting him as he attempted to pull this date off with his daughter in the back seat of his car. His entire consciousness zeroed in on the woman coming down the stairs, visible through the open doorway. What he saw first was legs—long, slender, beautifully curved, shamelessly flaunted legs. The woman descended another few steps and he saw the hem of her dress, a dark green sheath that ended somewhere above her knees and shimmied upward along her hips. Another few steps and he saw her hand clutching a small black purse. Another few steps and he saw the indentation of her waist, the swell of her bosom, the decadent spill of auburn hair against her shoulders, framing her pale, swanlike neck. Another few steps and he saw her face.

Allison Winslow was beautiful. So beautiful he was convinced his luck had changed. So beautiful he wanted to skip dinner and just stare at her...and then maybe strip off that seductively chic green dress and stare at her some more.

And then, when his eyes had had their fill, he wanted to make love to her, every inch of her, every way, until she was capable of only one coherent thought, and that thought was Jamie McCoy.

Far behind him, through the open window of the Range Rover, Samantha wailed.

Jamie McCoy immediately scratched lovemaking from his list.

CHAPTER SIX

THE MAÎTRE D' glanced down at the stroller and then back at Jamie. "Your reservation is for a party of two, not three," he said in a voice that sounded as if it was filtered through fourteen-karat-gold sinuses.

Allison might have made the same criticism. Whether or not she considered this dinner date a "party," she had definitely been under the impression that it was going be limited to her and Jamie.

Even without Samantha's presence, though, Allison had little hope of anything good coming out of the evening. Her entire day had hinted at doom. She'd put in a morning shift at the hospital that had included delivery of a borderline preemie—the baby's prognosis was good, but emergency deliveries at thirty-four weeks were always nerve-racking. At two o'clock, Allison's shift had ended. She'd raced home, washed her hair and discovered, only after the thick, tangled mop was dripping water down her back, that her hair dryer wasn't working. The phrase *bad-hair day* had been coined for just such disasters. She'd done the best she could to unravel the wet, tangled mess, but an hour of brushing, combing and towel drying had produced something resembling a cross between the Bride of Frankenstein and Medusa.

Giving up on her hair, Allison had tormented herself over her outfit. Jamie hadn't specified where they would be going for dinner, so she hadn't known whether to dress up or down. At six o'clock, staring at the array of outfits spread across her bed, she'd telephoned Molly, who'd spoken three words: "The green dress." Agreeing with Molly was always easier than arguing with her, so Allison had worn her green dress.

Now she worried that it was too short, too snug, too...suggestive. How could she think otherwise after Jamie had ogled her so blatantly when she'd come downstairs to greet him?

She would have been amply stressed out about this entire affair without his showing up late and presenting her with a bouquet nearly as big as he was. The flowers were flattering, but they put her on red alert. When she'd heard the feeble wail emerging from what appeared to be a huge military vehicle parked at the curb and then seen Jamie's guilt-stricken smile, the alarm system inside her ratcheted up to super-double red alert with siren.

Maybe it was just as well that Samantha was along to chaperon the date—and to help Allison maintain her perspective. Every time she glimpsed Samantha, or heard her, or smelled her baby lotion scent, Allison was reminded of why she should avoid any sort of involvement with Jamie. He was a man who had fooled around and been careless. He was a man who had flown off on a vacation and engaged in sex with a stranger. Allison shouldn't even have accepted his invitation for dinner.

Not only were his morals questionable, but his wealth made her uneasy. The military truck she'd spotted at her front curb had turned out to be the sort of vehicle billionaires drove to their ski chalets in

Aspen. And the restaurant he'd selected for their outing was the fanciest, priciest eatery in Arlington. Allison had read a review of Reynaud in the *Gazette* a few months ago. It had received three stars, and she'd been unable to identify most of the dishes the critic had named.

Perhaps the food was good, but the maître d' seemed of two minds about whether to let Jamie and Samantha enter. Dressed in a jacket that had to have cost more than Allison's dress, he gazed haughtily at the stroller and then at Jamie. "We don't serve chicken fingers here, you know."

"She won't be eating," Jamie said, adjusting his knapsack higher on his back.

"Nor do we have high chairs available."

"She won't be sitting, either."

The maître d' seemed skeptical. He discreetly signaled a waiter to join him in the dining room's foyer. Solemn and magisterial, they conferred over a seating chart for several minutes, discussing the situation with the intensity of United Nations negotiators working out new boundaries for the West Bank. At last they reached some sort of conclusion; the waiter lifted two leather-bound menus and a wine list and led Allison and Jamie to a table in the farthest corner of the room, near the painted silk screen that disguised the entry to the kitchen.

Allison sank into one of the deep armchairs flanking the table and observed as Jamie maneuvered the stroller against the wall, out of the path of passing waiters. He was dressed with casual elegance, in well-cut khakis, a linen shirt and loafers that looked soft enough to sleep in. Considering his car, his stroller and his choice of a restaurant, she could no longer deny that he was a very rich man.

He didn't *act* rich, though—at least, he didn't act snobbish. There was a tinge of self-mockery in everything he did, an ambivalence, a sense that he didn't take anything or anyone—particularly himself—too seriously. He didn't seem spoiled or polished or pedigreed. His hair was too long—not fashionably long, but long the way a man's hair got when he skipped his regular visit to the barber. His nails were short, his hands large and blunt. He just didn't seem upper crust.

Still, his column must earn him a pretty penny. Allison had read it devotedly since the *Arlington Gazette* started publishing it a few years ago, and it never failed to make her laugh. His approach in the column seemed to be that guys were jackasses, but they were so adorable women had to love them in spite of their brainless behavior.

He stashed his backpack on the shelf built into the stroller frame, took his seat across the table from Allison and sent her a smile that seemed to say she was all that mattered. But she wasn't and she knew it. His baby mattered, too. And if he didn't realize that, he was worse than a jackass. He was a lousy father.

"So," he said pleasantly. "Maybe the Daddy School should offer an advanced seminar in how to hire a baby-sitter. No one ever told me you have to reserve them two years in advance."

She understood his comment as attempt to put her at ease—and the fact that he felt it necessary to put her at ease emphasized how uneasy she was.

She wasn't sure what it was about Jamie that made

her nervous. He seemed to be handling the snafu with his baby-sitter well enough, even joking about it. His evening had started out as calamitously as hers: on the drive to the restaurant, he'd told her about Samantha's having soaked through her diaper and all but flooded her crib while he was trying to scrounge a sitter. Yet he seemed as relaxed as Allison was edgy.

It didn't make sense. She was the one used to babies and their demands. She was the one experienced with their bodily functions and their bad timing. Why was she so edgy?

She knew damned well why. She was edgy because of the way his gaze remained on her as if his thoughts were a kiss, his appreciation of her something full and whole and real. She was edgy because no man had looked at her *that* way in a long time, and Jamie wasn't just any man. He wasn't just a new parent, just her student, just a guy who got lucky nine months ago and unlucky nine months later.

He was a smart, funny, undeniably handsome man whose thick, tawny hair was neatly combed despite its length, whose jaw was clean-shaven but whose eyes still wore the shadows of sleepless nights. He was a man who could afford to take a woman to this restaurant—she had to swallow a shriek of protest when she opened the heavy menu to the first page and discovered a list of appetizers that cost more than burgers for two at the diner across the street from the YMCA. He was a man who could make her feel desirable...and desired.

"Other than baby-sitters, how are you doing?" she asked quickly, dismissing that last notion before it could take up permanent residence in her mind.

"Smooth as silk," he said, then let out a self-deprecating laugh. A patron at the nearest table, a good ten feet away, glared at him. "Oops. I guess we're not supposed to laugh here."

Allison leafed through the menu, cringing at the prices, which became more inflated with every page. Despite Grammy's advice, she couldn't bring herself to order the most expensive item. To do so might jeopardize Samantha's financial future. Some day, eighteen years from now, Jamie might find himself saying, "Sorry, Samantha, but college is out of the question. I squandered my life savings taking this nurse out to dinner at Reynaud when you were a baby, so now you'll have to spend the rest of your life bagging groceries at the supermarket."

Allison wondered if he actually ate at restaurants like this all the time or if he was merely trying to impress her. Not only did the menu display exorbitant prices, but the decor was exquisite to the point of disconcerting her. The high-ceilinged room was eerily quiet. Conversations at the other tables were muted. The footsteps of the waiters were muffled by the thick carpet. Elaborate chandeliers dribbled vague light through the room, and the table linens and place settings reeked of opulence. The clink of a crystal glass was jarring in the subdued atmosphere.

"I've never been here before," she finally said, lowering the menu. "You can order for me." Grammy would never condone such passivity, but Allison simply couldn't bring herself to order a forty-dollar entrée.

Jamie closed the menu and smiled. "I've never eaten here before, either," he told her. "Maybe we should have Samantha order for both of us." He peered down at her, then smiled at Allison again. "Would you like to place a bet on when she'll start screeching?"

"She wouldn't dare screech. Not in a dining room like this."

"If that's your bet," he warned, "you're going to lose."

"We could always go somewhere else," she suggested.

Jamie shook his head. "Just because the baby-sitter fell through doesn't mean I have to rearrange my life. We're managing, right? We got past the sentry at the door. We're home free."

"Maybe it's just as well you didn't hire a sitter you knew nothing about," Allison noted. "Leaving your baby with someone you don't know can lead to disaster."

"As opposed to bringing your baby with you," he countered, his smile expanding. "One thing I've learned about Samantha is that everything about her has the potential of turning into a disaster."

Allison smiled indulgently. "It can't all be disastrous. I'll bet you actually enjoy her sometimes, don't you?"

Jamie was spared from answering by the arrival of the waiter, inquiring if they would care to order drinks. Jamie glanced at her. She could hear Grammy's voice in her head, urging her to order an obscenely expensive cocktail. But something in the multicolored splendor of Jamie's eyes—something dangerously seductive, something that reminded her that this was a date and he was an undeniably sexy man—made her opt for safety. "Water would be fine," she said.

Jamie's brows dipped in a slight frown. "Water for me, too," he said, then added, "Also a bottle of the '88 Medoc. Two glasses." When the waiter removed the wine list and departed from the table, Jamie smiled with barely a hint of contrition. "No harm in getting an extra glass," he explained. "You might want a taste."

She hadn't looked at the wine list, but she could imagine what a bottle would cost. Allison hoped he wasn't expecting a reward for spending so much money on her.

With Samantha along, the kind of reward Allison was thinking of was probably out of the question. She ought to be relieved, but for some reason, she wasn't. Jamie was an incredible catch—or at least he would be if he hadn't done whatever he'd done to wind up with a daughter. Even if his eyes weren't so mesmerizing, his physique so lean and strong, his smile so roguish, Allison was a sucker for a man with a sense of humor.

But she was out of her depth with him. She was the working-class daughter of a working-class daughter. She'd grown up on the blue-collar side of Arlington. She didn't know one wine vintage from another. She didn't even know if a Medoc was red or white.

Having Jamie's infant daughter to chaperon them was probably just as well. The baby was sound asleep in her stroller, but her mere presence was enough to ground Allison, to prevent her from losing track of the kind of man Jamie was—and the kind of woman she was. She could admire his impish grin

and his cocky self-assurance, safe in the knowledge
that the evening wasn't going to end in a sweaty
clinch.

"You still haven't answered my question," she
prodded him.

"Do I enjoy Samantha?" He glanced at his slumbering daughter and shrugged. "I'm not sure *enjoy*
is the right word. Her communication skills suck, she
can't play tennis or chess, she has no interest in
books and she has this gross habit of stuffing her
hand in her mouth. *Enjoy?* I don't know."

Allison laughed, then touched her hand to her lips
to stifle the sound before the gentleman at the next
table glared at her. "You should read to her."

"Don't think I haven't tried," he complained.
"Yesterday I tried dissecting the contents of the *Gazette* with her. Not only couldn't she give me a co-
gent explanation for what's going on in Washington
D.C., but she kept kicking the paper. She actually
tore the sports section. I think she's got a talent for
karate."

He *was* enjoying Samantha. If he wasn't, he
wouldn't be able to describe her with such cheery
humor. His eyes wouldn't take on a special glow
when he spoke about her. "You ought to try showing
her books with bright, simple pictures in them."

"Like *Playboy?* I bet she'd like those pictures. I
know I would. Then again, all those naked breasts
might make her wish she was getting the real thing
instead of all that funny-smelling formula."

The sommelier chose that moment to return to
their table with a dusty bottle of wine, two crystal
goblets and his bottle-opening equipment. He wiped
the dust off the bottle, uncorked it, splashed a little

into a spoon-shaped metal receptacle, and poured a taste for Jamie. Jamie sipped and nodded his approval, and the sommelier filled the goblets.

Allison commanded herself not to drink the entire amount. She was going to need her full complement of wits to get through the evening without succumbing to Jamie's sense of humor. He tapped his glass gently against hers, said, "To women who understand babies," and took a sip.

She sipped and realized that Medoc was delicious. Rather than give in to the temptation to sip some more, she decided, for safety's sake, to change the subject. "What about Samantha's mother? Have you done anything to track her down?"

"I filed a report with the police," he told her.

"And what did the police say?"

"They'll do what they can." He sighed, glanced down at Samantha and gave Allison a crooked smile. "I really don't want to spend all evening talking about her. I'm trying very hard to keep a little sliver of myself child-free, if you know what I mean. I've been doing the baby routine every minute of every day since Monday. Maybe we could talk about something else."

"All right."

"Like you, for instance. You seem to know everything important about me—all the disgraceful, humiliating stuff, anyway. I don't know anything about you."

"I have no disgrace or humiliation in my background," she said demurely.

Jamie chuckled. "Right. And you've got a bridge for sale. Why don't you tell me about all the patients you've short-sheeted at the hospital? Or all the drugs you've administered wrong? Or how about that little old lady you kidnapped and locked up in your house?''

"She isn't little," Allison argued. "She's almost as tall as I am. She's my grandmother."

He knew that already. Allison had made the introductions. "She thinks I'm swine."

"She's an interesting judge of character."

The waiter arrived to take their orders. Allison smiled discreetly and said again, "Why don't you order for me, Jamie?"

He studied her over the edge of his menu, looking startled. Such humility was apparently the last thing he expected of her. "All right," he said, turning back to the waiter. "She'll start with an appetizer of escargot, and then—"

"No, no escargot," she interrupted, nudging him under the table with her foot. She might not know much about Continental cuisine, but she knew escargot were snails. At the waiter's questioning look, she explained, "No appetizer. I'm sure the entrée will be more than enough."

Jamie sent her a small, triumphant grin. "Bring her the cold cucumber soup, then," he went on, overruling her comment. "I'll have the lobster-sherry consommé. Mixed greens for both of us. And then she'll have—" he glanced at her again, searching this time for approval "—shrimp risotto with portobello mushrooms?"

She nodded, grateful that snails weren't involved.

"And for me, the swordfish with grilled vegetables."

"Very good, sir," the waiter said, staring down his patrician nose at the stroller and sniffing in disapproval. He took the menus and moved away from the table, cutting a wide route to avoid accidentally brushing the stroller handle.

"You don't like snails?" Jamie asked, his gaze mischievous.

She made a face. "I've never tasted them. I don't even like the idea of them."

"And here I thought you were open-minded."

"I'm not," she said, then realized how true that was. She was so eager to dislike Jamie because of the circumstances surrounding his paternity, she wasn't really giving him a chance.

"Why did you bring me here?" she asked. "You don't have to spend a fortune to impress me."

"Oh, I didn't bring you here to impress you," he assured her. "I brought Samantha here to impress her, and I brought Samantha to impress you—or maybe I brought you to impress her. But tell me more about you," he said before she could retreat to the safe topic of Samantha. "You actually live with your grandmother?"

"I actually do."

"Doesn't that put a crimp in things?"

What things? she wondered. Her sex life?

Why did that have to be the first thought that entered her mind?

"I like living with my grandmother," she answered. "She has some health problems, and I don't like the thought of her living alone. I'm able to stay out of her way enough that she doesn't realize I'm keeping an eye on her. And she's fun."

"I'll bet," he said, grinning crookedly. "It must be fun having her cut down your friends to their faces. Does she give all your gentleman callers a hard time?"

Allison should have guessed that he had a specific destination in mind for this conversation. He wanted to know about her "gentleman callers."

There simply wasn't much to tell. She'd had one big love in her life, and she'd tried to make it work, but after two years of trying, she'd concluded that she was trying a heck of a lot harder than Frank was, so she'd told him to take a hike. Since then, she'd kept herself too busy to be available for another heartbreak, another occasion where she did all the giving and got too little in return.

"Grammy gives everyone a hard time," she said tactfully.

Samantha made a peeping noise. Jamie glanced nervously at the stroller, but the baby fell silent and he looked up again. "See? This is why men don't understand women. They never say what they mean."

"Me or Samantha?"

"Both."

"She said what she meant," Allison countered. "So did I. For that matter, so did my grandmother."

The waiter approached the table with bowls of soup. Allison knew Jamie had ordered too much food, but the soup looked delicious. She took a small sip and sighed. It tasted even better than it looked.

"Good, isn't it," Jamie confirmed. "Here, try some of mine." He dipped his spoon into his consommé and extended it across the table. She parted her lips and he slid the spoon between them.

The gesture brought him close to her, and the intimacy of the moment unnerved her.

The soup tasted heavenly, warm and piquant, subtly rich with flavors she couldn't name but responded to with a shiver of pleasure. Jamie's gaze locked with hers, burned into her, made her drunk on the sherry in the broth. Suddenly she was ravenous—but not for soup or shrimp risotto or anything else on the overpriced menu. She was hungry for...things. Acts. Human contact.

Jamie McCoy.

An ear-splitting screech shattered the moment.

Throughout the elegant room, diners turned to gape. For a crazed instant, Allison believed they were staring at *her,* shocked by the passion she knew was shimmering in her eyes and darkening her cheeks. But then she realized they were staring at the source of the screams.

Samantha howled. She hooted. She hollered. Inside that small, soft infant lurked a sound system to rival the concert amps of a heavy-metal rock band. Allison glanced up toward one of the shimmering chandeliers, afraid the crystal would shatter from Samantha's shrill wails.

Cursing under his breath, Jamie dropped his spoon and dove for the stroller. He lifted his red-faced daughter into his arms awkwardly, trying to contain her squirming. She pawed at his face, grabbed at his collar, opened her toothless little mouth and bellowed.

Waiters from all over the room amassed into a tuxedo-clad army to descend upon the noisy invader. "Take her," Jamie whispered, rising from his chair and all but tossing Samantha into Allison's arms. She'd barely caught the child when he was on his knees, rummaging through his knapsack.

"Shh," she murmured, struggling to arrange her linen napkin around the baby to protect her dress. "Shh."

Samantha flailed. She sweated. Her scant eyelashes spiked into tiny points from her tears. Her hands groped Allison's hair, quickly becoming ensnared in the tangled locks.

"Here," Jamie said, stalking behind Allison's chair and trying to poke the nipple of a bottle into Samantha's pulsing mouth. "Maybe she's hungry."

"Jamie, I—" A dribble of moisture seeped through the fabric of her dress to her shoulder. She didn't know if it was formula or Samantha's tears. She tried to wrestle the baby down into her lap, but Samantha's hands were shackled by Allison's dense tresses.

Jamie dug his hands into her hair, laboring to extricate the baby's sticky fingers. She clamped her mouth shut to keep from yelping in pain as he tugged at the locks. Under other circumstances, she might love having him weave his fingers through her hair, but not with a baby shrieking into her ear and yanking fistfuls from her scalp.

She poked the bottle into Samantha's mouth. After a minute, Samantha began to suckle and the room fell silent. Sighing, Allison glanced up to see the maître d', three waiters, a bus boy and the sommelier gathered around the table, looking distinctly peeved.

"She was hungry," Jamie explained, smoothing Allison's hair down along her shoulders.

"That sort of outbreak disturbs the other diners," the maître d' chided in his expensive nasal voice.

"Well, having you guys all hovering over our table disturbs me," Jamie said mildly. "Why don't you all go back to whatever you were doing? Every-thing's under control here.''

The maître d' dismissed his staff with a crisp nod, then glowered a moment longer at Jamie, Allison and the baby. He rotated on the heel of his patent leather loafer and stalked off.

''Pompous ass,'' Jamie muttered.

''It's his job to be a pompous ass,'' Allison com-mented. ''And frankly, I think your claim that we have everything under control was a bit optimistic.''

''She's eating,'' he argued. ''Look at her. She's as happy as a clam. As quiet as a clam, too.''

''She'll be as wet as a clam by the time she's done with this bottle.''

''She'll calm down. She was just jealous because we're eating this incredible soup and she's stuck with the all-purpose neonatal cocktail. If I had to drink soya-protein deluxe day in and day out, I'd be screaming, too.''

Allison lowered her gaze to the baby in her arms. She really didn't want to be feeding Samantha. She wanted to turn the clock back five minutes, to be drawn into Jamie's charismatic gaze, to be running her tongue over the spoon where his tongue had just been.

Her pulse gradually slowed. Her cheeks cooled and reason returned. No, she *didn't* want to be think-ing erotic thoughts about Jamie. She wanted to hang on to her sanity.

Samantha began to relent, her mouth working the latex nipple in a slower rhythm. Her hands relaxed and curled, and Allison was able to pull from them the strands of hair caught between the tiny fingers. Samantha's eyes closed and her respiration grew deeper. "I think she's falling asleep," Allison murmured.

"Don't forget to burp her."

"You don't have to burp a baby after every feeding," Allison said. "If she's asleep, there's no need to wake her just to burp her."

"Really? I didn't know that."

Samantha let out a faint snore. Her lips stopped moving on the bottle. Allison left the nipple in her mouth, just for the tranquility it provided. With the baby held securely on her lap with her left hand, she reached for her spoon with her right and took another taste of her soup.

"You don't have to eat with her on your lap," Jamie said.

"She might wake up if we move her."

"We'll do it carefully." He wheeled the stroller over to Allison's chair, then plucked the bottle from Samantha's mouth. The baby started slightly, and he set the bottle back against her lips. But then she sighed and turned her face from the nipple.

"Okay," he mouthed, lifting the bottle again and placing it into the stroller. "I'm going to lift her very slowly." He reached his large, strong hands around Samantha's torso while Allison supported Samantha's head. His fingers wedged under the baby, brushing Allison's thighs. She tried to ignore the tingle generated by his touch. It meant nothing, she reminded herself. He was only trying to pick up his baby. It had nothing to do with her.

He lifted Samantha a fraction of an inch. His pinkie was caught on Allison's napkin, and she tried to ease it out of his clasp. The baby's head moved slightly, but Allison kept it propped up with her hand. With excruciating caution, Jamie raised Samantha another inch, and another, closer and closer to the stroller.

Abruptly Samantha's eyes flew open. She opened her mouth and let loose with the longest, loudest, most thunderous burp Allison had ever heard.

And when the burp had ended, Samantha smiled and spit out a horrifying cascade of semidigested formula across Allison's dress.

CHAPTER SEVEN

"I'M REALLY SORRY," Jamie said for the fifteenth time.

Allison plucked the damp green fabric away from her thighs and sighed. "It's okay, Jamie. Stuff happens."

"Yeah, but it happened all over you."

She shrugged. "It'll wash out. This dress is machine washable."

"And I'm going to wash it," he declared with such conviction she had to suppress a laugh.

If she thought objectively about the situation, she would have to concede that it was anything but laughable. Her first major date since forever had ended with a baby upchucking all over her, followed by the restaurant's snooty wait staff all but kicking her, Jamie and the baby out of the restaurant. Never had the maître d' been more solicitous: "Would the lady like to clean herself up before leaving? Might I have the chef wrap up the food you ordered so you can take it with you? Perhaps you would like to take the rest of the wine with you, as well?"

If it weren't for the restaurant's insistence that Jamie use Reynaud as an overpriced takeout joint, Allison might have asked him to drive her straight home. But dinner, packed in microwavable plastic containers and stacked inside a paper bag that Jamie had wedged into the storage space behind the back seat, awaited. He had argued that she couldn't strand him with all that food, and besides, she had to give him the opportunity to salvage the evening.

She'd considered stopping off at home to change her clothes before giving Jamie his chance at salvage work. But if she did that, Grammy would ask too many questions. Jamie managed to convince her that it would be easier for her to come back to his place, borrow a T-shirt and shorts from him and let him run her dress through his washing machine while they ate.

She didn't think it would be easier. But this date was obviously not destined to be easy. Yet the challenge of it whetted her appetite—not just for the gourmet food tucked into the rear of the Range Rover, but for adventure. Risk. Jamie McCoy.

"How are you feeling?" he asked, shooting her a quick glance while he stopped at a red light.

"Clammy."

Behind her, Samantha let out a whimper. She was no doubt feeling clammy, too. She'd spewed her dinner all over herself as well as Allison.

"No one ever told me," Jamie remarked, shifting into gear as the light turned green, "that having a baby was going to be so inconvenient."

"No one ever told you anything about having a baby," Allison remarked. "Having a baby can also be a joy."

Jamie snorted. "I need to keep being reminded of that. It's easy to forget." He steered west toward the fading mauve horizon, an outline of gently rolling hills as the city thinned out. "I will admit there was a moment or two when I almost thought Sam was, I don't know, a gift or something. Something special. Something precious.''

"She *is* precious," Allison said quietly, worried that Jamie might not recognize this.

"I know, I know. But…it was just before I left to pick you up, and I was thinking, okay, even without a baby-sitter, my life hasn't come to an end. I can still do things like a normal guy. I can still take a lady out for dinner. Ha!" he concluded with a snort.

If Allison had had any qualms about going back to his house, his words assuaged them. He had to learn not to resent his baby. He had to learn that "normal" was a very broad concept and that spending a Saturday evening at home with a baby and a female friend was just as acceptable as going out on the town.

Friend. It dawned on her that she was Jamie's friend. When he'd leaned across the table at the restaurant and slipped his spoon into her mouth, she hadn't felt like his friend. "Friend" didn't define the tremor of heat that had seized her at that moment, the shiver of yearning that had rocked her as she'd acknowledged her soul-deep attraction to Jamie.

But few things could squelch desire as effectively as an infant suffering from reflux. Whatever she'd been thinking of Jamie fifteen minutes ago, right now she felt more like his connection with reality—a reality that for the moment entailed being a father to a newborn.

He cruised along a winding two-lane road interrupted by an occasional house or unpaved driveway. This was the ritzy end of town, an area of old farmhouses and modern mansions seated on vast acreage. As recently as fifty years ago, most of the estates on the western outskirts of Arlington were working farms. But then word had reached frazzled New York City dwellers that a beautiful rural paradise existed in western Connecticut, less than a two-hour drive from their crowded apartments, and people began to buy the properties for weekend retreats. Old farmhouses became "antique restorations" and tripled in value.

Most of the estates were vacation homes, but some were occupied year-round. Some of the city folk fell so deeply in love with Arlington's environs that they gave up their city apartments and settled in permanently.

Allison couldn't blame them. The western edge of town boasted vast stretches of virgin forest, rolling meadows and stone walls that had stood for hundreds of years. Unlike Allison's neighborhood, where the houses were so close to one another that neighbors could converse from porch to porch without raising their voices, here a person had privacy and the beauty of nature, the sense of what Connecticut must have seemed like a century ago.

Apparently this was where Jamie lived. Allison supposed that if he could patronize a restaurant like Reynaud without balking at the prices, he must be able to afford a residence in the affluent west side of town.

He steered onto a gravel driveway flanked by a split rail fence. At the end of the driveway loomed an oddly sprawling shingled house. At its center was a simple fifties-style ranch, but wings and annexes spread from that center in several directions. The front yard was scruffy grass baking brown in the early summer heat. Random trees dotted the lawn;

the shrubs bordering the house grew unpruned and rambunctious.

Allison loved it.

Jamie navigated around one of the building's wings to a garage, pressed a remote garage door opener and drove inside. "Let me take care of Sammy first," he said as he turned off the engine, "and then we'll get you out of that dress."

His provocative phrasing jolted her. When she met his gaze and saw the devilish glint in his eyes, she realized that he'd chosen his words deliberately. Maybe she didn't feel like his friend, after all.

But before she could turn all huffy and give him a little lecture, he was out of the car, moving to the back seat to unstrap Samantha. For all his teasing, he must have known as well as Allison that with his baby daughter occupying center stage, a seduction was not going to happen tonight. Jokes about Allison's dress were as close as he was going to get.

She let herself out of the car while he hoisted his daughter into his arms. He still didn't seem quite comfortable holding her, but he did a good job of supporting her head even as he leaned over to lift his knapsack from the floor of the rear seat. "Come on in," he called to Allison over his shoulder. "Don't worry about the food—I'll come back for it."

He led her through a mudroom hall into the sort of kitchen that might be featured in a home decor magazine. The room was large and white with state-of-the-art appliances and grand windows overlooking the backyard. Without breaking stride, Jamie continued down a hall to Samantha's bedroom. Allison watched from the open doorway as Jamie carried his daughter into the room, dropping his knapsack en route, yanking the drawer of an old bureau open with his free hand and pulling out a clean outfit. He didn't ask for help and Allison didn't offer it.

Her gaze followed him to a small card table, which he used as a changing table. Despite the prominence of the crib and the menagerie of stuffed animals heaped on the chair in one corner, the room didn't seem like a nursery. The floor was covered in beige carpeting, the window shaded with vertical blinds, the walls bare white. Other than the animals, the only childlike decoration was a mobile of brightly colored helicopters hanging above the crib. A light breeze entered the window, setting the helicopters' rotors in motion.

"I'll be right with you," he promised without turning. He seemed to be struggling to get Samantha into her fresh outfit. It was quite a bout, and Samantha was ahead on points. From her angle, Allison could see Samantha flailing, capturing a forelock of Jamie's hair and yanking on it. He yelped, pried her hand away, and she kicked her feet into his wrist, almost causing him to lose his grip on her.

Allison could no longer resist the urge to help. She crossed the room in time to see Jamie's thumb get snared by the narrow sleeve he'd been trying to wrestle Samantha's arm into. Trying not to laugh, Allison reached over the baby and eased Jamie's thumb free of the soft fabric. The contact of skin against skin almost made her jerk her hand away.

She was used to touching people: holding patients' hands, rubbing their backs, massaging their feet during labor or brushing sweat-damp hair back from their faces. She believed skin contact was essential for patients—even patients who were healthy, as the maternity patients at Arlington Memorial usually were. As a nurse, Allison considered her work physical. She liked the tactile aspects of it, the human interaction.

But this was different. This was a man, a funny, sexy man. And the simple act of extricating his fingers from a garment designed for a child not much larger than his hand suddenly revived all those shivery, tremulous, not exactly friendly sensations she'd experienced in the restaurant.

Rescued from the baby garment, Jamie flashed her a smile of gratitude. "These outfits are ridiculous," he said. "Look at the size of the snaps! I've seen molecules bigger than that."

"Maybe you'd be better at this if you'd grown up playing with dolls," Allison suggested, sliding the baby's arms into the sleeves with no difficulty.

"Yeah, sure. Most guys have undressed Barbie a million times in their imaginations. It doesn't help."

"Barbie isn't a doll," Allison declared. "She's a three-dimensional pinup."

"My point exactly."

Clothed and dry, Samantha puckered her lips and sighed. "Just think, you might be buying Barbie dolls for Samantha someday," Allison said, brushing the gossamer strands of the baby's hair back from her forehead.

"That would be enough to kill the fantasy. I'd rather buy her a dump truck and a set of Star Trek action figures."

"Lucky girl," Allison murmured, grinning at Samantha. "Is that what you'd like? A dump truck and Ferengi?"

Samantha waved her hands toward Allison as if

asking to be picked up. Allison lifted the baby, kissed her cheek and then handed her to Jamie. His eyes seemed focused on Allison as if she'd done something profound, something he needed to learn through observation.

"I guess you want some dry clothes, too," he finally said, tearing his gaze from her. He walked out of the room, motioning for her to follow.

The room he led her to had to be his bedroom. She tried not to dwell on the implications of the king-size platform bed, the plush carpet, the thick beige terry cloth robe hanging from a hook inside the open bathroom door. She tried not to glance past that door to see if he had a sunken tub in the bathroom, a wall full of mirrors, a whirlpool. She didn't want to know, any more than she wanted to know just how soft the array of feather pillows spanning the head of the bed would feel beneath her head, how smooth the sheets would feel against her skin, how well she and Jamie would fit on that broad, inviting mattress.

He was too busy rummaging through the drawers of his Shaker-style dresser to look at her, which was probably just as well. She wouldn't want him to guess at the thoughts that were making her cheeks burn with color—specifically the thought that the only thing that would make his bed look more inviting would be him in it.

"Everything I own is going to be too big on you," he was muttering, slamming one drawer and yanking open another while simultaneously adjusting his grip on his wriggling daughter. "Here—these shorts have a drawstring...and here's a shirt. If you want to wash up, the bathroom's through there." He gestured vaguely with his hand, then fired a grin into the air and raced out of the room.

Maybe he *had* been thinking what she was thinking. Even with Samantha in his arms, maybe he'd been aware of the fact that he and Allison were in his bedroom and that more than once this evening erotic undercurrents had coursed between them. Maybe that awareness unnerved him as much as it unnerved her.

God bless Samantha, she thought, giving the baby full credit for keeping the date from slipping from a PG-13 rating right through R to X. Focusing her mind on the baby to the exclusion of anything else, she worked down the zipper of her dress and shimmied out of the damp garment. Her slip was damp, too, but she couldn't imagine handing the champagne-hued lingerie to Jamie for laundering. Instead, she carried it into his bathroom to rinse in the sink.

No Jacuzzi. No wall of mirrors. His bathroom boasted a feature more startling than that: a wall of glass rising up from the edge of the tub to the ceiling. She stifled a shriek and dove back into the bedroom. For heaven's sake—all she had on were her nylons and a bra and panties the same silky shade as her slip. And she'd marched right into a room with a wall of glass! Someone could have seen her!

Hiding her scantily clad body behind the door, she peeked into the bathroom. No, no one could see her other than perhaps a curious bird. The wall backed onto a dense, sunset-lit forest. Jamie's nearest neighbor must be quite a distance away.

Still, she found it peculiar that his bathroom would be so...exposed. Did he actually shower before that broad stretch of glass? Did he actually stand stark naked in the room, his body on full display?

Why was she thinking about him stark naked, anyway?

She hastily ran her slip under the faucet and then hung it on a towel rack to dry. It looked disconcertingly intimate there, but she wasn't going to carry it through the house in search of a more appropriate drying spot. For lack of a better idea, she left her stockings on the towel rack, too. They hadn't been touched by Samantha's eruption, but Allison would feel bizarre wearing them under a pair of athletic shorts.

Returning to his bedroom, she slipped Jamie's T-shirt over her head. The neckline was too wide and the sleeves fell past her elbows, but the soft gray cotton cuddled her. The shirt had undoubtedly been washed countless times—which implied that Jamie had worn it countless times. Maybe he'd sweated in it. Maybe he'd slept in it.

Maybe she needed to get back to focusing on Samantha real fast.

The shorts were gray cotton, too, and much too big, although she was able to cinch the drawstring tightly enough to keep them from sliding down her hips. She inspected her reflection in the mirror and decided she looked markedly less attractive than she had in the clinging green dress. The shorts came all the way down to her knees, and the shirt was so baggy she could swim laps inside it. It would take some clever guessing for a man to realize a full-grown, postpubescent woman was lurking inside all that fabric.

She pulled a comb from her purse and attempted

to neaten her hair, then gave up and padded barefoot out of the bedroom, bringing her dress with her. The mouthwatering aroma of food beckoned her down the hall. Reaching the kitchen, however, she found herself alone. The bag the restaurant had packed with their take-home dinners stood on a counter near the microwave oven, which was in use, but Jamie was nowhere in sight.

"Out here," he hollered.

She spun around and spotted the screened porch adjacent to the kitchen. He was on the porch, still dressed in his tailored slacks and crisp white shirt, although he'd rolled the sleeves up to his elbows. He leaned over a glass-topped table to arrange place mats and silverware before the two cushioned chairs that faced each other across the table.

Allison abandoned the warm tiles of the kitchen floor for the cool cement of the porch and inhaled another delicious aroma—the tart pine scent of the surrounding forest. Nearing the table, she noticed that the place mats featured scenes from Road Runner cartoons. Not exactly the classy ambiance of Reynaud, but frankly, Allison felt more at home with cartoons than with damask tablecloths and heavy sterling flatware.

"Where's Samantha?" she asked.

"The little twit," he muttered, placing a wineglass at each place mat. "Now she's asleep again. She waits until she's ruined everything and then she zones out."

"She didn't ruin everything," Allison argued.

He straightened up and turned to her. His gaze skimmed the length of her, scrutinizing her ridiculous, ill-fitting outfit. After reaching her bare feet he reversed direction, inspecting her calves, the drooping length of the shorts, the voluminous drape of the shirt and her disheveled hair. Closing his eyes, he shook his head and chuckled. "She ruined your dress," he remarked.

"No, she didn't. We just have to get it into the laundry."

"Laundry." He pulled the sodden green garment from her grip and strode into the kitchen. She followed, aware that he could ruin her dress more effectively than Samantha could. Allison couldn't believe a man so inept with a baby could handle a laundry chore without shrinking or bleaching or otherwise destroying what he was washing.

The laundry room extended off the kitchen, a narrow alcove scarcely big enough for two adults standing side by side. To give him more room—and to keep from hovering and micromanaging his efforts with the washing machine—she remained in the doorway, poised to leap into the fray the moment she felt a genuine threat to her dress.

He studied the dial settings on the machine intently. "I use soap, right?" he finally asked.

Her dress was definitely under threat. "Let me do it," she offered, venturing a step into the crowded room.

"No, no—I can do it. I was just checking."

"You were just checking whether to use detergent?"

"Detergent," he repeated, sending her a smile of amazement. "You know what I've learned since Sam's arrival? Soap and detergent are two different things. My neighbor Gloria told me not to use detergent when I washed baby clothes. She raised three

kids and they all survived to adulthood, so I figure
she knows more about this stuff than I do.''

Everyone knew more about that stuff than Jamie
did, Allison thought, though she kept her mouth shut.

"My suspicion is, women get obsessed with these
nuances so they'll feel like experts. Soap and detergent are probably the same thing, but if men figured
it out, women couldn't act as if they were wiser than
men.''

"Women *are* wiser than men in everything that
counts," Allison declared. "Let me do the dress."

He pressed against the wall, leaving her a few
inches of wiggling room to reach the washing machine. She felt the warmth of his body at her back,
the brush of his thighs against her bottom as she
wedged past him. The brief, inadvertent contact
caused heat to waft through her, treacherously soft
and intimate, like the too comfortable cotton of his
shirt against her skin. She narrowed her attention to
the array of buttons and dials adorning the top of his
washing machine.

There was nothing sexy about adjusting the settings, measuring the detergent, placing her dress into
the machine and pressing the On button. Nothing seductive about the white washing machine and its fra-
ternal-twin white dryer. Nothing the least bit amorous about the tangy scent of the detergent, the
churning rush of water into the machine, the glare of
the fluorescent light above her head.

Yet she was afraid to turn around, because once
she did she would be unable to avoid Jamie. He was
just inches behind her, much too close. The room
seemed electric with his presence, the air humming
with ominous energy.

Well, she couldn't spend the next thirty minutes pressed against his washing machine while it cranked through the cycles. Drawing in a deep breath, she spun around. He was as close as she'd feared, gazing at her with as much potent fascination as he had at Reynaud.

His eyes weren't smiling, though. The glow in his eyes was serious. Wicked but deadly serious. For a moment she found herself unable to move.

The clank of the washing machine jolted her nervous system back to normal. Jamie turned and sauntered out of the laundry room, heading straight for the microwave. "Can you grab the wine?" he asked, gesturing toward the breakfast table by the windows, where the open bottle of wine from the restaurant stood. He began to pull containers of heated food from the oven and arranged them on a tray.

Allison picked up the bottle. It might be the only thing he asked of her tonight that she could do without getting herself into trouble. She led the way out to the screened porch, holding the door open for him as he carried the tray of steaming food to the table.

The wine was poured, the plastic dishes distributed on the Road Runner place mats, and she and Jamie took their seats. She found herself less troubled than she ought to be under the circumstances. She was seated in a near stranger's house, wearing his clothes and feeling longings she wasn't accustomed to, longings that could lead to disaster when they centered on a roguish man with bedroom eyes who had accidentally fathered a child he was shamefully ill-equipped to handle, a child who had less than an hour ago regurgitated all over Allison in a three-star restaurant.

Molly would never believe this.

Grammy probably would. But then, Grammy had a unique way of looking at the world.

Seated across the table from Jamie, exerting herself to resist the dazzle of his gaze, Allison had the distinct impression that her own way of looking at the world was about to undergo a few alterations.

HE HAD NEVER realized that a woman in old, baggy workout clothes could look sexier than a woman in a hot little minidress. Something about the vision of Allison in his clothing made Jamie imagine Allison in his bed, in his shower, in his arms—and definitely *not* in his old, baggy workout clothes.

He dug into his food, rummaging through his memory for a safe topic of conversation. If he didn't start talking soon, he was going to vault over the table and kiss her silly. And he'd already botched enough of this evening to be extremely cautious about putting any fast moves on her. Making a major play for her while she was stuck in his house while his daughter's barf was being laundered out of her dress didn't seem like the right thing to do.

Not that he'd ever been all that concerned about doing the right thing, but he knew that if he pushed, Allison would push right back. She struck him as the sort of woman who knew how to protect herself from any man who dared not to do the right thing.

"So, what do you think of those Red Sox?" he asked.

Allison laughed. "I think baseball is boring."

Well, that sure lowered the flame under his libido. Any woman who considered baseball boring wasn't worth risking a bloody nose over. Even if she did have all that phenomenal hair spilling around her face and down her back, as thick and enticing as Lady Godiva's, and even if her hands were milky white and slender, and even if her eyes were just a bit too wide, too pure, too tempting a mixture of innocence and wariness...

Hey, if the lady couldn't appreciate baseball, what did he want with her?

Besides *that,* of course.

"Tell me about your column," she said. "I've read it—it's really funny. How did you get started?"

All right. He'd concede first place in the conversational gambit contest to her. Being able to make charming chitchat was one of those gender specific traits, like knowing the difference between soap and detergent. It came naturally to women.

But she'd given him a good opening, and he stepped through it willingly. "When I graduated from college," he said, "I took a job in the business department of the *Arlington Gazette* because they'd come to my college to recruit and I must have failed to unimpress them the way I'd unimpressed every other recruiter who came to campus. My job was in subscriptions. I was supposed to call people up and badger them. It's the sort of job you get when you're completely unprepared for any other job. I got hung up on a lot."

"That must have been rewarding," she said with a smile.

"Anyway, I did some writing on the side. The newspaper had a central computer system, and once when I thought I was deleting some inane jottings, I accidentally sent them into the great virtual stew, and they materialized on an editor's monitor. Next thing

I knew, I was called in to some muck-a-muck's office. I figured they were going to fire me for writing comic anecdotes on the job, but they told me to give them fifteen columns—they wanted to see if I had more than one week's worth of stuff in me. Apparently I do. I can make up a thousand words on any subject.''

"You're fortunate," she said. "Not that you can write on any subject, but that you stumbled into such a nice career.''

"It isn't nice," he corrected her. "Newspaper work is dirty and corrupting. Humor writing devours the soul. Making people laugh is a foul way to make a living.''

She laughed, and there was nothing foul about it. Her laughter was light and airy, like a breeze dancing through clover. Only breezes and clover didn't turn him on, and Allison's laughter did. "Tell me about you," he requested, wondering if she could hear the tightness in his throat, a reflection of the tightness in his groin. "How did you become a nurse?''

"My mother was a nurse, and my grandmother.''

"Family trade, huh.''

"That alone wouldn't have been enough," she went on. "I'm a nurse because I love the work. People...'' She paused to sort her thoughts. "People don't spend enough time and energy caring for other people. As a nurse, that's exactly what I do. I take care of others. I like it. It's necessary and it fulfills me. I know that makes me sound like some sort of saint, but I'm not.''

"I'm glad to hear you're not a saint," he remarked, then grinned as color flooded her cheeks.

"What I meant was, I'm a nurse for selfish reasons—because it makes me feel good doing things for others, taking care of others.''

''Why babies?''

''They need more care than just about anyone else.''

''I'm not so sure about that,'' he said. Through the porch's screen and the open window of Samantha's room, he heard a thin cry, as if the kid felt it necessary to refute him with a reminder of how high-maintenance babies could be. ''I'd better go check on her,'' he said, actually a bit relieved to get away from Allison until he could subdue the urge to ravish her with kisses.

Samantha had fallen back to sleep by the time he reached her crib. On those rare occasions when she was clean and dry and quiet, she didn't seem to demand much, and he felt adequate as a father. But when she was wet and fussy and obtrusive, he could appreciate the way Allison took care of her, never losing her temper or her poise. He wondered whether she liked taking care of men as much as babies.

En route back to the porch, he detoured to the laundry room. The washing machine had shut off, and he transferred her dress to the dryer. He reread the instructions printed on the inside of the lid—he was better at drying clothes than washing them, and he'd had a great deal of practice using both machines over the past week, but it didn't hurt to brush up. He doubted that shrinking Allison's dress was the quickest way to get her into his bed.

Back in the kitchen, he spied on her through the porch door. She was standing, gazing beyond the screened walls at the bucolic vista surrounding his yard. Usually he would be admiring that vista as well, appreciating the rose and lavender streaks left behind by the setting sun.

Right now, however, he had a more appealing vista: the sight of a tall, slim woman with a cascade of copper-tinged curls spilling down her back. The borrowed male clothes she wore only emphasized her femininity. And her bare feet...oh, yes. Her bare feet were slim and pink and unbelievably pretty.

She turned as he pushed open the porch door, and he saw she was holding her wineglass, which was nearly empty. He tried not to take her wine consumption as a gauge of how lucky he was going to get tonight.

"Is everything okay?" she asked.

He wondered for a moment whether he looked as if everything *wasn't* okay, then realized she was asking about Samantha. "She was just talking in her sleep," he reported. "Telling all her nasty little secrets. Too bad she doesn't speak English."

"You were gone awhile."

"I put your dress in the dryer. Thirty minutes and you could be out of here if you wanted."

She smiled hesitantly. "Is that a hint?"

He approached her slowly, not wanting to spook her. "I don't do hints well. Subtlety isn't my long suit."

"I noticed."

"So if I wanted to get rid of you, I'd say, 'Gee, Allison, why don't you wear your dress wet?' Although, come to think of it, I bet if you put that dress on wet, I'd never want you to leave." Like now. Like the way she wore his shirt and shorts, her eyes so wide and luminous as she gazed at him, her cheeks still flushed with telltale pink. He never wanted her to leave.

He saw a tinge of panic in those beautiful, expressive eyes, but she bravely lifted her glass to her lips and took another sip. As he moved a step closer, she took another sip and discovered that her glass was empty. She glanced down at the goblet, scowling as if it had betrayed her.

"I have more wine," he offered.

"No, thanks."

Before she could scoot past him to place the glass on the table, he took it from her and set it down on the nearest end table. He could reach her easily now; she was less than an arm's length from him.

"Jamie...?" Her voice twisted up into a question.

"You are the sexiest nurse I have ever known," he said, resting his hands on her shoulders.

To her credit, she didn't flinch. "How many nurses have you known?"

"Billions. Maybe trillions."

"Oh, my. Trillions," she said, her speech accelerating, her voice rising again. It was the only sign of how nervous he was making her. He wished she would relax, because he had a pretty good idea that she wanted exactly what he wanted. She just didn't seem sure how to accept that wanting, whether to rush headlong into it or flee.

All right, then. He would do the rushing. If she fled, she fled, but he hoped to heaven she wouldn't.

His hands tightened slightly on her shoulders, and he drew her toward him. "You're not going to make a pass at me, are you?" she asked, her eyes meeting his, searching his face.

"As a matter of fact," he said, proving exactly how unsubtle he could be, "I am."

CHAPTER EIGHT

KISSING ANY MAN would have been a novelty for Allison after such a long stretch of celibacy. But kissing Jamie was unlike anything she'd ever experienced before. His hands were both rough and tender, gentle enough to cradle a baby but awkward in their gentleness. His eyes were blindingly bright, a dazzle of silver and emerald barely dimmed by his lowered lids. And his lips...oh, his lips.

His kiss was strong the way a wind could be strong. You couldn't see it, but you could feel the strength of it, be moved by it, be caught up or knocked down or torn apart by it. You could stand your ground, resisting its fierce pull, or you could yield to the tempest and let it carry you away.

She yielded, letting the sensation storm inside her, deep and swirling, creating tiny whirlwinds and eddies that spun her emotions until she was reeling, her balance undermined. She leaned back and found Jamie's arms wrapped around her, holding her up, protecting her from the very force he had unleashed within her.

He had such strong arms.

His entire body seemed strong. Not uncomfortably tall, not overly muscular, but solid as granite and utterly male. His shoulders were broad, his chest sleek, his waist trim. His hips were a few inches away from hers, although that narrow space didn't make her feel at all safe. Then again, how safe could a woman be with a gale-force wind whipping at her from inside and the most heavenly mouth caressing her lips from the outside? She was clearly under siege.

And she loved it.

"I've been wanting to do this ever since the first time I saw you," he murmured.

"The first time you saw me, you were barging into my class ten minutes late."

"That's right." Even though he was smiling, he continued to kiss her, touching his lips to her cheek, the corner of her mouth, the tip of her nose. "If I'd had any decency—which I don't—I would have been thinking about what a terrible thing it was to be late for class. But all I could think of was that you were beautiful, like a skinny Botticelli angel."

She ought to have been insulted. But she laughed instead. "I'm not skinny."

"Compared to Botticelli, you are. Those Renaissance angels could have used a bit of liposuction and a three-month membership at the local gym."

"You really think I'm skinny?"

"I think you're perfect." He freed his hand from the heavy fall of her hair and trailed his fingers down her back until he reached the hem of the T-shirt, which he lifted to stroke the skin at her waist. The light friction of the contact dazzled her.

Slowly, seductively, he moved his hand higher, tracing each ridge and indentation along her spine, the hollows on either side of it, the curve beneath her shoulder blades, the span of her bra strap. His

hands were broad and hard, and his caresses seemed
to burn right through her flesh.

She was going to have to take a breath soon. If
she concentrated, she might recall how that particular
life skill was performed. But before her memory
could clarify itself, his mouth was covering hers
again, coaxing her lips apart, her teeth. His tongue
filled her mouth with a hungry surge, and she decided
remembering how to breathe wasn't really all that
important, after all.

Anyone who could create such torrid sensations
with his kisses ought to be avoided. Jamie was dangerous. But she couldn't draw away from him. The
deep thrusts of his tongue, the erotic play of his fingers against her skin, the light yet insistent pressure
of his hips against hers, sucked her into the eye of
the storm, luring her into that magnificent center
where nothing but Jamie existed. No logic, no self-
preservation, no accidental pregnancies. Just Jamie
McCoy.

Wait a minute. That last item *did* exist, and Allison
would be wise to remember it. He'd gone on a Caribbean vacation and met a woman, and if he'd used
precautions, he'd used them carelessly. And now
there was a baby.

That was the kind of man Jamie was.

It hurt to break from him, but Allison found the
strength to lean away. Her respiratory instincts took
hold as she pulled deep lungfuls of air into her body.
Her mind resumed functioning and she regained her
bearings. She was standing barefoot on a screened
porch in Jamie's house, wearing Jamie's clothes,
feeling Jamie's arms tight around her and seeing his

eyes spill their yearning silver light down into her face.

"We can't do this," she murmured.

"We can't?"

She shook her head and tried to swallow her regret. If she made the slightest move to slip out of his embrace, she was sure he would let go of her. The problem was, she didn't want him to let go. She wanted to hurl herself back into the hurricane, to forget everything she was supposed to remember and let him have his way with her.

As if it sensed her ambivalence, the dryer announced the end of its cycle with a loud buzz. "My dress is done," she said.

Jamie didn't move. He obviously didn't care that her dress was done. He brushed a light kiss on her forehead, then leaned back and peered into her face. "Okay. Tell me why we can't do this. Have I overwhelmed you with my charm?" he guessed, his grin indicating that he knew exactly how charming he was.

"I'm not sure *overwhelmed* is the word I'd use." Even if it was damned close to the truth, she conceded silently.

He regarded her in the dim light, his smile beckoning. "Maybe it's because you don't believe in kissing a guy on the first date—except that it's too late to throw that one at me. We've already kissed."

"Jamie—"

"Or that you don't think it's right to develop a personal relationship with your students. God knows, if this thing goes any further, I could bring charges of sexual harassment against you. Although I promise I won't if you give me an A."

She smiled in spite of herself. "Jamie—"

"Because I could drop out of Daddy School if that would make things easier for you. We could do private tutorials. No one would have to find out."

If he didn't have that deliciously wicked grin, if his pleas were truly serious, she would have jerked free from his embrace and stalked off in a huff. She didn't like pushiness in a man, especially when the pushiness was about sex.

But she knew Jamie was only kidding, disguising his disappointment behind a few jokes. Graceful in defeat, he didn't deserve to be castigated. "Let's back up a bit, okay? No, I don't usually kiss guys on first dates."

"But this first date is an exception, right? Or should I say it's exceptional? Now there's a term that works for me."

"I hardly know you," she said tactfully. "And what I do know isn't all good."

He seemed to take her words less as a criticism than a dare. "You only kiss men who qualify as all good?" he asked. "Gee. You must not kiss very often."

"Maybe I don't," she said bluntly.

Her comment seemed to take him aback, but it didn't scare him off. He loosened his hold on her, sliding his hands up to her shoulders and then down her arms until his hands were clasping hers. "All right. I'm taking things too fast for you. No problem. I can downshift." He wove his fingers loosely through hers. "Tell me what's so bad about me. Besides the fact that I came late to class and I'm so irresistible that despite my baby's unruly behavior at the restaurant, you tossed your principles out the window and kissed me on our first date.''

She sighed. If she told him the truth, she would come across as sounding like a judgmental prig. But lying seemed pointless. ''It's not your baby's behavior. It's just your baby, period. You're an out-of-wedlock father. You had a child with a woman you don't even know.''

''Oh. Right.'' His smile faded. ''I guess that would make me irredeemably evil.''

''I didn't say you were evil. I just think maybe...well, you were a little thoughtless. I mean, in this day and age—''

''You're absolutely right,'' he agreed a bit too briskly. ''Caveat emptor. Let the buyer beware. It was my own fault for not realizing I was using a defective condom. Forgive me, for I have sinned.''

''I didn't say—''

''No need to get defensive, Allison. You're right. I was a bad boy and I deserve to be punished. Castration might be good for starters.'' His hands dropped from her and he took a step backward, forcing her to realize why she hadn't moved back herself. She didn't like losing the warmth of his arms around her. She didn't like losing the warmth of his smile.

''Jamie, I never said—''

''No, you're right. We're in complete agreement, sweetheart. I'm about ten notches below scum of the earth. I did a very naughty thing.''

''You shouldn't kid about it, Jamie. I didn't say it was a naughty thing, but—''

''But it isn't good.''

She sighed. She *had* come across as a judgmental prig, and Jamie was obviously infuriated. His eyes had lost their lovely radiance; his playful grin had transformed into a harsh frown.

Yet she wasn't entirely wrong. Judgmental, yes, but the truth was, Jamie had made a serious mistake nine months ago, and she wasn't sure he recognized it. Still, as severely as she was judging Jamie, she had to do something to rescue the moment. "What happened happened," she allowed. "And maybe what happened wasn't good. But it resulted in Samantha, so maybe it wasn't all bad, either."

"Meaning what? Samantha is cute, so maybe I'm only five notches below the scum of the earth?"

Allison had done her best to sprinkle water on the burning tinder, but Jamie seemed determined to fan it into a bonfire with his sarcasm. It was her turn to frown, her turn to purse her lips with impatience.

Maybe he *hadn't* come to terms with what he'd done. Maybe Samantha wasn't quite real to him. She was a collection of body fluids and whimpers, an assortment of tiny outfits and enormous needs. Maybe Jamie was already planning to give her up for adoption. Maybe he believed the police were going to locate the mysterious mother and return the baby to her.

And maybe Allison's imagination was running wild, just as minutes ago her passion had been running wild. Jamie had the ability to throw her mind and her heart out of kilter with his kisses and his screwed-up logic.

"I don't think you're taking me seriously," she said, wishing she could come up with a better argument. Jamie was the one blessed with wit and a flair with words. Allison was just a nurse who cared too much about babies.

"Of course I'm taking you seriously," Jamie retorted, pushing his hair back from his brow with a restless hand. "You seriously think I'm an evil man for having slept with a woman in Eleuthera. You seriously think it was all my fault. My fault that the woman from Eleuthera decided she wanted nothing to do with me. My fault she's hidden herself so successfully neither the police nor I have any idea who she is, let alone where to find her. You know how it is with guys. We're goofs. We're irresponsible turkeys. The instant you leave, I'm going to stick Sam back in that baby seat of hers, leave her on the deck where I found her and hope some kinder, nobler person will come along and take her away."

"I didn't say that!"

"You thought it."

How had the mood become so hostile? Was Jamie assailing her with his anger simply because she wasn't ready to tumble into his bed? What had happened to the funny, wonderfully sexy man she'd been kissing?

He'd become defensive, and apparently he believed that the best defense was a good offense. If getting Allison into bed wasn't in the cards for him, he might as well lash out at her.

Well, maybe she wasn't as clever as he was. But she wasn't going to stand quietly by while he assailed her with his scathing words. Whether or not Samantha's conception was *his* fault, it certainly wasn't *hers,* and she wasn't going to let him take his frustrations out on her.

"Are you done?" she muttered. "Because I'd like to put on my dress and leave."

"I'll get your dress," he snapped none too graciously. Before she could stop him, he stalked into the house, abandoning her on the porch.

In his absence, she felt the stillness close around her, cold and hollow. She closed her eyes and breathed deeply, willing away her own seething anger. When she opened her eyes once more, her vision took in the leavings of their delightful dinner: the wineglasses, the plastic containers, the plates, the silly place mats.

Tears stung her eyes. She had never before given any consideration, pro or con, to Road Runner place mats. But now she couldn't imagine a finer way to decorate a table.

Or maybe she just loved the place mats because of Jamie's company.

All right. So her hot date had gone down the drain. At least she'd learned something valuable about Jamie and about the slim-to-none possibility that she and he could ever have a relationship. He was Samantha's father, and he hadn't the foggiest idea what that meant. As useful as Allison's Daddy School class might be to him, she couldn't teach Jamie that vital lesson. The only way a man could learn what it meant to be a father was to find the truth for himself.

Until Jamie McCoy did that, Allison couldn't allow herself to be a part of his life.

"YOU BLEW IT, AL," Molly summarized.

Twelve hours had passed since she'd left Jamie's house wearing her newly laundered dress and sitting silently, stiffly next to him as he drove her home. She'd spent just about every waking minute of those twelve hours analyzing the time she'd spent with him, and she'd come to the same conclusion as Molly: she'd blown it.

She was in the kitchen of Molly's condominium, a cozy, bright first-floor unit in a town house complex. Molly's older sister, Gail, was there, as well. Gail had dropped by to discuss how much money to spend on the flowers they planned to wire their parents for their anniversary. When she'd discovered Allison and Molly hunched over steaming mugs of freshly brewed chocolate-raspberry coffee, she'd decided to stay awhile.

For ten minutes, Molly fretted over how much money she could contribute to the flowers. Gail generally had more money than Molly, since Gail was a lawyer in a world where lawyers were considered more valuable, in dollars and cents, than children and the people who cared for them. But since Gail was the kind of lawyer who specialized in lost causes, she wasn't exactly rich, either.

Clad in faded denim overalls a size too big for her, she *looked* like a lost cause. She tended to favor large, body-disguising clothing when she wasn't at work. Although Allison could see a definite resemblance between the two sisters—both had heart-shaped faces, angled eyes and petite builds—she knew them both well enough to be conscious of their differences, which extended past their coloring. Gail had inherited their mother's fair hair, while Molly took after their dark-haired father; Molly was naturally more bubbly, Gail more reserved.

Both were mercilessly blunt, however. When they'd run out of things to disagree on concerning the flowers, they returned the conversation to the subject of Allison's dismal date with Jamie. Gail nodded at Molly's succinct critique of her performance last night and said, "She's right, Winslow. You blew it. Royally."

"It's not a problem of misunderstandings," Allison tried to explain. "I think we understood each other just fine. I mean…there's an attraction. And I *do* like a lot of things about Jamie. But he resents the fact that I can't view Samantha as a minor inconvenience."

"He said that?" Molly exclaimed. "He thinks she's a minor inconvenience?"

"He didn't say it. But the way he acts sometimes…" Allison shrugged. "He's got an attitude."

"He's a man," Gail summed up, her tone leaving no doubt that men and their attitudes ranked mighty low on her list. "I've read McCoy's newspaper column. You know what it is? A celebration of testosterone with a few jokes tacked on."

"You're being a little harsh," Molly argued. "I think his column is hilarious."

"Of course you do. You spend the better part of every day talking to three-year-olds. A journalistic essay written on a six-year-old level must represent the height of sophistication for you."

"Now, now," Allison mediated. Not that Gail and Molly Saunders really needed her to run interference. They bickered with that special fervor reserved for sisters who passionately adored each other. She realized that Gail's jibe was directed more at Jamie than at Molly. "I don't think his column is that bad, Gail," she argued, venturing politely into the fray. It wasn't that she wanted to leap to Jamie's defense, but she honestly didn't think his column was written with a six-year-old mentality. If his observations sometimes seemed juvenile, his point was that men were juvenile, not that his readers were.

Gail shrugged. "Well, whatever. The man is earning a fortune writing his column, so who am I to say whether his stuff is valid or not? The key issue is, if you never see him again, will you slit your wrists?"

"Of course not." It wasn't as if Allison were in love with him. "But I will see him again. I have to. I have a Daddy School class tomorrow. He'll be there."

"How do you know?" Gail asked as if she were cross-examining a witness. "Maybe he'll drop out."

"Oh, he'll be there," Molly declared with unjustifiable certainty. "I'll bet that deep down he loves his baby and wants to do everything he can for her. He just hasn't figured out how to deal with this unexpected, unfamiliar emotion. Besides, he's rich and he's cute. What more could you ask for?"

"You could ask for someone whose brain is bigger than his gonads."

"Okay," Allison interjected, although the Saunders sisters' argument amused her. "I haven't measured Jamie's gonads. For that matter, I haven't measured his brain. His anatomy isn't the problem. It's the circumstances surrounding his becoming a father."

"Knocking up a total stranger sure doesn't win a guy too many points in my book," Gail remarked.

"It takes two to cause a pregnancy," Molly remarked. "Jamie didn't do it by himself."

"He could have chosen a more compatible woman. I'd say he has lousy taste in women, except that he took Allison out for dinner. What do you think?" Gail asked her. "Are you better off now that you had dinner with him or would you have been better off if you hadn't?''

"I don't know." Allison sighed. "He's so much fun to be with, even when things are going wrong. I could really like him—if I could only get past the baby thing. Which I can't.''

"You know what your problem is?" Gail said. "You're horny. You need a good, sizzling affair. Maybe Jamie's the one to have it with and maybe he isn't. But he sure as heck isn't Mr. Right. Did you read that column he wrote about why guys like professional wrestling? Sheesh. It was stupid.''

"I thought it was funny," Molly argued, shooting her sister an impish smile.

"Gee, I thought I was going to find some tender loving care here," Allison complained, although she was smiling, too. "I could have gotten more useful advice if I'd stayed home with Grammy.''

Molly sprang to her feet and patted Allison on the shoulder. "You want TLC? You got it," she promised, topping off Allison's half-full mug with hot coffee, then pulling a package of chocolate-glazed butter cookies from a cabinet and setting it on the table. "What did Grammy say about your date?''

"Well, I didn't go into all the details," Allison admitted. "But she said she thought he was damned good looking and it was too bad he had the morals of a tick.''

"A tick?" Gail askcd, her eyebrows arching.

Allison grinned. "She was impressed that he managed to wash my dress without destroying it. She was horrified that I could fit into his gym clothes. She figures I either need to lose a few pounds or else I was really lying around the house naked.''

"No!" Molly and Gail chorused, reminding Allison of why she adored the Saunders sisters.

"Anyway," she continued with a shrug, "none of it matters. I *did* wear his gym clothes, and nothing happened that would have required me to lounge around naked, and now I'll have to get through the next few weeks of Daddy School and send him off to cope with his baby."

"What if he signs up for another Daddy School class when this one is done?" Gail asked.

Allison pulled a face. "There won't be another Daddy School class. I'm losing my funding."

"What?" Gail's eyes grew round, her expression indignant.

"The hospital won't fund me after I finish this class. It was an experiment, they said, and now the experiment is going to end."

"Oh, for heaven's sake." Gail drummed her polished nails on the table impatiently. "That's so myopic of them. The program is worthwhile. Molly, weren't you going to branch off into a class for fathers of toddlers?"

"That was the plan," Molly confirmed with a scowl.

"Ridiculous." Allison could almost hear the gears whirring in Gail's head as she assessed this information. "Have you investigated alternate sources of funding?"

"I don't even know how to begin," Allison lamented. "I'm a nurse first, a teacher second. Fundraising is beyond me."

"I'm no expert," Gail said, her pale eyes glinting as if to announce that she was about to set herself up as an expert. "But it seems to me that if you want to raise money, you need to go where the money is. Foundations. Government agencies. Rich people.''

"Like Jamie McCoy," Molly suggested helpfully. "He's rich."

"Oh, great!" Allison rolled her eyes heavenward. "I'm supposed to go to him, tell him I don't want anything to do with him, mention in passing that my grandmother thinks he has the morals of a tick, and oh, by the way, would he mind writing me a check for fifty thousand dollars?''

"Why not?" Molly asked, then laughed.

"*You're* the one who wants to open a second Daddy School class," Allison muttered. "Why don't *you* go hit Jamie McCoy up for money?''

"Because—'' Molly's grin grew sly ''—you're the one who got into his pants.''

"They were shorts," Allison corrected her. "And anyway, I can't possibly go to Jamie for anything. I thought we agreed unanimously that I blew things with him. Royally,'' she added, glaring at Gail.

"Do you want money for your Daddy School or don't you?'' Gail asked.

"If I were that desperate for money, I'd stand on the corner of Althorpe Lane in a pair of leather hot pants and a bustier.''

"Gee,'' Gail said, peering past Allison at Molly. "She really must have the hots for the tick man if she can compare asking him for a donation to becoming a streetwalker.''

Allison groaned. Of course asking for money to keep the Daddy School alive wasn't the same as prostituting herself. She knew that every day, men and women badgered friends, relatives and total strangers for contributions to various causes. Allison had once sent a donation to a museum in Hartford, and that donation had led to her name being added to dozens of mailing lists. Over the next year, she'd received innumerable solicitations to help this or that organization. Zoos, research centers, dance troupes in Seattle, societies for the protection of endangered species in the Gulf of Mexico—all of them hoped she could send a small contribution.

Given that she was supporting both her grandmother and herself, as well as paying off some educational loans, she couldn't afford to endow research centers and art collections on a regular basis. But Jamie... If he could afford dinner for two at Reynaud, he could surely afford a donation to the Daddy School.

If Allison could muster up the guts to ask him.

"You'll see him tomorrow," Molly added, as if she knew Allison needed some help in guts mustering. "After class you could ask him. He probably has rich friends, too. He lives west of town, right? Everyone living on that side of town is rich. Plus he's probably got buddies in the syndicated-columnist business, all those Pulitzer prize winners and the like. Maybe he could convince the *Arlington Gazette* to sponsor the Daddy School."

"Forget that," Gail muttered. "The *Arlington Gazette* is the cheapest, most reactionary publisher in the world."

"I think their news coverage is fair," Allison argued, eager to be distracted from thoughts of Jamie.

"Their coverage of news is okay," Gail allowed. "But the business offices are for the birds. You wouldn't believe their salary scale—especially what they pay their secretaries, who are conveniently all women. There's a class action suit lurking in there somewhere."

"If they pay low salaries, then they must have huge profits," Molly reasoned. "So they could support the Daddy School."

The Saunders sisters' bickering helped diffuse Allison's bitterness over her evening with Jamie. She'd much rather think about the Daddy School's financial problems.

"I'll just go back to the hospital and see if I can squeeze another nickel out of them," she said, aware that a nickel wasn't going to do her much good. Disappointed as she would be if the Daddy School had to end after its current session, she simply could not imagine herself trying to wheedle money from wealthy benefactors.

Especially Jamie. Especially after Allison had kissed him, and fought with him and all but walked out on him.

She couldn't even imagine herself facing him in class tomorrow night. Asking him to support her beloved project with a nice, fat check? That would be impossible.

CHAPTER NINE

GUY STUFF by James McCoy—

I got a call from my mother yesterday. "Jamie," she said—she's the one who tagged me with the nickname, since my father's name is Jim and he kept getting confused during my first few weeks of life, when my mother would say, "Now, Jimmy, stop fussing and put this in your mouth like a good boy...." But I digress.

Anyway, my mother said, "Jamie, I've just met the perfect girl for you."

Sharpen your pencils, folks, put on your thinking caps and follow along with me as I deconstruct that sentence.

Let's begin with "I've just met." Understand, please, that my mother lives about twenty-five hundred miles away from me and she was calling me from her home. So if she says, "I've just met," it means that the person she met must be located twenty-five hundred miles away. In other words, "the perfect girl for me" is currently situated in my mother's neighborhood, not mine, which in turn means either that my mother wants me to move closer to her or else she believes that the only girl who could approach perfection in relation to me would be one who maintains a distance of several thousand miles between us.

Moving on: "perfect." Now, this is a loaded term. In my mother's mind, "perfect" would have nothing to do with bra size. It would have even less to do with lifestyle. My definition of "perfect" as an adjective to describe a woman would be a professional dog walker who wears cropped T-shirts and low-slung, high-cut denim shorts and, perhaps fifty percent of the time, can string together enough words to fill a sentence.

My mother's definition of "perfect," on the other hand, is someone who likes her.

"Girl." We're not supposed to use that term in reference to anyone over the age of three anymore. Kindergarten females are now called "potential women," or sometimes "very small women," or, on occasion, "PMS apprentices." And my mother isn't an idiot. She knows this. She actually read *The Feminine Mystique* in hardcover when I was still called Jimmy and got my mouth plugged with something to suck on whenever I fussed.

Therefore, we must deduce that my mother used the term *girl* deliberately. Her reason probably has something to do with her fear that describing this perfect female as a *woman* would scare me off.

By the way, why didn't anyone ever tell me it's impossible to use a computer keyboard when you've got a squirming little PMS apprentice on your lap and she's trying to suck on your mouse....

HE PRESSED A KEY to delete the last sentence and cut loose with a string of colorful expressions he hoped he'd never hear Samantha using.

He wished he could delete her that easily.

No, that was a terrible thought. A brief spasm of insanity must have brought it on—or, perhaps, a brief spasm of *sanity*.

He hadn't told his mother about the baby when she'd called Sunday afternoon. Thank God Samantha had been asleep on the screened porch in her stroller where Jamie could hear her if she awakened but his mother, twenty-five hundred miles of fiber-optic cable away from him, could not.

He should have told her. He had always gotten along with his mother, and he'd kept dishonesty to a minimum in their dealings. She was a remarkably tolerant woman. She'd had to be, to survive the nearly insurmountable task of raising Jamie. He'd been one of those kids with a knack for making messes and breaking fingers, who never got into trouble at school for failing tests but always got in trouble for clowning around. He'd been the kind of boy who had a little bit of difficulty taking things seriously. But his mother had done her best, and Jamie respected her for that. That she'd emerged from two decades of child rearing with her sense of humor intact made him actually like her.

Still, informing her that she had become a grandmother might push her beyond the limits of her tolerance and humor, especially once she'd learned the circumstances surrounding Samantha's birth. Jamie's mother had been dropping hints since his twenty-ninth birthday that, as he was approaching his thirtieth, he might want to think about getting married and starting a family.

Of course, she never put it so baldly. Instead, she found any and every excuse to mention worldwide epidemics of sexually transmitted diseases. She breezily noted in passing that one or another of her acquaintances had just become a grandparent *for the third time*. She mailed him articles about the high rate of infertility, dire reports clipped out of magazines called *Health for Today* or *The Journal of Reproductive Statistics*. Jamie had no idea where she found such magazines. He suspected she might be publishing them herself, just to provide her with official-looking articles, all of which coincidentally reached the same conclusion: Jamie McCoy needed to settle down and start a family immediately.

He knew his mother would be thrilled to have a granddaughter—but not this way. Not as the result of such unfathomable irresponsibility on Jamie's part.

He was trying to be responsible, for gosh sake. He'd contorted himself all sorts of ways to keep his date with Allison after his baby-sitter had copped out on him. If he wasn't responsible, he could have just left the baby home and gone off with Allison, right? But he'd done the responsible thing and brought Sam with him. And then, when Sam had flouted every law of etiquette by spitting up all over Allison at the restaurant, Jamie had done the responsible thing and brought Allison home with him, had her remove her clothing and made a pass at her.

Okay, so he was a jerk. He deserved everything she'd given him—and everything she *hadn't* given him. He was going to have to accept responsibility for everything that had gone wrong Saturday night. But at least he was more responsible than Sam's mother. He wasn't the one who'd abandoned a baby on someone's back step and stolen away without even leaving the baby's birth certificate or social security number. Responsible parents made sure the paperwork was in order.

Samantha kicked his keyboard again. A row of Zs zipped from the left margin to the right. Jamie yanked her foot away and shoved back from his desk. Sam gurgled. Jamie cursed again. "I'm in a rotten mood, toots. Ten guesses whose fault it is."

She gazed up at him with her pretty gray-green eyes. Damned if her eyes weren't exactly the same color as his. Damned if he didn't interpret her stare as some sort of answer. Or, more accurately, an indictment.

"Yeah, it's my fault. My fault the most exciting woman I've ever met walked out on me because she thinks I'm a brainless stud. How could she think such a thing just because I wanted to tear my old gray shirt off her and kiss her breasts? How could she possibly think... Ah, what do you care, anyway? Not that I'd stand quietly by if you let a guy do that sort of thing to you. Any guy even tries to get near your body, sweetheart—any guy even *thinks* about your body, and he answers to me and my fists. You got that?"

She blinked. Her poochy little mouth seemed to turn up at the outer corners.

"You think I'm kidding? Sammy, old girl, the next diaper I put on you is going to have a lock and key—and I get to keep the key in my safe-deposit box until your wedding day. Or longer if I don't trust the guy you're marrying.''

She made a squeaky sound.

"Who am I kidding?" he groaned. He couldn't imagine defending Samantha's honor against hordes of male jerks like him. He couldn't imagine raising her to the age when she'd be attracting male jerks. When he projected into the future, he could see no further than perhaps a month. Beyond that, he simply could not picture Samantha being a part of his life.

He couldn't picture Allison being a part of his life, either.

He wasn't sure which of those two ideas upset him more.

"Okay," he said, aware that he wasn't going to get any work done as long as Samantha was practising her backstroke on his lap. "Here's the deal. We're going for a drive. Think you can handle that without puking all over my Miata?"

She reached for his nose and pinched it.

"Ouch!" He pried her tiny fingers away. "Cripes. Look at those claws," he muttered, examining her pale, sharp fingernails. Was he supposed to cut them? How? How could someone with big, thick guy fingers—fingers adept at wielding a screwdriver or throwing a curve ball or maybe making love to a full-grown woman with curly reddish brown hair and pale green eyes—cut a baby's fingernails without cutting her fingers off, as well?

He would have to have Samantha's nails groomed by a professional. He wasn't going to risk mutilating his daughter's hands by trying to trim her nails himself. He supposed a trained nurse would be up to the task, but he couldn't go to Allison. It was bad enough that he'd ruined what should have been a magnificent evening with a magnificent woman—a woman who looked a hell of a lot better in his clothing than he did, a woman who could cast spells with her kisses, who could bewitch a man merely by standing in the circle of his arms.

He wasn't pleased by the prospect of facing that woman tonight at Daddy School class. But to go and beg her for help in taming his daughter's fingernails?

Forget it.

THE STAFF AT Maison Christophe didn't seem particularly interested in Jamie—at least the women on the staff didn't. They walked around the faux country decor of the beauty salon with their noses aimed skyward. One had green hair; another had short black hair glued so smoothly to her skull it looked like a patent leather bathing cap; still another had brown hair that appeared to have been shaped with a machete. All the women tended toward anorexic proportions, and none of them looked at all thrilled by the prospect of taking on Jamie as a client.

The two men, on the other hand, looked friendly. One was dressed in an orange jumpsuit that reminded Jamie of those protective coveralls worn by people who worked with nuclear waste. The other had hair as long and wild with curls as Allison's. If one of them was Christophe, Jamie couldn't guess which. Neither looked old enough to own a hair salon.

A fashionably undernourished woman behind the pickled-pine desk near the entrance gazed up at Jamie superciliously. "Do you have an appointment?" she asked.

No, he did not have an appointment. And if luck

gazed kindly upon him, he never would. Although he could afford a barber expensive enough to call himself a stylist, Jamie preferred to get his mop trimmed at the West Street Barber Shop, a defiantly old-fashioned place decorated with mirrors, lit with fluorescent ceiling fixtures and carpeted in wads and tufts of unswept hair clippings. Located next door to a deli that sold the best bagels in town, the West Street Barber Shop charged twelve bucks for a haircut, politics and sports talk thrown in for free. The only woman Jamie had ever seen in there was Angie, a gum-cracking, wiseass fiend with scissors who knew more about sports than all the male barbers combined.

He gazed about him at the stridently charming interior of Maison Christophe: hardwood floors, chintz curtains, mirrors framed in puffy floral print fabric, classical music and muted lighting that was supposed to make everyone look good but in fact made most of the people in the joint look like the living dead. Some of the women had chalky makeup on, too, and thick black gunk outlining their eyes, adding to their zombielike appearance.

"Sir?" the receptionist prodded him with her snooty voice. "Do you have an appointment?"

"No."

"I'm afraid we don't accept walk-ins here," she declared, sounding anything but afraid. The place wasn't hopping with customers—more chairs were empty than occupied—but a rule was a rule, and obviously, by his presence alone, Jamie was threatening their entire appointments-only system. The receptionist glanced through thick layers of mascara at the stroller where Samantha lay dozing. Jamie was tempted to point out that, given how much he'd spent on the damned stroller, these hoity-toity stylists ought to treat him with a little more respect.

If anyone at the West Street Barber Shop ever learned how much money he'd spent on the stroller, he'd be laughed out of the joint. Angie would squawk, "I'd sell my kid before I'd spend that kind of money on a freaking stroller."

"I'm not here for a haircut," he said. The receptionist eyed his mop of hair with obvious disdain, as if she'd been absolutely certain he'd come in to be tonsorially redeemed. "I'm here to get my kid's nails done."

"A manicure? For the child?" She rose from her seat and peered into the stroller. Her sepulchral face broke into a smile. "What a darling idea. Martina? This gentleman would like to have his daughter's nails done. Can you squeeze her in?"

The woman who responded to the name Martina had been loitering on a gingham-covered settee with a cup of coffee that smelled like one of those cloying flavored brews. She sauntered over to the stroller, peeked in and let out a squeal of delight.

Her shriek must have somehow liberated the other salon employees, because within a second Jamie could no longer see the stroller at the center of a crowd of terminally chic beauticians. They issued a chorus of "oohs" and "aahs" and "Isn't she adorables!" while Jamie backed away, wondering whether he ought to dive into the swarm and rescue Samantha or let her newfound fans have their way with her. "She's gorgeous!" one stylist crooned.

"When she gets hair, I want first crack at it!" another declared.

The receptionist eyed Jamie curiously. "Where's her mother?" she asked.

Good question. "We aren't married," he answered vaguely.

"Oh." The receptionist's meticulously tweezed eyebrows arched. "How interesting. What's your name?"

He opened his mouth, then shut it and assessed the situation. If he wasn't misreading things, the receptionist's antennae had quivered to life, searching for signals. Boy-girl-type signals. He'd just announced that he wasn't attached to Samantha's mother, and this anemic woman was interested.

Jamie scrambled for a diplomatic way to squelch that interest. He wasn't looking to strike up a flirtation with the receptionist or any of her bony colleagues. Only one woman occupied his mind, and she hated him for the very reason the employees of Maison Christophe were gurgling and gushing: Samantha.

Martina had unstrapped Samantha and lifted her out of the stroller. "Oh, you cutie, you! What shall we do with you today, my little sweet? Should we give you French nails? Would you like that? Or perhaps some nice silver appliqués? Your fingers are so tiny!"

She seemed to have that inbred female instinct for knowing how to say appropriate things to an infant. And how to hold one. With grudging admiration, Jamie observed how easily she supported Sam's head, how securely she held the body that less than an hour ago had been squirming so crazily in his lap she'd managed to type more with her flailing feet than he had with his fingers.

"I'd go with bright red," the woman with the patent leather cap of hair said. "Scarlet. Give her a thrill, Martina."

"How much is this going to cost?" he thought to ask.

The receptionist's eyebrows dropped. "Twenty-five dollars for a straight manicure. French costs more."

"I just want her nails cut," he said.

"Cut? Oh, no, no, no, no," the receptionist clucked as if he were an ignoramus, which, on the subject of manicures, he was. "Her nails will be smoothed and shaped. Some nice scent-free lotion will soften her cuticles. You want her to have nice nails, don't you?"

"I want her to have nails that can't open a vein," he muttered. "She's dangerous enough without claws."

"You're a thumb sucker, aren't you," Martina chattered to Samantha with a hint of reproach. "Now promise me you'll stop that nasty habit. Can you promise me? Oh, you piece of sugar, you!" And with that, she carried the baby off, trailed by a retinue of stylists.

Jamie pursued them with his gaze as they trooped across the hardwood floor to a small, mirrored table covered with tiny bottles of polish. "Where are they taking her?" he asked the receptionist apprehensively.

"To have her nails done. Sit and read a magazine," she advised him. "We'll let you know when it's time to pay."

He bet they would. With a sigh, he lowered himself onto the gingham settee, which was hard with

horse-hair stuffing and obviously designed for people
eight inches shorter than he was, and flipped through
a copy of a magazine called *Hair Styles*. The entire
magazine was devoted to that rather limited subject.
One article discussed shampoos, another color stripping, yet another the pros and cons of relaxed per-
manents. A special section confronted the complex
subject of hair accessories, which, Jamie learned,
comprised a great deal more than bobby pins.

Twenty minutes passed. Twenty minutes of
Jamie's skimming articles about the virtues of natu-
ral-bristle brushes and the benefits of rinsing one's
hair in ion-free water, whatever the hell that was.
Twenty minutes of a high-pitched babble rising like
champagne bubbles from the little mirror-topped table in the corner of the room. Of all the voices he
heard, none was his daughter's. Not a wail, not a
roar, not a hiccoughy bout of weeping. Evidently she
liked being surrounded by women. Or else she just
liked having her nails done.

He was going to have to find Samantha's mother.
A girl needed her mother at times like this. Cripes,
Samantha's first manicure! What was Jamie doing
here?

Where was Luanne Hackett? *Who* was Luanne
Hackett? Why had she stranded him without a hint
of how one took care of a baby's nails?

Why could he not even remember what she looked
like? They'd enjoyed each other just fine in Eleuthera. If only she hadn't gotten pregnant. If only he'd
been a little more careful with the twentieth or thirtieth condom. If only she'd stuck around when she
did get pregnant and given Jamie the chance to make
things right....

If Luanne hadn't run away, Jamie would never have met Allison. He would never have taken that solemn, statuesque woman in his arms and kissed her. He would never have wound up becoming obsessed with her and berating himself for his failure to live up to her too high standards.

Sheesh. Who gave a rap about her standards?

Jamie did, unfortunately. Somewhere, in a remote corner of his brain, he harbored the suspicion that Samantha was fate's revenge on him for having had too much fun in Eleuthera. Samantha, and Allison's condemnation. His double whammy punishment.

The woman with green hair materialized before him like a nightmarish weed. "We just wanted to tell you," she said in a husky contralto that surprised him after all the shrill giggling and jabbering, "that you have the best-behaved little baby any of us has ever seen."

"You're kidding!" he blurted out, wondering whether adding compliments to the manicure would jack up the price even further.

"Oh, no." Green Hair shook her head earnestly. "She's adorable. And I understand you're unattached?" Either she had a tic or she was winking at him.

"Uh...well, actually, I *am* attached."

"To that adorable little girl. Of course. I understand." The way she said "I understand" sounded like the come-on of a hooker.

"No," he insisted, assuring himself he was speaking only in self-defense and not because there was any truth to it. "I'm actually involved with someone. A nurse," he added, as if to clarify for Green Hair that his tastes ran to wholesome Norman Rockwell type women. Allison, however, made him think of anyone but Norman Rockwell, and he wanted to believe she wasn't too wholesome—on the chance that she ever decided to forgive him for being human.

"Oh." Green Hair smiled and shrugged, apparently giving herself a few points for effort. "Well, the other woman in your life, that little sweetheart over there, is almost done."

"She hasn't spit up on anyone, has she?" he asked nervously.

With a flourish, the other stylists swept across the room, bearing Sam like a princess on a litter. She looked stunned, her mouth open, her hands doing their usual reflexive furling and unfurling. A preliminary inspection informed him she had her full complement of fingers. Obviously he'd been right to entrust this hazardous task to people who knew what they were doing.

At least they knew what they were doing with nail scissors. As far as taste, they were operating in another galaxy from Jamie. Samantha's nails had been painted a ghastly pink, the color of raspberry sherbet. They were short, thank God, and smooth...but purplish pink?

The worst part was that she seemed pleased by the garish effect. She kept flinging her hands in front of her eyes and blinking, startled but not upset. None of her usual fretting, no bawling, no emissions of bodily fluids. Just a narcissistic fascination with her digital extremities.

Paternal dread nipped at him. "She does suck her fingers sometimes," he told Martina. "Is that stuff going to make her sick?"

"Oh, no, no, no," the receptionist interjected.

"We use only organic products here. There's nothing toxic in the polish."

"Plus, I softened her cuticle areas with a little baby oil," said Martina. "What could be more apropos? Now, she's probably going to want a little touch-up in a week, so you just keep bringing her to me and I'll make sure she's got hands to die for. And if you have any questions, anything you want to talk about—" batting her eyes coquettishly, she stuffed a piece of paper into the chest pocket of his shirt "—here's my home phone number. Just in case."

"I've really got to go," Jamie said, removing Samantha from her entourage. She gave him one of her who-the-heck-are-you? stares, making him feel totally inadequate. No, he couldn't trim and polish her nails. No, he didn't know how to get together with a bunch of ladies and do cosmetic things. No, he didn't feel comfortable in beauty salons like Maison Christophe, reading magazines about fifteen different ways to make a French braid work for you.

He was always doomed to fall short in his daughter's eyes. Fool that he was, he gave her helicopter mobiles, not pink nail polish. What did he know?

What he knew, he thought after forking over twenty-five dollars to the receptionist and a five-dollar tip to Martina, was that he was going to have to find Luanne Hackett. Samantha needed a mother—a better one than Luanne, but at least if he could track her down, he'd be moving in the right direction. He'd be proving to Allison that he did take his predicament very seriously, and that he was responsible, and that he was doing everything within his power to settle his daughter's life.

Sighing as he strapped his elegantly manicured

daughter into her seat in the car, he resolved to pay a call on Detective John Russo. Given how much Jamie paid in municipal taxes every year—taxes that went to support the police department, among other things—Russo had better have dug up some information about Samantha's reckless, feckless mother.

If not for Sam's sake, then for Jamie's, Russo just better have tracked that woman down.

ALLISON HAD BEEN positive Jamie would come to class. She'd been sure that, no matter what had gone so abysmally wrong on Saturday night, he cared enough about his baby that he wouldn't just drop out of the Daddy School. No one else in Arlington offered a class so perfectly suited to his needs, and Allison couldn't believe he would quit the class when he still had so much to learn.

But as the clock in the YMCA community room inched from 6:00 p.m. to 6:05, and from there to 6:10 with no sign of Jamie, she was forced to accept that he was less of a man than she'd hoped.

The room's bland decor grated on her. The scuffed linoleum floor, the wooden chairs carved with a generation's worth of initials, and the buzzing overhead lights irked her. The full day shift she'd already put in at Arlington Memorial fatigued her. If her students—the diligent ones, the ones who cared enough about being good fathers to show up, the ones who would have gotten A's from her if the Daddy School gave out report cards—hadn't been seated in their usual semicircle, staring with curiosity at the carton of baby dolls and disposable diapers she'd brought for them to practice on, she would have driven home and spent a quiet, sulky evening with Grammy, eating a spinach salad and watching reruns on TV while Grammy criticized her anemic social life.

But her good students were there, talking about how Damien's lady had had false labor over the weekend and, man, it was spooky. "She's, like, screaming her effin' head off," Damien related, playing to his audience, who gazed at him with the sort of awe the privates back at base camp might bestow upon a soldier who'd just returned to camp after engaging in hand-to-hand combat. "She's like, 'Oh, Damie, Damie, it hurts!' I had to spoon-feed her rocky road ice cream to keep her from freaking."

Damien's woman was no fool, Allison pondered, choosing not to inform him that Braxton-Hicks labor wasn't anywhere near as painful as the real thing and that ice cream had no analgesic power when it came to labor pain. It sounded as if the woman had figured out how to get the most from Damien. Allison had to give her credit.

"False labor can occur on and off throughout the entire ninth month of pregnancy," she lectured the class. "It's fairly common. It isn't a sign that anything's wrong. But it does mean a baby is on its way. And when that baby comes, you are going to have to be ready for it. So I've brought some dolls for you to practice on."

"Dolls!" one of the guys hooted. "Oh, wow. And after we're done with them, let's go outside and play hopscotch!"

The class hooted with laughter. Allison smiled to show she was a good sport. And then her smile waned when the door squeaked open and Jamie entered, pushing Samantha in her stroller.

"Oh, man!" one of the others bellowed. "Check

out those wheels, man! My car's got fewer options than that carriage!''

"What kind of mpg you get on that thing?'' another one shouted, while a third one said, "Power steering, power brakes—that baby's loaded.''

"Sorry I'm late,'' Jamie mumbled into the air. Allison could hardly hear him, and she wasn't in the mood to forgive him.

She waited with barely contained patience while he wheeled the stroller across the center of the room to the only empty chair in the circle. He looked haggard, his eyes dark with shadow. Samantha, on the other hand, looked effervescent. As the stroller glided by, Allison caught a glimpse of pink—several teardrop-size dots of it speckling her fingers.

Nail polish? What on earth...?

As if he could read her thoughts, Jamie sent her a glower that seemed to say, "Don't ask." She nodded slightly to show she understood, but her imagination quivered with possibilities. Had Jamie, in his rage at having failed to get Allison into bed, gone berserk and attacked his child with a bottle of nail enamel? Or had he invited another female friend to his house to quell the flames of passion Allison had ignited, and this other woman had just happened to have a bottle of polish in her overnight bag? Or had Jamie taken Samantha to a street fair where they had a clown doing face painting and the like?

Or was he just a bit...odd?

"All right, class,'' she said, refusing to let Jamie, his late entrance and her memories of Saturday night distract her. "Let's get started on diaper practice. Jamie, since you've already had plenty of practice with this, why don't you demonstrate for us?''

"Sam's dry," he said. The admiring comments of his classmates had done nothing to leaven his mood. He was still glowering, still looking melancholy and angry and mildly ill.

"I meant you could demonstrate on one of the dolls." She handed him a life-size doll and a small disposable diaper. As he took the doll from her, his hand accidentally brushed hers. She accepted the contact stoically, refusing to let her body react the way it had when he'd touched her Saturday night.

He touched her again when he took the diaper from her—only this time it didn't seem accidental. His gaze met hers as his fingers brushed her palm. She read a question in his eyes, a pleading, a panic different from the new-baby panic she'd read there when he'd attended his first class.

Allison knew her soft spots. She was a sucker for anyone who needed help, whether it was her grandmother, her friends or her patients. Or her students, she supposed. If Jamie needed help, she would help him.

She just wouldn't kiss him. Or let him stroke his fingers against her skin and gaze at her with an intimacy that turned her innards into warm, sweet syrup. She wouldn't laugh at his jokes or sympathize with him over his problems or agree to have dinner with him ever again.

She would help him in her capacity as his teacher. Period.

He demonstrated his diapering technique well enough to convince her that he'd been performing the task an average of ten times a day, which meant Samantha's bottom was being properly attended. The baby's manicured fingernails still mystified Allison,

though. Why in God's name was a three-week-old
baby wearing nail polish?

"Remember," she instructed the class, supple-
menting Jamie's demonstration, "there are differences between diapering boys and girls—because, of
course, there are differences between boys and
girls."

"You said it," one of the students murmured, inviting a chorus of snickers.

"When it comes to diapering a boy, you have to
work fast. Boys can spray in all directions."

"That doesn't make sense," Damien commented.
"You change the kid's diaper because the kid's just
taken a leak. So when the diaper's off, the kid ought
to be empty, you know? How can some little guy be
spraying you when he's just taken a whiz?"

"Babies are funny that way," Allison explained.
"You think they're empty, and then they surprise
you by proving they aren't."

"Allison's right," Jamie grumbled. "The minute
you put a dry diaper on them, they wet it. It's their
sadistic idea of a joke."

"Yeah? But then, you must be paying a fortune in
diapers. I mean, you put a diaper on, the kid pees,
you put another diaper on, the kid pees...."

Allison saw this as a good way to introduce the
subject of diaper economics. She discussed diaper
services, the pros and cons of laundering one's own
cloth diapers, the strategies of bargain hunting and
coupon clipping when it came to disposables. The
class seemed intrigued by this aspect—but then,
money seemed to fascinate them more than the nitty-
gritty of how to clean a baby's bottom and treat diaper rash.

As Allison moved around the room, watching as her students practiced on their dolls—not just changing diapers but holding them, supporting the dolls' wobbly necks, feeding the dolls with bottles and practicing burping strategies—Allison felt the hour stampede past her. The second fifty minutes of the class went faster than the first ten minutes. Something happened to time when Jamie was around. Her perception of it—like her perception of *him*—got skewed.

Why did she find him so irresistibly sexy? Why did he so appeal to her? Why did his eyes, roiling with weariness and worry, tweak responses deep inside her? Why, whenever she passed within his orbit, did she wish she could go back to Saturday night, back to their kisses on the porch? Why did she wish she could pretend the details of Samantha's conception were irrelevant to her?

Maybe Gail and Molly were right. Maybe she was just horny, her body crying out for a little amorous exercise.

But she could get that exercise any time she wanted. The hospital was teeming with young, handsome residents looking for a good time but allergic to commitment. If a fling was all she was after, she could have had dozens of them.

She wasn't after Jamie, that was for sure. And yet...

And yet her pulse tripped in double time whenever she glanced his way, whenever she got close to him. Apparently, being in the same room with him was as close as she needed to be, because by the end of the hour she felt overheated, as if too much blood were rushing through her veins.

"Okay, guys, that's it," she said as the big hand crossed the twelve, marking the end of the class. "Bring your babies back up here. *Gently,*" she warned Harold, who had tucked his doll under his arm as if it were a newspaper. "Always support the baby's head." Her cautions seemed a little silly as the fathers-to-be carefully carried their "babies" to the front of the room and dumped them into the carton. She would have to return the dolls to the hospital that night. As if having them back on the shelf in the childbirth class closet before tomorrow morning would make any difference in the hospital's decision.

Margaret had told her earlier today that the hospital had made its decision based on budget constraints, that although everyone believed Allison had come up with a great idea, it was more important to train mothers than fathers. "Face it," Margaret had observed. "Some of those daddy students of yours are going to light out for the territories first chance they get. If they were stick-around types, they'd be married and making arrangements for the christening, not hanging out at the Y. And the older ones are going to be out the door and at their desks the minute they realize how much work child rearing is. They'll be dumping the babies on their wives and screaming for nannies. You're wasting your time and the hospital's money trying to turn sows' ears into silk purses."

Allison believed quite the opposite—that by teaching fathering skills and imbuing her students with confidence in their own abilities, she could transform even the most reluctant father into an involved, caring parent. But with Margaret and the rest of the hospital's senior staff denying her the support she needed, the Daddy School students were all doomed to end up sow's ears.

Except for Jamie. He might end up resembling some part of an animal. But it wouldn't be a sow. And it certainly wouldn't be an ear.

While the rest of the class filed out of the room, joshing and nudging each other and making uneasy jokes about labor pains and dirty diapers, Jamie remained behind, pretending to be extremely busy adjusting the seat belt that held Samantha in her stroller. Allison knew the baby didn't need his ministrations. He was lingering in the room for another reason—and Allison had a strong sense of foreboding about what that reason might be. He wanted to talk to her, rehash Saturday night, make her feel even worse than she already felt, about herself as well as him. She honestly didn't want to have that talk. But as his teacher she had to make herself available on the minuscule chance he might have a legitimate child care question for her.

Not likely, she thought, bracing herself as he approached her at the front of the room, where she was cramming her folder of lecture notes into her canvas tote.

"Hi," he said almost shyly.

Glancing at him, she was once again jarred by the turbulent shadows darkening his eyes. Something was up. Something beyond Samantha's rendering him sleepless night after night. Something beyond his ghastly dinner date with Allison.

Something big.

"You look terrible," she blurted out. She recalled all the warnings she'd always heard about the risks of medical personnel becoming personally involved with patients. Jamie wasn't exactly a patient, but it didn't matter. She was already involved, and she couldn't keep herself from caring about him. "What's wrong?"

He allowed himself a wan smile at her blunt critique of his appearance. The smile didn't last long, though. "I went to see my buddy John Russo at the police station today."

"John Russo? Is he the detective assigned to Samantha's case?"

Jamie nodded. "He's found out some interesting stuff about her mother."

"Oh?"

"Yeah." Jamie scrubbed a hand through his hair, then turned and observed his daughter resting in her stroller, as if he needed to reassure himself that she was all right. "Samantha's mother isn't the woman I thought she was."

"Meaning…?"

"Meaning…" He sighed plaintively, and his eyes glimmered with emotion as he met Allison's gaze. She saw desperation in them, and yearning. "I'm in a hell of a fix, Allison. I've spent the past how many days going without sleep, going without peace, going without—" he hesitated, his gaze sweeping meaningfully down Allison's body and then back to her face "—going without you."

"Jamie—"

"I didn't think it could get any worse. I thought having you walk out on me Saturday night was as bad as it could get. But…" he sighed again. "It's worse. It seems Samantha's mother has money, she has power and…she has a husband."

CHAPTER TEN

SHE HAD PROMISED herself she would never go out for dinner with him again, but this was different. This was the coffee shop across the street from the Y. It was inexpensive sandwiches and attitude-free waiters, and the emotions flowing between her and Jamie were entirely different from what they'd been on Saturday night.

Well, no, not entirely different. She couldn't look at him without imagining him standing naked in the glass-walled shower of his master bathroom, wet and glistening beneath the spray and framed by a backdrop of trees and sky. She couldn't talk to him without recalling the heat of his mouth against hers. She couldn't be in his presence without wishing he'd managed his life with a little more prudence, because if he had...

There was no point in dwelling on ifs. What mattered was now, his baby's future.

They were seated at the same booth as a week ago. In the narrow space between the banquette and the table, Jamie tried to juggle Samantha, her bottle and his hamburger, and he was in serious danger of dropping at least one of the three. But Allison had learned her lesson Saturday night. She wasn't going to risk her clean white slacks and knit top by volunteering to hold his baby for him.

Biting her lip to keep from offering assistance, she watched as he propped Samantha on his knee, with his right arm hooked around her and his wrist contorted to get the bottle's nipple into her mouth. With his left hand he reached for the plastic ketchup bottle, squirted a dab of red onto his hamburger patty and closed the bun around it. Allison was dying to hear what the police had told him about Samantha's mother, but she was at least as anxious to see if he could take a bite without spilling ketchup or formula down the front of his shirt.

He managed a hungry bite, leaning so far over his plate Samantha came dangerously close to getting squished. As soon as he had a mouthful of food, he settled back against the banquette and chewed. Samantha flapped her hands, flashing the luminous pink of her nail polish, but she didn't stop sucking at her bottle.

"Which would you rather tell me about first?" Allison asked once he'd swallowed. "The nail polish or the police detective?"

"There's nothing to tell about the nail polish. I just felt like wasting thirty dollars on a beauty treatment for her."

"Of course." She smiled.

He smiled, too, and conceded with a nod. "The truth was, I was afraid I'd hurt her if I tried to cut her nails, and they were getting so long she looked like Fu Manchu. So I took her to a manicurist."

"You're joking," Allison said dubiously.

"Her nails aren't important," he responded, which was enough to inform her that he hadn't been joking at all. "What's important is..." He leaned forward precariously once more, this time to sip some iced tea through a straw. "I had quite a chat with John Russo over at the Arlington police station. First thing, her mother's name isn't Luanne Hackett. Not anymore."

Not anymore? Then she'd changed her name? Why would she do that? Because she was in hiding? Hiding from Jamie and her baby? Exercising great willpower, Allison held her questions and nibbled on her turkey sandwich, giving Jamie the chance to proceed in his own way.

"Hackett was her first husband's last name. Her current name is Luanne Pierson."

"She went back to her maiden name?"

Jamie shook his head grimly. "She's on her second marriage. She was married when I met her."

Allison's appetite evaporated. Even giving Jamie the benefit of the doubt—that he hadn't known the woman was married when he'd had his fling with her at that Caribbean resort—the idea still bothered her deeply.

Obviously, it bothered him deeply, too. He seemed to have lost interest in his burger. Sinking back against the vinyl upholstery, he eased Samantha into a more natural position in his arms and concentrated on holding her bottle at the right angle, watching her guzzle her formula.

"I mean...hell, you probably think I'm some sort of degenerate, messing around with a married woman. But I swear to God, I..." He couldn't seem to finish the sentence. Instead, he peered down at Samantha, who was devouring her meal with gusto. Slowly, trying not to jostle her, he reached for the napkin dispenser at the end of the table, plucked out a napkin and dabbed dribbles of formula from her chin.

The sight made Allison's eyes blur with tears. She didn't want to become involved with him, honestly she didn't—and yet his plight moved her. No, he wasn't a degenerate. He was simply a man who had botched things up splendiferously just because, like the typically brainless guys he celebrated in his column, he'd let an available woman paralyze his intellect for a few idyllic days on a resort island ten months ago, and now the consequence lay snuggled cozily in his arms, drooling and making tiny, contented grunts as she guzzled her formula.

"What else did the policeman tell you?"

Jamie sighed. "Her maiden name is Luanne Eldridge. She's from the Washington D.C. area. Her father made a fortune investing in real estate, and now he gets even richer by investing in congressmen. He's a very powerful guy, apparently."

"What does it matter how powerful her father is? If his daughter abandoned her child—"

"She registered at the resort in Eleuthera using her first husband's name and her father's home address. Detective Russo told me he could arrange to have the D.C. police pay a call on Mr. Eldridge and find out his daughter's whereabouts, but if he did that, Eldridge owns enough people to protect his daughter and make Russo's life hell. And my life, too. Not to mention Sam's." He gazed down at the baby in his arms again.

"So," he continued, "Russo's trying to track Luanne down without dragging her father into it. She paid for the hotel room on a credit card; Russo thinks he might be able to get information on her from the issuing bank. But that could also draw suspicion, plus he would have to get a search warrant and all that. Meanwhile, he was able to find out the address of a condominium she and her husband own in Boston No one's there, though. The building manager thinks they're at one of their vacation homes.''

''So she's with her husband? In spite of what happened in Eleuthera?''

''It's possible he doesn't know what happened in Eleuthera.''

''How could he not know? She spent nine months being pregnant, didn't she?''

''They were separated when I met her. The way I figure it, I was some sort of revenge. She was mad at her husband, so she had an affair with me. Apparently they remained separated for another nine months. She dumped Sam on me and now she's reconciling with her husband.''

''Oh, Jamie.'' Allison gnawed on her lip to keep from saying what she was really feeling: that anyone who would hide a pregnancy from her estranged husband, give birth and abandon the baby and then get back together with her husband had to be the most selfish, coldhearted person imaginable. She wanted to leap across the table and gather Samantha in her arms. She wanted to vow that she would never let anyone so horrible gain custody of that precious little girl.

But Samantha wasn't hers to protect. That was Jamie's job—if he decided he wanted it. For all Allison knew, he might ultimately prefer not to be stuck with custody of the baby. That he had accepted his responsibility for the time being didn't mean he wouldn't jump for joy if the multimarried Luanne Pierson reappeared to claim her child.

But Jamie wouldn't really give up Samantha, would he? Not after buying that adorable mobile, the finely constructed crib and the most expensive stroller in the world. Not after he'd sat through Daddy School classes. Not after he'd bonded with his daughter, learned to juggle her dinner and his own and found a way to adapt to fatherhood even at the cost of his sex life.

Which, as far as Allison knew, might have already resurrected itself, rising like the phoenix from the ashes of Saturday night. Just because things had gone poorly with her didn't mean Jamie had any intention of living like a monk, or even a near-monk, while raising his daughter.

She took a bite of her sandwich even though her appetite hadn't returned. Every time she glimpsed Jamie she saw too much: his ambivalence, his anguish, his anger...and other emotions, intimate emotions, emotions that had less to do with his baby and that baby's mother than with Allison. Or maybe it wasn't Jamie's emotions she saw; maybe it was her own emotions, reflecting off him and returning to her.

She was ambivalent, too. The notion of falling for Jamie filled her with dread. She'd already had the dismal experience of loving a man too caught up with himself and the complications of his own life to give her what she yearned for. Frank had been charming, he'd been handsome, he'd been endowed with his share of sex appeal—and he'd lived from crisis to crisis, challenge to challenge, always just a bit too busy concentrating on those things to remember that Allison was supposed to matter to him, too. She'd always been supportive, serving as his sounding board, listening to him complain and analyze and work out every last detail of his life. By the time he'd finished contending with this crisis or that challenge, he'd never had any energy left for her.

At first she hadn't minded. Helping people was her profession and her passion. Few things satisfied her as much as giving of herself so a person in pain could hurt a little less—or even heal if luck was running the right way. And so she'd helped Frank, advising him on a job switch, counseling him through his conflicts with his father, listening patiently as he bounced ideas off her and sought her approval.

But when Grammy had fallen and bruised her bad knee and Allison had been shaken and upset by this evidence of her grandmother's growing frailty, Frank had offered little consolation. "She's old," he'd summed up. "What do you expect? Look, if you're down in the dumps, let's go grab some pizza and take in a movie. That'll get your mind off your grandmother."

She hadn't wanted to get her mind off her grandmother. But Frank had wanted her to, because he hadn't wanted to listen while she worked out her feelings. If it wasn't about *him*—or about good food or good times or good sex—he wasn't interested.

Allison didn't need to be the center of a man's life. But if she was going to love a man, she wanted him to think of her as his lover, not his crutch. And she certainly didn't want to love a man who needed to give so much of his attention to himself that he was never going to have anything left to give her.

Jamie had only one thing going on in his life—

but it was the most important thing in the world. A baby, his daughter.

"You hate me," he muttered.

She was sure she'd misunderstood him. Lowering her sandwich, she frowned. "I beg your pardon?"

"You're sitting there thinking I'm the biggest moron ever to walk the earth. I go off on a vacation, make a fool of myself over some stranger simply because she's tosses some bait my way and then I find out she's not what I thought."

"I'll admit you showed a lack of judgment, Jamie. That doesn't mean I hate you."

"It means you don't respect me."

She startled them both by laughing. "I thought only women cared about being respected."

"Men need respect, too—especially after they've done something stupid. Which, if you're a regular reader of my column, you know is a common occurrence. All that testosterone makes it hard for us to be respectable, you know? But we try so hard." He attempted a plaintive smile.

She was still laughing. To her great pleasure, Jamie joined her, his cheeks denting with dimples and the skin at the corners of his eyes pleating with smile lines. "I think I understand—men are trying, so women are supposed to respect them."

He wiggled his eyebrows lecherously. "No, Allison. Women are supposed to respect men because they're so hard."

She would have blushed if she weren't enjoying his palaver so much. The truth was, she *did* respect him, for his honesty and his willingness to do the right thing in the face of such upheaval. "What steps does your policeman plan to take?" she asked, deciding to focus on Jamie's tangled life so she wouldn't start thinking about specifically what he wanted to do to deserve her respect.

"He's going to find Luanne if he can. If he can't, he'll go after her husband."

"Not her father?"

"Her father is a last resort, given the old man's clout and connections. The husband knows where she is. And if he finds out about the baby, he might be more inclined to help the police. Her father would be more inclined to try to fix things for her."

"Do you think the policeman knows what he's doing?"

"Yeah." Jamie shifted Samantha slightly and took another bite of his burger. "Russo's a father himself. He cares about kids. He also seems smart. And organized." He took a long sip of iced tea, then sighed. "He said something, though..."

"What?"

"He brought up that whole issue of whether Sam was really my daughter."

"You don't even want to consider that, do you?"

"I don't know." His voice was low, thick, pushing through a knot of tension in his throat and emerging barely louder than a whisper. "I had a good talk with Russo. I was pleased that he'd found out so much about Luanne. I mean, I was shocked, but I was also impressed. I figured, if anyone can straighten this thing out, John Russo can." He drained his glass and adjusted Samantha in his arms once more, easing the empty bottle out of her mouth and placing it on the table. "But then, when I was getting ready to leave, he hit me with his parting shot. 'It's always possible,' he said, 'that Luanne Pierson's husband could be the baby's father.''

"But they were estranged."

"Maybe they did the deed just before they split. I don't know. I'd think that if she thought there was a chance the baby could be her husband's, she would have told him. But maybe she was still angry with him and didn't want him to know." He shrugged. "I'm just guessing."

"She could have gotten an abortion," Allison noted.

"She didn't," he said fiercely, holding Samantha a bit more snugly, as if to protect her from the very idea.

It dawned on Allison that in his own way, Jamie loved Samantha deeply. "If your dream could come true," she asked, "what would you want? Would you want it to turn out that Samantha wasn't your daughter?"

"If my dream could come true..." He mulled over his response, his eyes drifting until he was staring at something no one else could see, something deep inside himself, that secret place where his dreams were stored. After a long moment, he brought his gaze back to Allison. "Sam would be mine—but she wouldn't be Luanne Eldridge-Hackett-Pierson-Whatever's. The mother would be someone I could trust, someone I could marry. Someone who would love Samantha with all her heart."

Allison trembled slightly, pinned by the sharpness of his gaze. She told herself he was looking at her that way only because she was challenging him to think, to consider things he might not wish to contemplate. It had nothing to do with her personally.

Yet for a brief, insane moment, she couldn't escape the comprehension that in his dreams, *she* would be the mother, the woman who loved Samantha with all her heart.

Interesting that he wouldn't want any part of that woman's heart for himself.

Still, that he would put his daughter's need for love ahead of his own softened Allison's opinion of him in a dangerous way. She watched him eat, watched him hold Samantha, watched him watch her—and she wondered what she could do to make his burden easier...besides take Samantha over, onto her lap and into her heart.

Allison wasn't going to do that. She wasn't going to risk her heart on Samantha—or Samantha's father—when the odds of losing were so great.

HE WASN'T READY to leave Allison when they departed from the diner. The evening was mild, the sky a watercolor of bleeding pastel shades as the sun inched down toward the western hills. Unlike the sticky midday heat, the air had grown dry and balmy.

It was a night for a walk. A night to take Sammy cruising in her spiffy stroller—and a night to keep Allison by his side for a little while longer if she would let him.

He'd already revealed too much of himself to her. He'd let her glimpse beneath the wisecracking facade of the witty columnist. She'd seen his fear and confusion. Things had gotten extremely personal.

He was used to giving a woman everything he had physically. But not emotionally, not the way he just had with Allison. It frightened him a little, opening up to her like that, letting her in on the real James

McCoy Jr., putting her in touch with the guy who
wanted to do the right thing but seemed to have done
too many things wrong, who liked being in control
of his life but wasn't in control of it now. She'd seen
the scared soul behind the cocky smile.

So far she hadn't shown any inclination to reject
him, even knowing that he wasn't exactly perfect. In
fact, she seemed a whole lot friendlier than she'd
acted Saturday night, when he'd thought he and she
both were performing pretty close to perfect. If she
liked the flawed reality of Jamie better, he'd go with
that for as long as she let him.

"Do you have to be anywhere?" he asked as they
stood on the curb waiting for the light to change.

"Now?"

"I was just wondering…" Damn! Why did he feel
so insecure? He wasn't used to so much self-doubt,
first as a father, then as a potential suitor. "Maybe
we could take a walk or something?" he half asked.

"Now?"

"Well—" desperate, he resorted to humor "—either now or sometime next year."

She cracked a smile. "I think I'm booked solid
next year, so it's going to have to be now."

He smiled, too. He'd spent all of their dinner
whining about his meeting with Russo. He wanted to
laugh about something, think about something other
than his own screwy life.

The traffic light turned green, and they crossed the
street. The downtown stores and offices were mostly
closed for the day, but the slanting sun glazed the
building facades and windows with a copper sheen,
and the city seemed almost restful. Cars weren't
jammed bumper to bumper along the streets as they'd

been an hour ago; rush-hour traffic had thinned, leaving the downtown district almost peaceful.

In her stroller, Samantha snoozed. "I really like her when she's sleeping," Jamie commented.

"Sleeping babies are enough to make a person believe in angels," Allison agreed.

"And screaming babies are enough to make a person believe in Satan."

"Tell me about it." Allison slid the handles of her tote higher on her shoulder and dug her hands into the pockets of her white slacks. "I had a riot in the neonatal nursery today. One little infant got the others all revved up. A real rabble-rouser. In ten seconds flat, he had them all bellowing at full volume."

"Why?"

"Does there have to be a reason?" She chuckled. "It's their way of exercising. They can't work out on an Exercycle or jog five miles, so they scream."

"And they give you a chance to get your exercise, too—sprinting out of the nursery faster than an Olympic gold medalist."

Still chuckling, she shook her head. "After a while, you learn to tune out a lot of the noise in the neonatal nursery. I imagine construction workers who've been on the job long enough don't notice the rumble of jackhammers."

"I can't wait till I reach the point where I can tune out Sam's screaming," he groused.

"By the time you get used to it, she'll be much bigger. Newborns are actually pretty quiet compared to older children."

"Oh, no!" He gasped in pretended shock. "I guess their vocal cords grow along with the rest of them, huh."

"Their vocal cords and their lungs."

Jamie ushered Allison around the corner, passing a darkened candy store, a darkened coffee shop and a darkened shoe boutique, the shoes neatly segregated into men's and women's in the showcase windows. A couple of young office workers bounced past, whispering and giggling. Across the street, a man in a hotshot business suit and a bike helmet glided past on a racing bike. The building that housed the *Arlington Gazette* was still alive, its windows lit up as the evening staff settled in for their shift. Except for his brief stint working there, Jamie had managed to avoid commuting to a downtown district to earn his living. And until Samantha's arrival, he'd managed to arrange his work environment so he didn't have to listen to anyone screaming— either a boss or a baby.

"Nurses must be a brave lot," he surmised, genuinely impressed by Allison's courage in tolerating screaming babies every day.

She shrugged. "No braver than lots of other people. Nurses put in their hours just like everyone else. Most of the time we just do routine tasks. Every now and then we've got a high-risk preemie, and then it's really rigorous. But usually the work I do is happy work. It's not like hospice care or ICU, where you're dealing with critical patients all the time."

"Yeah, but you put in your hours with the screaming babies—and the occasional high-risk preemie— and then you come and teach bozos like me in the Daddy School."

"Well, that won't last long," she muttered.

He shot her a quick glance, then eased the stroller

over the curb as they crossed to the next block. "You can't wait to get rid of us," he said.

"That wasn't what I meant."

Her mood had changed markedly, whetting his curiosity. "Are you talking about taking a break between semesters? How much time do you take off between this class and the next one?"

"There isn't going to be a next one," she said laconically.

He gave her a longer, more attentive perusal. She remained in profile to him, her hair pulled back from her face and held with a tortoiseshell clip, although the thick locks seemed to be straining for freedom. Her chin was high, her eyes squinting slightly against the angle of the setting sun. She looked both proud and resigned and extremely peeved.

Suddenly he felt unforgivably self-centered. He'd been crabbing about his problems the whole time they'd been at the diner, and meanwhile she clearly had problems of her own. He should have talked less about himself and asked how things were going with her. He should have remembered that whether or not they ever got around to finishing what they'd started Saturday night, they were still friends—at least he hoped they were.

"Why isn't there going to be a next class?" he asked.

"No support."

"What do you mean, no support? I support what you're doing—and you could ask any one of those guys in the class. They all support you—Damian, Leon, Harold, all of them. All the guys adore you for what you're doing." And at least one of the guys had a serious case of lust for her, too.

She turned to him, nearly singeing him with the exasperation burning in her eyes. "The hospital won't support me. They won't fund me. They think I'm stretching myself too thin. They're downsizing the staff and they want the nurses to put in more hours. They think I should be devoting my energy to training mothers. They think I'm wasting my time working with fathers, that the younger ones are going to walk away from their babies and the older ones are going to wind up hiring nannies."

"They think that?" Jamie was offended. Even if, every now and then, he got to fantasizing about how nice and easy his life could be without Samantha in it—and even if most of his classmates probably harbored similar fantasies at times—he was doing his best. He'd bet some mothers harbored the fantasy of walking away from their babies, too. "That's incredibly sexist," he remarked, amazing himself. Jamie McCoy, the consummate guy, was protesting sexism!

"Believe me, I'm not happy about it. I had hopes of expanding the program, introducing a second level of classes my friend Molly was going to teach. She runs a preschool, and she wanted to develop a class for fathers of toddlers. Now it looks as if the whole thing is going to die as soon as your class is finished."

"That stinks," he said, indignant on her behalf—and on his own, and on behalf of the entire Daddy School. "Who's in charge there? I could talk to them, write a testimonial—"

"It's not your problem, Jamie."

"The hell it's not. You're working wonders for fathers like me. I'm sure there are hundreds of them out there."

In spite of her obvious anger, she laughed. "Oh, sure—hundreds of men who wake up one morning and find the result of a vacation fling sitting in a basket on their front step."

"It was the back step," he corrected, then grinned. "Okay, maybe not hundreds. But there are lots of fathers like the other guys in the class. Kids who need to understand what's in store for them. I mean, they don't have a clue." He thought about it a moment, then reluctantly added, "As if I were any better prepared than they are. I didn't have a clue, either."

She dug her hands deeper into her pockets. He could make out the ridges of her knuckles through the cotton fabric; her fingers were curled into fists. "Well. I appreciate the vote of confidence, but it isn't going to do any good. My supervisor gave me the final word today. The hospital's pulling the plug."

"Not a good metaphor for what a hospital should do." He veered around a fire hydrant, taking a moment to appreciate the stroller's suspension system. "What kind of money are you talking about, anyway? Thousands of dollars?"

"It's a matter of time as well as money. The hospital wants me in the neonatal unit for longer shifts."

"Time *is* money," he returned. "They want you in the unit because it costs them less if you're in the hospital than if you're in the YMCA teaching a class and someone else has to take your place in the unit. I'm just wondering what the bottom line is. What's your time worth to them?"

"I don't know. The business department doesn't share information like that with mere nurses."

He mulled over the idea taking shape inside his

brain and decided he liked it. "People could donate money to make up the difference, couldn't they?"

She fired him a quick, resolute look. "You're not donating money to the Daddy School."

"I'm not?" Even more than he liked his idea, he liked the way her eyes blazed when she was revved up, the way energy seemed to crackle like an electrical field around her. He liked the way she pursed her lips—as if she were challenging him to kiss her mouth back into a smile. He liked the way she squared her shoulders, the way she tossed back her hair, the way she pulled her spine taut. The old cliché about how some women looked beautiful when they were angry was definitely true in Allison's case.

"No," she said vehemently. "You're not going to donate money to the Daddy School."

He suppressed a smile. "How are you going to stop me?"

"Jamie." Her voice was gritty. "We have—" she picked over her words carefully "—enough complications in our relationship right now without adding money to the mix. I won't let you do that."

"What complications?" he argued, even though he knew exactly what she was talking about. "All I want to do is keep a worthwhile program from going down the tubes. What does that have to do with our *relationship?*" He hated that word, but he couldn't come up with a better label for whatever was going on between him and Allison.

"If you gave money to the Daddy School, I would feel indebted to you."

That would suit him fine, but he could see how a woman with her overabundance of pride wouldn't care for it. Her pride shouldn't enter into it, though, any more than the fact that it was his money they were talking about. What mattered was keeping the Daddy School afloat.

He didn't want to detour into a fight with her, though. If he extricated himself from the whole idea, maybe she would view it more objectively, without having her vision clouded by all that "relationship" nonsense. "There have to be other sources of funding. Have you looked into city grants? State money? Private foundations?"

"I did get some money from the city for this first class. But that grant hinged on the hospital's support. With the hospital backing away from the program, I won't see any more money from the city. As far as the state goes, I made some inquiries and was told that the governor is in a tax-cutting mood and there's no way the legislature will fund any new projects when so many of the old projects are scrambling for pennies. And private foundations—I wouldn't even know where to start."

"Then you're going to have to figure it out. Maybe someone at the newspaper would know," he said, noticing the *Gazette* building looming ahead as they completed a circuit around the block. "I could ask around."

"Thanks, Jamie, but no."

"Why not? You're accomplishing something significant here. You're saving a lot of guys from blowing the most important job they'll ever have. This program shouldn't die." She didn't dispute him—she couldn't, since he was only saying what she already knew—so he pressed ahead. "Let me just ask around. I know people at the newspaper. I used to work there. They'll know how to get the money."

"I told you, Jamie, I don't want to be beholden to you."

This was not the voice of Allison, the noble young nurse. It was the voice of Allison, the woman who had come dangerously close to being seduced by Jamie two nights ago. Allison, the woman who had stood in Jamie's clothes on Jamie's porch and returned Jamie's kisses with a passion that bowled him over just thinking about it. That other woman, the noble nurse, would have no compunctions about being beholden, unlike this woman, the alluring lady, the almost-lover...

Beholden. Bad choice of words, he thought, stopping and turning fully toward her. It made Jamie realize whom he wanted to be holding.

As he slid his hands over her shoulders, turned her to face him and brought his mouth down hard on hers, he had no compunctions at all.

CHAPTER ELEVEN

SHE KNEW SHE mustn't let this happen. Bright red flags of alarm waved wildly in her mind, sirens clanged, warning flares shot into space like fireworks....

Or maybe it was his kiss that was igniting the fireworks. Maybe it was his strength—the strength of his arms around her, the strength of his mouth claiming hers, the strength of a man who wasn't afraid to let a woman see he wasn't always strong.

If only he didn't kiss so well.

If only this didn't feel so right.

If only Allison could find enough strength in herself to back away, to tell him to straighten out his life before he lured her into it.

But she had already decided that it was futile to dwell on ifs. Ifs could not change the fact that Jamie was the most intriguing, most delightful, most downright sensual man she'd ever met, and if one kiss was going to lead her to her doom, well, so be it.

Far in the distance, a car horn honked. A summery breeze gusted down the street, amplified by the office buildings and shops lining the sidewalks and carrying the scent of hot concrete and urban dust. In the stroller, Samantha slept, oblivious to the activities of the two adults casting their merged shadows over her.

For all Allison knew, the entire world was oblivious. Nothing existed beyond the circle of Jamie's arms, the heat of his lips on hers. Nothing existed but the pressure of his hands on her back. Nothing existed but the warm pool of arousal that gathered below her belly.

She felt safe within his embrace, even though it was probably the most dangerous place for her to be.

He moved his hands down to her waist. She felt the contours of his palms through the fabric of her sweater. She was aware of how powerful his hands were as they came to rest above her hips, his fingertips digging lightly into the small of her back and his thumbs venturing around her sides and forward. They were hands that could turn a woman on merely by thinking about them, that could obviously turn her on much more by stroking, exploring, possessing with a subversive gentleness that made it impossible for her to think at all.

She barely felt herself moving, yet suddenly she was standing closer to him, much closer. His hands had ordained it. They had guided her, and she'd gone willingly.

Those same magical hands glided around her ribs and upward, coming to rest beneath her breasts. She caught her breath and sighed, wishing she and Jamie weren't standing on a public street, wishing they were somewhere private where he could tear off their clothing, and really touch her.

How on earth could she feel safe in his arms? Nothing was safe when she was with him.

He skimmed his hands higher, his body shielding hers, lending privacy to his touch. She moaned as he swept his fingers over her breasts. Her nipples swelled painfully, and heat massed in a fierce knot between her thighs. "Jamie," she whispered, though she couldn't hear herself. Her heart was beating too loudly. Her voice was too faint.

"Come home with me," he murmured, stroking her breasts, lightly pinching her nipples.

"I don't know, I..." She damned well *did* know. She couldn't go home with him, because going home with him would mean going to bed with him. She couldn't risk sharing so much of herself with him. Her heart was already too open to him, too ready to let him inside. Sleeping with him would somehow make all her feelings irrevocable. She wouldn't be able to extricate herself without getting destroyed.

"Allison, it's me, Jamie. You know who I am, where I'm coming from—you know more about me than anyone else. You know I wouldn't hurt you."

Not deliberately. But she could wind up hurt, anyway. If she let him make love to her, she would become too caught up in his life, in his problems. She knew he was heading into a dangerous, dizzying maze. And neither he nor she knew whether he'd ever find his way out. She wasn't ready to enter the maze with him, to lose herself inside it for him.

Still, when he rubbed his thumbs so tenderly against her breasts, teasing her flesh as his tongue teased her trembling lower lip, she could scarcely breathe, let alone explain calmly and coherently why she thought it would be better if she didn't go home with him. He had a way of making her feel tiny even though she was taller than average, a way of making her feel petite and protected even when his erotic caresses stripped her of every protection she had. He bent his knees slightly and leaned his hips into hers, letting her know the effect the kiss was having on him.

"We're standing on a street corner," she managed to say.

She could feel the curve of his smiling mouth against hers. He rocked his hips against hers, slowly but emphatically. "I'm so turned on, I don't even care."

"I care."

"Then let's go home."

"I can't." It emerged as a lament, her tone shimmering with regret.

Slowly, terribly slowly, he let his hands fall from her. He bowed his head, resting his forehead against hers, and closed his eyes. His respiration was uneven, and his expression—what she could see of it—resonated with disappointment. "Can you tell me why? Is it the same stuff as Saturday night? I'm a sinner and you can't forgive me?"

"No," she said honestly.

"Ah, so I've received absolution."

"Jamie, listen to me." She cupped her hands over his shoulders and leaned back until she could peer into his face. "You've got a lot of things going on in your life right now, what with the baby and the information your police detective dug up. You don't know where you're going. You can't know until you've given it some thought. There's no room for me in all that."

He offered a tentative smile. "I was hoping maybe you could help me figure out where I'm going."

He might as well have doused her with icy water. She felt her spine go slack, her spirits plummet. "That's what I was afraid of."

One of his eyebrows quirked upward in puzzlement. "What do you mean?"

"I can't tell you how to handle your life, Jamie. And I don't want to. You've got to work that out on your own."

"Why? I mean—I value your opinion, Allison. You're a lot more clearheaded than I am. You know how to talk to babies. You know about women and their moods. I'm splashing around in the middle of the ocean without a life vest, and you're a coast guard cutter."

Her spirits fell further. "I am *not* a coast guard cutter, Jamie. Do I look like a boat to you?"

He drew back and eyed her up and down. "You look like a woman," he murmured, his voice hoarse with revived passion. "Forget the boating metaphor. You look like the most tantalizing woman in the world."

"Save your breath," she muttered, ordering herself not to let his flattery get to her. "The issue here is, maybe you've been in a shipwreck, but I don't want to save you." Not true—she *did* want to save him. Saving people came naturally to her. She enjoyed it. And if anyone was ever worth saving...

No. She wouldn't give in to the impulse. She wouldn't let herself become involved with a man who depended on her to solve his problems for him. For her own sake, she wouldn't do it.

"I'm sorry, Jamie," she said quietly, forcing resolve into her words. "I like you and I want things to work out for you. But you've got to work them out for yourself." She swallowed to still the quiver in her voice. Gazing into his beautiful, stormy eyes made her want to weep, to hurl herself back into his arms and worry about the consequences once the damage was done. But that would make her no better than him, acting without a thought for the aftermath. If she became involved with him—more involved than she already was—she would wind up devastated. She wasn't going to let passion blind her to that truth.

"I don't know if I can work things out without you," he confessed.

"You'll have to," she said, then brushed her fingertips lightly over his lips. "Let me know the minute you do. I'll be waiting."

Before she could change her mind, before she could yield to her pleading heart, she spun around and raced across the street to the parking lot behind the YMCA. She didn't dare look over her shoulder to see if he was watching her, following her, reaching out to her. She didn't hear him call her back.

YOU'LL BE WAITING, will you? he thought bitterly, watching her vanish behind a row of cars parked in the lot across the street. Well, maybe I won't want you waiting. Maybe I won't want you at all.

Anger seared him, as caustic as battery acid. How could she walk away from him like that? Whatever burned between them went way beyond lust, although there was certainly plenty of that, too—on her part as well as his. She wanted him, he wanted her, and they were grown-ups. This should be a no-brainer.

Except that it went beyond the obvious. What connected him and Allison wasn't just an aria of harmonizing hormones like the duet he'd sung with

Luanne Whoever in Eleuthera. This was complex. It was serious.

He needed Allison. That would be bad enough—but he'd made it even worse by letting her know he needed her.

How could she walk away?

All right, then. He was going to have to stop needing her. The hell with her big green eyes and her long, luscious body. The hell with her expertise. He would get a book on fatherhood and learn everything there was to know about raising a daughter—or, God help him, he'd fess up to his folks and get some pointers from his mother. Because he was never ever going to Allison Winslow's damned Daddy School class again.

And she could go scrounge her own funds, too. He didn't want her beholden to him, that was for sure.

He gave her a few more minutes to drive out of the parking lot, then crossed the street. Samantha woke up and started to bawl. It figured. Jamie already felt like crud—why shouldn't Sammy add to his misery? Actually, he found her caterwauling kind of cathartic, in a way. She was only doing what he wanted to do.

That, he acknowledged, was yet another thing babies had over adults. They could pee whenever and wherever they wanted without the risk of getting arrested for public indecency or health code violations. They could take naps whenever the urge struck. They got carried everywhere or pushed around on a wheeled throne. They didn't have to do their own burping if they didn't want to; adults would manipulate their burping mechanism for them.

And they could scream. When they were upset, when they were hungry or uncomfortable, when life wasn't giving them what they needed the instant they needed it, they could holler to high heaven. When they were sad. When they were hurting. When they were afraid.

"Scream away," Jamie murmured, pushing the stroller through the parking lot to the Range Rover. "Scream your sweet little heart out, Sam. You've got to do the screaming for both of us tonight."

A DAY PASSED without Allison in it. Twenty-four long, dreary hours. Amazingly, Jamie experienced a few minutes here and there during which he actually thought about something else.

As days went, it really wasn't so bad. Samantha actually slept for six hours straight overnight, which meant Jamie could spend those six uninterrupted hours in his own bed, blaming his inability to fall asleep on everything but the kid's midnight hunger pangs and elimination habits. He lay on the bed, which suddenly seemed much too big for him to occupy alone, and contemplated what it was about Allison that had grabbed his imagination and refused to let go.

It wasn't just her appearance. He'd known women who were arguably prettier, or more curvaceous, or cuter. He'd certainly known women who dressed better. Except for their one dinner date, Allison was always clad in nurse's white. White was such a virginal shade.

It wasn't just the way she kissed, either. She kissed both deeply and shyly, and it was an intoxicating combination. She always seemed a bit startled when

Jamie kissed her, as if she weren't sure she was supposed to experience such a rush of pleasure. But she did experience it, and she didn't retreat. She gave back all the pleasure she got and then some.

The way her body moved against him when they kissed, the softness of her breasts, the sleek shape of her. The way her hips had found his, the way her thighs had cradled him... But it wasn't just her sensuality that got to him.

So what was it? Her priggish, prudish morality? That was usually the sort of thing that turned him off.

Her competence? Yeah, right.

It was something else, and he spent his rare six-hour stretch of tranquility in bed trying to figure it out. Fragments of ideas snagged in his brain. The way she talked to Samantha. The way she held the baby and studied her face and seemed genuinely taken with the kid. That was part of it.

The way he'd felt, all warm and tight in the region of his solar plexus, when she'd asked him what he would want if his dreams could come true, and he'd almost blurted out, "You. If my dreams could come true, I'd want you in my house, in my life, helping me to raise my daughter. I'd want you to be Sammy's mother and my wife, and the three of us would pull this gig off together."

He still couldn't believe she would walk away from him when he was feeling that way. It just didn't seem possible that she couldn't have felt as attached to him as he felt to her.

Thus he'd endured the night, alternately awestruck that he had found a woman who could help him through the greatest challenge in his life and infuriated that the woman didn't want to be bothered with him until he'd gotten through that challenge on his own. By the time Samantha did her impersonation of an air-raid siren at around five that morning, he'd given up on his one big chance for a restful night.

He tried, he really tried not to think about Allison all day. He spent some time at his computer, pushing and pulling concepts for his column in the hope they would take a shape he could recognize. He tried feeding Samantha while he wrote, holding her in his lap, propping her on his shoulder and leaving her on a blanket spread across the floor of his office, but she wouldn't have any of it. She fussed and fussed. She was cranky and crabby, red-faced and moist-eyed. Nothing satisfied her. After a while, Jamie started to view her as the physical incarnation of his mental state.

"What's with you, toots?" he asked her at one point. She was lying on her belly across his knees, and he'd actually managed to write a few good paragraphs for his essay about a mother's notion of a perfect female companion for her adult son. Samantha seemed determined to prove that she was *not* the perfect female companion for Jamie. She wept and slobbered so much, he had to change into fresh jeans because the ones in which he'd started the day were soaked at the knees.

He held her against his chest and she whimpered. He'd learned through trial and error that this was one of her preferred positions, with her face pressed to his sternum and her hands pawing his pecs. He wondered if she was looking for lactating mammaries, but she never complained about the lack of them when he held her that way, with his hands cupped securely around her well-padded bottom and his chin resting against her pale, downy hair. Usually she piped down within a minute when he held her on his chest, as if just resting against his beating heart was enough to soothe her.

It wasn't enough today. She continued to fuss. She clawed at him, her shiny pink nails pinching his T-shirt. She mewled and left patches of saliva on the front of the shirt. Sweat seeped through her scalp and left her hair matted and damp.

Something was bugging her, and he didn't know what. Allison would know, but he pushed that thought from his mind. Samantha was warm, probably from all her squirming and fretting. He ran his hand gently over her hair, brushing the wet locks back from her face. She peered at him, her face scrunched into a scowl, her complexion mottled.

"Okay, pal. You don't want me to work? We'll do it your way." He saved what he'd written, rolled back in his chair, hooked his pinkie through the handle of his empty coffee cup and carried Samantha out of his office, down the hall to the kitchen. He refilled the cup, then journeyed on to the den. If he couldn't finish his column, he might as well vegetate for a while in front of the tube.

He sank onto the oversize couch, slouching deep into the cushions so Samantha was practically horizontal as she cuddled against his chest. Wielding the remote, he switched on the TV. He rarely watched daytime television, and he was mildly amused to find it every bit as wretched as he'd always heard. On one talk show, three young men were gleefully discussing how they'd cheated on their girlfriends with their girlfriends' best friends. Another talk show featured a young woman who boasted of having had three breast augmentation surgeries and was planning to have a butt lift soon. A third talk show had as its theme X-rated dentists. Jamie didn't even want to think about that.

He pressed the channel changer button, and the screen filled with professional wrestlers. A bulky gentleman dressed in what appeared to be a caveman's animal skins pontificated into the camera about the many savageries he was hoping to inflict on his opponent. "Hey, Sam, this looks good," Jamie remarked, turning her so she could watch. "See that guy? That's Waterloo Walt Riley. Listen to him. He says he's going to tear Pit-Bull Howland's head off. What do you think, Sam? Can he do that?"

She issued a teary sigh.

Jamie recalled the last time he'd watched pro wrestling on the tube. It had been at Steve's cabin on Lake Waramaug on Jamie's thirtieth birthday— that glorious weekend before his life had been reduced to changing diapers and indulging in adolescent dreams about a prickly, uptight nurse with gorgeous hair. He had staggered into the cabin's living room late Saturday morning, after having slept in, and he'd found Steve nursing a cup of coffee and watching Waterloo Walt go at it in the ring with the Mongoose. The two overfed, grunting men had tossed each other around, pretended to yank each other's hair and stomped their feet for a sound effect every time they threw a punch. Jamie had scarcely paid attention; he'd been intent on mainlining some caffeine, after which he and Steve were going to take the boat out on the lake.

He could use some caffeine now, but to get it

would require leaning forward to reach the cup he'd left on the table in front of the couch. He finally had Samantha semicalm, and he didn't want to jostle her. He satisfied himself with the robust aroma wafting up from his mug and adjusted the baby more comfortably on his torso.

She wriggled against him, her hair still damp, her eyes blinking and her hand working its way into her mouth. On the screen across the cozy, paneled room, the two wrestlers were jawing at each other. Jamie wondered what Sam thought of those guys yelling that way. No one had ever yelled at Samantha, at least not since she'd arrived in Arlington. Occasionally Jamie wanted to yell at her, but mostly he kept his complaints to an assortment of grumbled curses.

He didn't have to yell at her, but he was supposed to talk to her. That was Allison's advice to new fathers. Jamie couldn't talk to Samantha the way Allison could, but he could share his thoughts on this professional wrestling show with her.

"Okay, now see that guy?" he explained, pointing at the TV. "That's Pit-Bull Howland. He's the bad guy. How do I know that? You might well ask."

Samantha thumped her head against his chest and poked her foot against the buckle of his belt.

"I hate to be the one who tells you this, honey, but if you can't trust your father to be honest with you, who can you trust? So, here's the down and dirty—professional wrestling is fixed. It's all a show, not a sport. These guys work out together, they choreograph their moves, and everyone knows in advance who's going to win and who's going to lose. I know, it's really sad that you have to learn the facts of life at such a tender age, but I'm not going to lie to you about this. Professional wrestling is bogus.''

She gurgled.

''All right, so I haven't turned you into a cynic yet. Now Waterloo isn't really going to tear the Pit-Bull's head off. They just talk like that. It's a lot of verbiage. Totally meaningless.''

She gurgled again.

''Yeah, kind of like the way you talk. Unlike Allison, who doesn't open her mouth unless she's going to say something so reasonable it makes you sick. That's a real problem with Allison. She's always so gosh-darn reasonable. Gosh-darn is a euphemism, by the way. Can you say euphemism?''

Samantha slurped on her thumb and forefinger.

''You know, I try to talk to the woman, I try to invite her to go with the flow, listen to her body, do what comes naturally. It's not like she needs a whole hell of a lot—I mean, a whole *heck* of a lot—of persuasion. She's as interested in getting up close and personal with me as I am with her. This is definitely a mutual situation. The only problem is... Holy-moly, did you see that? The Pit-Bull just threw Waterloo across the ring. You know how much that guy weighs? Two-fifty, easy. Maybe more. Jeez, did you see the way the Pit-Bull tossed him? Like he weighed no more than a tennis ball.''

Samantha grunted. That meant that either her digestive system was pushing her most recent meal through the final inch of her intestine or she was choking on her thumb. Her thumb still seemed to be attached to her hand, though, and he smelled no foul odors emanating from her diaper area. Maybe she was just grunting in imitation of the two wrestlers.

"So, where was I? Allison." He took a deep breath and shook his head. "Allison wants to make love with me, Sammy. I know she does. I hope I'm not shocking you—when you hit puberty, I'll make sure someone explains this stuff to you. But in the meantime... The trouble with Allison is, she thinks I have to have every last detail of my life worked out before she can get close to me. Does that make sense?"

Samantha's attention was riveted to the television screen, where Waterloo was now prevailing. He was faking punches to the Pit-Bull's blubbery stomach, growling and stamping his foot and creating a grand, dramatic impression of brutality. Samantha growled right along with him.

Great. His daughter was going to learn her linguistic skills from a televised broadcast of professional wrestling. "I think I'd better switch the channel," he conceded. But just as he positioned his thumb on the channel button, Waterloo started pulling the Pit-Bull around the ring by his hair. This was too good to miss. "Don't ever pull someone's hair, Sam," he lectured her. "Remember, those guys are professionals. Don't try this at home."

Samantha chirped. For a kid who couldn't utter a single recognizable word, she certainly had quite a vocabulary of noises. And given that professional wrestling was kind of preverbal anyway, Jamie supposed it was just as well that he let her watch the mayhem. She was probably the perfect age for it intellectually.

"See that?" he said as the referee leaped into the fray and started counting the Pit-Bull out. "Once he counts to three, the bout is over. Pay attention,

Sammy. It's time for you to learn your numbers. One…two…three.''

"Fee!" Samantha squawked.

Jamie bolted upright. "What did you say?" he demanded, turning her to face him.

Her head bobbled, and he quickly cupped his hand behind it to hold it steady. Her eyes flickered open and shut, and she screwed up her face as if revving up to cry. But although her cheeks turned red, she didn't cut loose with a scream as Jamie expected. "Fee!" she babbled.

"That's right! Three." He planted a loud, smacking kiss on her forehead, then lowered her back against the cushion of his chest and grinned like a druggie on a high.

"Fee," she'd said. One, two, *fee*. Scarcely more than a month old, his daughter could count.

Maybe she was a certified genius. And maybe he wasn't such a bad father, after all.

"I CAN'T BELIEVE you did that!" Molly groaned.

Allison sighed. The shoe store was glaringly bright, as if to compensate for the fact that it was nearly 10:00 p.m. and dark outside. But she'd been putting in long shifts at Arlington Memorial the past few days, and Grammy needed new shoes, so this was the only time they could shop.

She probably shouldn't have brought Molly along. But Molly had phoned just as Allison was ushering Grammy out the door, and when Allison had told her where they were headed, she'd invited herself to join them. They'd already had supper—bad pizza at a shop in the minimall, a few doors down from the shoe store. The pizza crust had been rubbery, the cheese dripping with grease. A half hour after consuming only half a slice, Allison's stomach continued to churn.

"The program is about to go down the drain, Jamie offered to help you find some money to keep it going and you said no. How could you do that?" Molly said in a harsh stage whisper.

"I told you," Allison repeated for the umpteenth time. Not only was her stomach churning, but her back ached from the hard bench where she and Molly sat, waiting while Grammy paraded around in a pair of leather sneakers to assess the fit. "I don't want to be indebted to him."

"You wouldn't have been indebted to him. At worst, you would have been indebted to the bank or the funding organization or whatever. I don't get it, Allie. He was only trying to help you."

"He wants— Well, he wants a lot from me," she said vaguely. "If I let him help me, then he might expect something in return."

"What? What might he expect?"

Fortunately Allison was spared from answering by her grandmother, who appeared before them. She peered down at the sneakers, then glowered at Allison. "I hate these shoes," she announced.

Ignoring Grammy's declaration, Allison rose from the bench, hunkered down and prodded Grammy's toes through the soft white leather. "They're the right size, Grammy. They seem to be a perfect fit."

"I don't care." Grammy poked at the floor with the rubber tip of her cane. "They're ugly as sin."

"They're sneakers. What's ugly about them?" Allison pointed to her own plain white sneakers. She owned several pairs. Nothing was more comfortable for work, where she was constantly on her feet, running down the halls, leaning over beds and pushing isolettes.

"They look like something a sweaty, smelly marathoner would wear. I found another pair of shoes I want to try on." Grammy held up a strappy gold tone sandal with a narrow two-inch heel.

"You can't wear that," Allison said, straightening up and trying not to laugh.

"Why not?"

"You've got arthritis." She took the sandal from her grandmother and scrutinized it. If the sneakers Grammy had tried on looked like the sort of footwear designed for a long-distance runner, the sandal looked like the sort of footwear designed for a runway model—one who didn't have to walk more than a few steps at a time in the real world. "Look at this heel, Grammy. You'd break your neck wearing shoes like this. *I'd* break my neck in them. That's why I wear sneakers. Do you really think my shoes are ugly as sin?"

Grammy eyed Allison's feet and then her own. "Yours look better than mine. At least they've got real laces."

"I picked out the pair with Velcro straps for you because they're easier to fasten."

"What, you think I'm too old to tie a bow?" Grammy turned from Allison and glanced at Molly. "You don't think I'm too old to tie a bow, do you?"

"I think you're the perfect age for who you are," Molly answered tactfully.

"A diplomat. This is what I'm stuck with—a nurse and a diplomat. I want the sandals," Grammy declared.

"And I want a grandmother who's just a little bit sensible," Allison countered, carrying the sandal back to the display shelf from which Grammy had removed it.

"The heck you do. You're sensible enough for both of us," Grammy called across the store.

The criticism resounded inside Allison as she paid for the new sneakers and placed Grammy's old, worn-out oxfords in the box the sneakers had come in. Yes, Allison was sensible. Sensible enough to want to steer clear of Jamie until he'd worked out his problems. Sensible enough not to want to get into another relationship where it became her job to make everything better for her man.

As if Molly could guess her thoughts, she lit into Allison as they walked through a chilly drizzle to her car. "I don't think you're too sensible," Molly murmured. "In fact, I think you're an idiot. If you had half a brain, you'd let Jamie raise some money for the Daddy School."

"Molly, I told you—"

"You don't want to be indebted to him," Molly recited. "Well, you know, I've got a vested interest in all this, too. If the Daddy School goes under, I'll never be able to set up the toddler program."

"Fine. *You* go to Jamie and beg for money," Allison snapped, as impatient with her best friend as with her grandmother.

"I just don't see the big deal. You don't want to date him, so don't date him. You're both adults. You could still work together on fund-raising for the Daddy School."

"I don't want to work with him on anything right now." If she worked with him, she'd fall in love with

him—and with his little daughter. And then, if he
decided to give his daughter up, she'd be doubly
heartbroken. It wasn't even her business whether or
not he retained custody of Samantha. She didn't want
to be a part of the decision. And she didn't want him
leaning on her for support. She didn't want to be
telling him what to do and then doing it for him when
he couldn't manage to do it himself.

"All you ever want to do is help everyone else,"
Molly said, her shorter height forcing her to take
three steps to every two of Allison's. "You have no
trouble being the one giving the help. But when it
comes to letting anyone else help you, you just can't
take it."

Allison's retort died before it could take shape.
She knew Molly was speaking out of her own frustration—she wanted to be able to work with floun-
dering fathers in a class of her own, and as the sole
owner of a small preschool, she had even less access
to institutional support than Allison did. But behind
her anger, Allison heard truth in her accusation. She
did devote most of her energy to helping others because she genuinely enjoyed helping people. But
Molly was right: she had a real problem accepting
help from others.

Especially from Jamie. To accept his help in raising money for the program would throw the precar-
ious balance between them way off. If she could demand that he take care of his own problems, then she
couldn't very well turn around and ask him to take
care of hers. They simply shouldn't be depending on
each other for these things. She wanted their relationship simplified, each of them having resolved

their own issues before they attempted to become a couple.

She unlocked the car door for her grandmother, helped her onto the seat and handed her the box containing her old shoes. Then she turned to Molly and sighed. "You're right. I have trouble accepting help from Jamie McCoy."

"Why?"

"Because I—" Allison swallowed. Even though Molly was her best friend, it was still difficult to admit the truth. "I'm half in love with him already, Molly. And I shouldn't be. I need to put some distance between us."

She'd forgotten her grandmother was sitting within earshot. "She's a wreck, Molly," Grammy reported. "A lovesick little puppy. No appetite. You saw the way she picked at that pizza."

"The pizza was too oily," Allison argued.

"And she's mopey and surly. I don't see what the hang-up is, myself. The boy is rich, he's handsome, and so what if he's made a few mistakes? Find me a man who's never made a mistake and I'll call the *Guinness Book of World Records*."

"Grammy." Allison smiled in spite of herself. "You were the one who said he had the morals of a tick."

"At my age, I can say whatever I want. For all I know, ticks operate by their own strict moral code. As for this man's problems with frisky sperm, well, there are worse things a man can do in the world than knock up a woman by accident. It's not like he ever raised a hand to you," Grammy continued, naming the one evil no Winslow woman would ever tolerate. "At least he's doing right by his baby."

So far. Unless he decided to give up the baby, to send her back to her rich, spoiled, irresponsible mother.

"This isn't a topic open to general debate," Allison declared firmly. "It's my life."

"It's my Daddy School class," Molly muttered.

"It's my ugly new shoes," Grammy added.

Allison couldn't help herself. She succumbed to a laugh. "You two are going to drive me crazy!"

"As long as you drive us home," Grammy said, buckling her seat belt around her and smiling complacently.

LATE THAT NIGHT, Allison was still awake, staring at the shaft of moonlight that spilled through the dormer window into her bedroom and wishing it could illuminate her tangled musings. Was Molly right? Was it a sign of weakness on Allison's part that she couldn't accept help from Jamie? Would it have been easier or harder for her to accept his help if she had gone back to his house Monday night?

She had wanted to. Three days later—three long, lonely nights later—the ache of denying herself what Jamie had offered still gnawed at her. She replayed the memory of his kiss Monday night over and over, masochistically. How had she ever found the integrity to walk away from him?

Why had she?

Wisely or foolishly, she *had* walked away. She'd done the right thing. She wanted to believe that Jamie understood, that once he'd come to terms with his paternity and with the woman who'd given birth to Samantha, he would contact Allison and they could pick up where they left off.

But she doubted he would do that. She read his column, and it gave her a pretty clear hint of how a guy like Jamie would respond to a woman's turning from him. He would most likely go out in search of a woman more flexible and less hardheaded than Allison.

She'd made her choice, and it would probably save her some emotional wear and tear in the long run. But it was the short run that was causing her pain. The short run of long, lonely nights.

The silver sheen of the moon burned her eyes—or maybe what was burning them was tears. She squeezed them shut and rolled away from the window. The telephone beside her bed rang.

She jumped, and her heart pounded. When a telephone rang at midnight, a person—especially a nurse—had to assume bad news loomed at the other end of the line.

Grammy was safe and sound, asleep downstairs in her first-floor bedroom. It must be Allison's mother or her stepfather. Or maybe an emergency at the hospital, although the head nurses on night duty would have used her pager to summon her.

Before the phone could ring a second time and awaken Grammy, she lifted the receiver. "Yes?"

"Allison?" Jamie's voice came through the wire, breathless with tension.

She didn't need him to identify himself. She'd been hearing his voice in her head for days. "Jamie?"

"I'm sorry to call you, Allison—especially so late, but—"

"What happened? What's wrong?"

"It's Sam." His voice cracked slightly. "I don't

know what's bothering her. She won't stop whimpering and she won't take a bottle—I've been trying all day, but she won't eat. She just keeps clinging to me and whimpering, and she's so hot. It's like she's on fire or something. She's burning up. I'm scared, Allison. I don't know what to do.''

"Get her over to Arlington Memorial right away,'' Allison ordered him. A baby with a high fever could be suffering from any number of different ailments, the majority of which weren't emergencies requiring a hospital's care. But it didn't pay to play guessing games with Jamie over the phone or to try to diagnose the baby without seeing her. Better to get Samantha into a doctor's hands immediately.

"The hospital?''

"Yes. Take her right into the emergency room.''

"And then what?''

"And then give her to me. I'll be there, waiting for you. Just bring her to me and I'll take care of everything.''

It wasn't until she hung up that she realized what she was doing—exactly what she'd sworn she wouldn't do. She didn't want to sweep in and take care of everything. She didn't want to solve Jamie's problems.

But this was Samantha. The baby was obviously sick. Jamie was desperate. And no matter what Allison felt about him, what she wanted, how much she needed to protect herself, she had to help him with this.

CHAPTER TWELVE

AT MIDNIGHT, the emergency room at Arlington Memorial Hospital was an eerie place. The daytime-bright lights illuminating the room glared; the daytime energy of the staff glared even more. Nurses and orderlies swarmed and stalked around the area with purpose, ducking in and out of curtained examining areas, transporting impressive-looking equipment and appearing terribly important. They chatted and joked among themselves, their eyes clear and focused. Unlike Jamie, they were completely awake.

Jamie was sort of awake, but he was running on adrenaline, not the healthy power derived from eight hours of sleep. Only two things kept him from reeling outside through the glass double doors and collapsing on the grass that bordered the parking lot. One was Samantha. The other was Allison.

She'd been at the hospital, as promised, when he'd arrived. Cradled in his arms, wrapped in a thick blanket, Samantha had been sweating profusely, and he wasn't sure that the blanket was necessary. But without it, she might get a chill, pneumonia or something. As if he knew what caused pneumonia in babies. As if he had any idea what to do with a child running a high temperature.

Hell, he didn't even know what Samantha's temperature was. He had a thermometer at home, but it was designed for adults. He couldn't imagine explaining to Sammy that she had to hold a fragile glass rod under her tongue for three minutes. This was something she could not be expected to do, especially given that she was so obviously distraught. She'd been whining and crabbing for several days now—long enough that he could no longer rationalize her mood.

He shouldn't have phoned Allison tonight. She had made it clear that she didn't want to hear from him. But it had been late, Sam had been sobbing inconsolably and he'd been frantic. His baby was obviously sick, and he didn't know what to do.

He'd considered calling his new pediatrician, but the alignment of the hands on his wristwatch argued against that. So he'd called Allison—because she was an expert when it came to babies, he told himself, even though he knew the real reasons he was reaching out for her: he trusted her and he needed her. He had absolute faith that she would know what to do, and she would make sure it got done.

She'd come through for him. She'd been there in the emergency room when he skidded the Range Rover to a halt near the entrance and charged inside with his forlorn little girl. Allison had taken Samantha from him, pointed him in the direction of the admitting clerk and sent him a smile that said, *Don't worry. Everything will be fine.*

He *knew* everything would be fine as long as Allison was with him, with his baby.

Right now, medical practitioners were doing things to Samantha. They'd carted her off somewhere to examine her, leaving him to thumb blearily through month-old magazines while all those live-wire hospital workers strutted around him. On the opposite side of the waiting area sat an aromatic gentleman, swatting at imaginary flies and singing a ditty about saints and streetwalkers. None of the orderlies paid him any attention as they scurried past, pushing carts and gurneys and shouting chipper greetings to one another.

Above the admissions desk, a wall clock announced the time: nearly one. It occurred to Jamie that he could catch a few winks while Allison and her colleagues figured out what was plaguing Sam. But the room was too well lit and noisy, and Jamie was too keyed up.

Middle-of-the-night emergencies hadn't been covered in the Daddy School, but he supposed it wasn't all that rare for parents to find themselves in such a situation—not necessarily hospital emergency rooms, but long, dark hours sitting up with a sick child or chasing away nightmares or slaying the monsters under a tot's bed. And parents would probably have to contend with daytime emergency-room trips, too, thanks to tumbles out of tree houses and spills from bicycles. Years would pass, and there would be more long, dark hours of pacing while one's adolescent progeny stayed out past curfew, like the baby-sitter Jamie had tried to hire last week. Once a parent made the commitment to raise a kid, twenty-four-hour-a-day crises were bound to be part of the package.

He wasn't sure he wanted to accept delivery of that package. He was only thirty. Admittedly that placed him squarely in the "adult" category, but he wasn't even married. He had never sworn before God and family to love someone else in sickness and health. How had he gotten stuck with a sick daughter?

Lifting his gaze from the magazine, he spotted Allison approaching from a hallway, and all his ambivalence evaporated. He must have awakened her when he'd called—if she'd been working a night shift, she wouldn't have been home to answer her phone—but she seemed as alert and animated as all the other health care professionals bustling through the room. Her hair was pinned back into a ponytail, but stubborn tendrils had escaped the clasp and drizzled about her face, softening the sharp lines of her nose and cheeks. Her eyes were wide and glowing, her lips curved into a smile.

He wanted to grab hold of her and hug hard. But he restrained himself, burying his hands in the pockets of his jeans and allowing himself a halfhearted smile in response to hers. "How is she?"

"She has an ear infection and she's dehydrated. Has she been eating?"

"No, I couldn't get anything into her all day."

"Sometimes when a baby won't eat, you have to force her to. You can use a syringe without a needle to squirt fluid down her throat. Fruit juice would be good. She needs the liquid and the sugar and vitamins. Even better, you should try one of those fortified sports drinks."

"Really?" When he thought of those beverages, he thought of international soccer stars kicking balls in slo-mo on TV ads. He didn't think of month-old babies with ear infections.

"The doctor put her on an antibiotic," Allison continued. "She's kind of young to get an infection like that. The bad news is, she may turn out to be one of those babies with chronic ear infections. You'll just have to monitor it.''

"So... She gets an antibiotic and what else?"

"Liquids. We've got her temperature down to a shade over a hundred and one. Baby acetaminophen will help with the fever. It comes in a syrup base, like the antibiotic.''

He nodded mutely. Syrup base. Acetaminophen. It was an awful lot of jargon to absorb this late at night. "So what happens now?''

"You take Samantha home and she gets better.''

He almost guffawed. Allison made it sound so simple—just as she made all aspects of child care sound simple. The weirdest part was, gazing into her luminous eyes, he almost felt as if he *could* handle syrup base and acetaminophen and child care. He *could* make sure, through sheer force of will, that his little girl got better.

But the source of his certainty was Allison. It wasn't an internal, natural part of him, and he knew that the instant he left Allison he would feel utterly helpless.

"What if she cries?" he asked.

"You hold her, sing her a lullaby and rock her in your arms.''

As easy as ABC—or one, two, "fee." "What if her temperature goes up? How will I even know it's gone up, anyway? I don't have a thermometer—''

"I'll get you a baby thermometer," Allison promised. "And if her temperature goes up, you can give her a little more acetaminophen or a cool bath.''

A cool bath? Now things were getting complicated. "Allison," he began, then hesitated. He was about to ask her an unfair question, and he searched her face for a clue as to how she would react. "Would you hate me for the rest of your life if I asked you to stay with me tonight? Not for me, but for Sam. Could you..."

Noticing the shadows falling across her eyes, he drifted off. No, she could not stay with him, not even for Sam. She didn't trust him enough. She didn't like him enough. She thought he was evil incarnate because of the circumstances surrounding Sammy's conception. Allison had judged him and found him worse than wanting.

She averted her gaze, apparently fascinated with the checkerboard pattern of the floor tiles. "I think you can handle Samantha," she said in a hushed, husky voice.

He thought he could handle having Allison in his house much more easily than he could handle giving Samantha cool baths and sports drinks with a syringe. "I swear to God, this isn't about you and me," he whispered, wishing he dared to take Allison in his arms. It would only be to reassure her, but he suspected that if he touched her, she would be anything but reassured. "The truth is, I *can't* handle Samantha. Not with an ear infection. I'm completely out of my depth with this. What if I do something wrong?"

"There's nothing you could do wrong. Just hold her and comfort her and get fluids into her. If she starts getting worse, you can always bring her back here."

"Oh, right. That's exactly what she needs—another Indy 500 speed drive to the hospital emergency room."

"You won't have to come back here," she told

him, refusing to let his sarcasm rile her. "You could take her to your own doctor in the morning if you—"

"What the hell do you think I'm going to do to you?" he erupted.

He hadn't thought he was speaking loudly, but the fragrant fellow on the other side of the room quit singing his little aria about a hooker on Canal Street and said in a flimsy Bogey imitation, "Go ahead and kiss her. You know she wants it."

"She doesn't want it," Jamie shouted over his shoulder. When he turned back to Allison, he found her smiling ruefully. "You don't, do you?"

"Right now," she confessed, "I want some sleep. And I want Samantha to get well. Do you really think you can't get through the night without me?"

She couldn't have meant the question the way it had come out, so he didn't answer by informing her that the past four nights were proof that he couldn't get through the night without her. "What I'm worried about is Samantha getting through the night without you," he rationalized. "She's just a baby, Allison. What if I did something wrong? What if she choked on the syringe or her eardrum burst or—"

"All right," Allison said, sounding more resigned than pleased. "I'll stay at your house. Just for tonight, to help out."

Dropping to his knees in gratitude would have been a tad melodramatic. "Thanks," he said, which barely began to express how relieved he was. Despite his own selfish desires, having Allison spend the night at his home to oversee Samantha's convalescence was the most important thing. Allison wasn't going to abandon him in his time of need. She wasn't going to leave Samantha at the mercy of his incompetence.

Allison eyed him dubiously. "I'm doing this for Samantha," she stressed.

"Of course." With Allison monitoring the baby's recuperation, Jamie might actually relax enough to fall asleep. He was too exhausted to get anything going with Allison, anyway. She would be perfectly safe with him.

"I'll have to swing by my house to pick up a few things and leave a note for Grammy so she won't panic when she wakes up tomorrow and I'm not there."

"No problem."

She studied him for a moment longer, as if scrutinizing him for a hint of his true intentions. He wanted to hold his hand over his heart and pledge his integrity, but he doubted that would convince her. As far as she was concerned, his integrity was less than one hundred percent reliable. So, for that matter, was any pledge he might make.

Either she'd found the reassurance she was looking for in his face or she'd given up hope of finding it. She pursed her lips, shrugged and aimed her chin at the corridor leading out of the emergency room. "Well," she said, "let's go get your baby signed out."

SHE WAS ONLY doing this for Samantha, Allison told herself as she steered up the gravel driveway to Jamie's rambling house. He had left lights on for her all along the route: post lights along the driveway, porch lights, lights in the wide living room window. He obviously wanted to make her feel welcome.

Frankly, she would have preferred to feel a little less welcome. She knew Jamie wasn't going to make a pass at her tonight—he wouldn't dare. Too much was at risk, starting with his daughter's health.

But still, Allison needed to keep her guard up. Her treacherous heart increased the risk many times over.

She set the parking brake, climbed out of her car and lifted her overnight bag from the back seat. She wasn't sure she'd get much sleep tonight, but she intended to try—in Samantha's nursery, or on a couch, or on a chair on the screened porch. She would sleep anywhere but in that decadently broad bed in Jamie's bedroom, just a hop and a step from the bathroom with the glass wall that had played too prominent a role in her fantasies of late.

By the time she'd reached the front porch, Jamie had the door open for her. He looked drowsy, his hair tousled, his eyelids at half-mast and his chin stubbled with an overnight growth of beard. His T-shirt was untucked and he had Samantha on his shoulder. She was wide awake and cantankerous. The poor thing. How could an adult explain to an infant that her discomfort wasn't anything serious, that it would go away, that it would go away even more quickly if she would only go to sleep?

As Allison crossed the threshold, Jamie fell back a step, giving her a wide berth as if to prove that he intended to stay out of her way. "I stopped at an all-night convenience store on the way home," he reported, closing the door behind her and beckoning her toward the kitchen. "I bought two bottles of Gatorade, grape and lime. I don't know which flavor she'll prefer. I was going to try shooting some down her throat with that syringe thing the hospital gave me, but I was afraid she might throw up."

"She's been known to do that," Allison remarked

wryly, following him into the kitchen. Once there, she dropped her overnight bag and lowered herself onto a chair. "Hand her over. I'll get some juice into her."

Jamie placed Samantha carefully in Allison's lap, then gave her the two bottles of Gatorade and the wide syringe. He watched attentively as she drew some of the grape-flavored drink into the syringe, glided the tip gently between Samantha's lips and squirted the juice into her mouth. Some dribbled out and down her chin, but Jamie handed Allison a paper towel before the purple liquid could drip onto her clothes. It wouldn't be a tragedy if her jeans got Gatorade on them, but she appreciated Jamie's vigilance. Perhaps he remembered what happened the last time Samantha had made a mess on Allison's clothes. Like Allison, Jamie was apparently in no rush to relive that night.

"See how easy it is?" she told him. "Now, you try it."

Jamie concentrated hard as he poked the syringe into the bottle of Gatorade and filled the tube. "I'll have you know," he muttered, easing the syringe out of the bottle and frowning, "that I never had anything to do with drugs as a kid. It's not like I've had a lot of practice using syringes."

"You're a lucky man. Now just wedge the tip into her mouth, nice and slow... There you go."

His face broke into a proud smile as Samantha swallowed his dose of Gatorade. Because Allison was still holding Samantha in her lap, he had to lean against her to squirt the juice into Samantha's mouth. Allison felt his warmth, his muscular breadth, as his body bowed above her to feed Samantha another dose. She smelled the last, lingering traces of his spicy aftershave and the familiar fragrance of the laundry detergent he'd used to wash his shirt. She'd grown accustomed to that smell. Every time she opened her closet, the green minidress he'd run through his washing machine offered a hint of the same scent.

"She isn't going to choke on this, is she?" he asked.

"No. She's thirsty, Jamie. She wants the stuff. It's just that nursing is hard work for a baby, and she's too weak and tired to go to all the effort of tugging on a nipple. This juice, with all those minerals and electrolytes, ought to get her through the night. Tomorrow, if the antibiotic hasn't upset her stomach, you can try her on a little formula."

For the next twenty minutes he fed his baby, a few cc's at a time, until she'd consumed half a cup of juice. All the while Allison held Samantha. All the while, Jamie pressed close to her, his attention fully on the baby. There was nothing erotic about his position, no pressure, no insinuation of romance...yet Allison responded to him just as she should have known she would. She was affected not only by his nearness but by the sight of his big hands wielding the tiny syringe, the pinch of his brows as he frowned in concentration, the worry tugging at his mouth. He was trying so hard to do the right thing for his daughter, and his efforts touched Allison.

She gave herself a stern silent lecture. Merely by running to his side when he'd phoned her, she'd started down the slippery slope of becoming involved with him. She would have to work hard to climb back up that slope.

"I think she's had enough," she said when the baby twisted away from Jamie's gentle probing with the syringe. "Why don't we see if we can get her down to sleep."

Jamie lifted Samantha from Allison's lap. Allison was gratified to see how well he'd learned the Daddy School technique, steadying the baby's head and supporting her with his arms. He trudged off to the nursery, and Allison didn't follow. She didn't want to be gratified by anything he did. She didn't want to think positively about him in any context. She was already too vulnerable to him.

After a couple of minutes, he returned to the kitchen. "She's in her crib," he reported, "but she isn't asleep. She's lying there, whining and acting really ticked off."

"Give her some time. She may settle down."

"God, I hope so." He raked a hand through his hair and groaned. "I'm so tired, it hurts."

"Why don't you go get some sleep, then?" Allison suggested, thinking that if he was out of sight and unconscious, she might have a chance of surviving the night at his house. "I'll keep a close watch on her."

His eyes, glazed though they were, zeroed in on her. "What if she falls asleep?"

"Then I'll take a nap, myself. Just tell me which couch I should use."

A flicker of understanding glinted in his eyes. If there had been any doubt in his mind about where she would sleep, her comment clarified the issue.

"I've got a sofa bed in the guest room," he said evenly. If he was so tired he hurt, he was surely too tired to argue with Allison over the sleeping arrange-

ments—and too tired to care where she wound up
spending the night.

He lifted her small bag and extended his hand to
help her off the chair. She took it, accepting the gesture in friendship. He didn't squeeze her hand, didn't
stroke his thumb over her palm. He was probably too
exhausted to remember that she was a woman, let
alone a woman he'd once hoped to seduce.

As they passed the open door to the nursery, Allison heard Samantha sniffling and sobbing in her
crib. The guest room was across the hall, a compact
square of space with a sofa, a wall of bookcases
crammed with books, a dresser and a small television
set. "Nothing fancy," he said apologetically, "but I
can open the sofa into a bed. The mattress isn't bad."

"Leave it for now. The way Samantha is carrying
on, I may not be needing it."

He let go of her hand but remained inside the doorway. "If she keeps you up more than an hour, come
get me. We can take turns sitting up with her."

"No, that's all right. You get some sleep now. I
can sleep tomorrow."

"What about work?"

"I pulled a Saturday shift last weekend. I'm off
this weekend. I'll catch up on my sleep tomorrow."

"Are you sure?"

"Go to bed, Jamie. I'll take care of Samantha."

He was clearly too tired to argue. "Thanks."

"Forget it."

He hesitated for a moment, leaning slightly toward
her, his soul reaching for her even if his arms didn't.
"I won't," he warned, at last dropping back a step.
His smile was pensive, weighted with unreadable
thoughts. "Good night, Allison."

She watched him turn and leave the room, then listened to his footsteps as they moved down the hall. She heard the thud of his bedroom door closing, then shut down her imagination before she could start visualizing his bed, his shower, his body. Fortunately, Samantha squelched any libidinous thoughts by bleating her misery loudly enough to echo through the hallway.

Allison crossed the hall to attend to the distraught baby. This was what she ought to be thinking about, she reminded herself as she leaned over the crib and massaged Samantha's warm back through the soft cotton of her one-piece nightie. Here in this nursery, with this sick little girl, was where Allison's mind needed to be. Nowhere else but here.

JAMIE FOUND ALLISON on the floor of the nursery at nine-thirty the following morning. She was fast asleep.

Back in his youth—until he was, oh, about twenty-nine—he wouldn't have minded sleeping on a floor. He'd done some camping as a teenager, and he'd slept on the floors of dorm rooms during various outings to parties and concerts on other campuses. He recalled a wild weekend in New York City a few years ago when eight guys from school all went down for a classmate's bachelor party, followed by his wedding at a fancy Park Avenue synagogue. All eight of the guys had crashed at a ninth pal's studio apartment on the West Side. Not only had they slept on the floor, but they'd had to arrange their sleeping bags to interlock like jigsaw puzzle pieces so they could all fit into the twelve-by-sixteen-foot space.

The party and the wedding had been so much fun, he hadn't even noticed the hardness of the floor.

But now he was thirty, fast approaching geriatric condition. Floor sleeping was a sport for youngsters. And dedicated nurses, apparently.

Seeing Allison on the floor caused him a pang of guilt. He felt better rested than he'd been since Samantha first started acting funky a few days ago, and there lay Allison, the person responsible for his renewed energy, lying on her side with her knees drawn up and one arm bent under her head. Her shoes were off, her shirt untucked, and her hair was a luscious mess splayed out across the rug.

He tiptoed past her to check on Samantha, who was also sound asleep. He was pleased, for reasons he felt it best not to analyze, that the faint snoring he'd heard from the doorway came from Sam and not Allison.

He pulled Samantha's blanket up over her, then crept back out of the room. Across the hall the guest room door stood open. Peeking in, he noticed that the sofa had not been slept in—or on. Allison's overnight bag lay open on the floor, and a nylon toiletries case sat on top of the suitcase's few contents. She must have washed up and then returned to the nursery to keep vigil over the baby.

His baby. Yet Allison had taken care of Sam the way a mother might. Gratitude barely began to describe what he was feeling.

His feelings were irrelevant, though. He ought to be thinking about Allison's feelings—specifically her feelings of aching bones and stiff muscles from having fallen asleep on the floor.

He returned to his bedroom, smoothed out the

sheets on his mattress and plumped the pillows. The least he owed Allison was a few hours of serious sleep on the most comfortable bed in the house.

Returning to the nursery, he studied her for a moment. She hadn't moved in his absence. She was obviously in a deep slumber. Was it deep enough for him to be able to carry her to his room without waking her up?

There was only one way to find out. He squatted down beside her, slid one arm under her shoulders and the other under her knees and hoisted her into his arms. Her height made her unwieldy, and she weighed more than he'd expected—dead weight, since she remained fast asleep. Carefully, he hoisted her higher against his chest and straightened up.

Without opening her eyes, without acknowledging that he was holding her, she looped her arms around his neck and rested her head against his shoulder. A quiet sigh escaped her.

Her hands felt surprisingly sensuous at the nape of his neck, cool and soft. How soothing they must have felt on Samantha through the night. How soothing they must feel on all her patients. He wouldn't mind being one of her patients right now, even if it meant regressing to Sam's age. Allison would cradle him in her arms and cuddle him and peer intently into his face and say things to him, things he wanted to hear. And those smooth, capable hands of hers would stroke him and clasp him and...

These were the kind of thoughts that made it difficult for him to walk. He let out a slow breath, then lugged her out of the nursery and down the hall to his bedroom. He lowered her onto the bed and did one of the hardest things he'd ever done—eased her hands from the back of his head and walked away from her.

Feeling rather noble, he stalked to the kitchen and prepared a pot of coffee. While it was brewing, he ducked into his office, turned on the computer and called up the file containing his current column, about mothers selecting allegedly perfect mates for their sons. He returned to the kitchen to fill a mug with coffee, then headed back to the office to finish the column, all the while knowing that his mother could not possibly have met the perfect woman for him, because the perfect woman for him was lying in his bed right now, and he was being shamefully decent and moral and staying away from her.

The column practically wrote itself. It contained cerebral chuckles and belly laughs, wry irony and droll wit. It was brilliant, or at least passable. When his mother read it in her local Arizona newspaper in a couple of weeks, she would never see herself in it.

He printed a hard copy of the article for himself, then faxed a copy through his computer to his syndication company. His mug was empty, and he went back to the kitchen for a refill.

The clock on the wall said ten-thirty. Allison had said she didn't have to work at the hospital today, but even so, she might want him to wake her up so she could go home. Her grandmother might need her or she might want to buy groceries...or she might just want to get away from him.

He filled a second mug with coffee and carried both mugs down the hall, stopping along the way to check on Samantha. She was still snoring, evidently making up for the several sleepless nights she'd suffered along with Jamie.

Past the nursery, he entered his bedroom. Allison had rolled onto her side. Her hair spread in a riot of auburn locks across his pillow, and her shirt had ridden up slightly to reveal a sliver of skin above the waistband of her jeans. Her lips were parted slightly, pursed into the shape of a kiss.

Bringing her the coffee had been a mistake. If this was a test of his willpower, his willpower was mighty close to flunking. The only way he could get out of the bedroom with his decency intact would be to leave the coffee on the night table without awakening her and sprint through the door as quickly as possible.

He stole across the room, silent in his bare feet, and set the mug down with a muted thud. Just as he started to straighten up, her eyes flew open.

"Jamie?" Her voice was hoarse, muffled by drowsiness and the pillow.

He took a giant step backward. "I brought you some coffee."

She blinked and slid her hand along the surface of the sheet, exactly the way he'd imagined her sliding her hand across the surface of his skin. "Why am I in your bed?" she asked, sounding less troubled than curious.

"You fell asleep on the floor of the nursery. I carried you in here because I thought you'd be more comfortable. That's all there is to it, I swear."

"Don't swear." She pushed herself up to sit and reached for the coffee. With the mug halfway to her mouth, she hesitated and shot him a startled look, as if her mind were only just coming into focus. "You *carried* me in here?"

"I told you, you're a skinny Botticelli angel."

"And you're an Olympic weight lifter." She put the mug back on the night table and studied him. "I was in your arms?" she asked in a small voice.

He swallowed, feeling certain parts of his anatomy do the guy thing as he picked up her radar. "Yeah," he said just as softly.

"And I didn't even wake up?"

"You put your arms around me," he told her.

She sighed, obviously embarrassed. Her cheeks grew pink.

"I know you didn't mean anything by it," he told her.

She shot him another piercing look. "How do you know that?"

If his willpower hadn't already failed, this was enough to push it into the D-minus column. He wasn't even aware of walking back to the bed, but in less than a second he was there, practically dropping his mug on the night table next to hers and offering himself for her to put her arms around again. She did, without hesitation, without explanation. She did it as if she understood that it had to be done, that not putting her arms around him would kill them both.

"I don't want to want you," she whispered as he rained kisses over her face. "I don't want to feel this way."

"It's okay," he assured her. He had no idea what *it* was, let alone whether it was okay. All he knew was that he felt the exact same way she felt, and pretending otherwise wasn't doing either of them any good.

"I dreamed you were carrying me to your bed," she confessed. "I didn't think it was real."

"It was. It is," he said, touching his lips to her cheeks, the bridge of her nose, the delicate, narrow tip. "This is so real, Allison. It doesn't get any more real than this." Her skin was like velvet against his lips, velvet dipped in fresh berries. Did his soap really smell so good or had she brought her own soap with her in that toiletries bag?

He kissed a path down to her mouth and held his breath, waiting for her to come to her senses and push him away. But she didn't. She closed her arms more tightly around him and moaned in resignation, in relief, in pleasure as he sank onto the bed beside her and took her mouth with his. She opened to him, welcoming his tongue, burying her fingers in his hair and arching against him.

He knew what she meant about not wanting to feel this way. The feelings were too uncontrollable, too massive to contain. The tenderest, toughest woman he'd ever met was kissing him as if her life depended on it, and maybe it did. Her tongue did wicked things to him, her legs shifted to accommodate his weight between them and she arched again, pressing herself against him. He felt the sweet curves of her breasts as she moved, and the tautness of her nipples. That physical sign of her arousal short-circuited the wiring of his psyche, rendering him unable to think of anything beyond now, anyone but Allison.

This was dangerous. It wasn't fun, it wasn't a lark—it was, as he'd warned her, as real as it got. He wasn't sure he was ready to accept so much reality at one time—but he couldn't stop. He couldn't stop wanting her even more than she wanted him, couldn't stop kissing her, leaning into her, nestling between her thighs and feeling her shudder, hearing her gasp.

"Allison," he groaned, tearing his lips from hers. His heart was pounding like a jungle drum, sending urgent messages throughout his body. "Allison, if you want me to stop, say so now. Because if I keep kissing you, I'm not going to be able to stop."

"Don't stop," she pleaded, tightening her hands at the base of his neck and pulling him down to her. "Don't stop."

This was it, then. Reality at its most compelling. She had told him not to stop, so he started.

He pulled back enough to reach for her shirt and draw it up. She released him and slid her arms through the sleeves, then circled her arms around him once more as he brought his hands down along the narrow straps of her bra to her breasts. Through the cream-colored lace he could see the dark circles of her nipples, plump and straining at the fabric. He teased them with his fingertips, loving the way she sucked in a breath and writhed beneath him, loving even more the way she looked once he'd undone the clasp and shoved away the fabric. Her breasts were soft and round, golden flushed with pink. If he kissed them, he expected to taste peach.

He lowered his mouth to the tantalizing flesh and tasted not peach but Allison, lush, ripe Allison. The way she moaned when he closed his lips over one nipple made him wonder whether he could make her come just by doing this. The temptation to try was great, but she clearly had other ideas. She groped at his shirt, tore at it until he shucked it and tossed it across the room, and then he realized he was the one in danger of climaxing from nothing more than her touch, the erotic brush of her fingertips against his skin.

She caressed him as if he were a sculpture and she were a blind person. She traced each rib, each sinew, each curve and hollow. She stroked his nipples, his sternum, the dusting of hair that daggered down to his navel. She explored his back, his shoulders, the bunched muscles of his upper arms as he propped himself above her. She touched the small of his back, and he had to bite his lip to keep from groaning.

"This was part of my dream, too," she admitted, following the edge of his jeans forward to his fly.

"Quite a dream. I wish I'd been there," he joked, although his voice was too ragged to sound particularly funny.

"You were there. You *are* there." The button at the top of his fly came loose, and she slid the zipper open.

"Allison," he whispered, his voice all but gone. She traced his hardness through his briefs, and he didn't bother to smother his moan this time. "You do that again and I won't be responsible for my actions," he cautioned her, though he did nothing to stop the tentative motion of her hand on him.

"You'd better be," she warned.

He laughed. She smiled. He hadn't expected her to be this unselfconscious—not that she was overly aggressive, but she wasn't behaving like the prim and proper nurse he might have expected. She was adventurous, playful, bold. Hotter than he'd dared to imagine.

He worked off her jeans and panties. When he reached between her legs, she lurched and bit back a cry. He slid his fingers down over her, into her, and she clamped her lip between her teeth and closed her eyes, as if to focus all her attention on his hand.

She felt like heaven, slick with arousal. Again he was tempted to do nothing but this until she came. Her hands tensed against his thighs; her head fell back against the thick down pillows. She was so close, so very close.

He wanted to be as close as she was. He wanted to be with her when she peaked. He wanted— God help him, he wanted her more than he wanted to want anyone.

He was scarcely able to pull back enough to reach into his night table drawer for protection. Scarcely able to tear open the envelope and ready himself for her. She flexed her fingers against his thighs and hips. Her fingernails pinched just enough to launch him into orbit.

He cupped her hips with his hands and plunged into her. He heard himself mouth her name, heard her breathe his. Almost instantly he felt the magic, her magic, that miraculous moment when her body turned from mortal flesh into blazing sensation, action and reaction. She felt so good, so good. So good...

He was lost. Deep inside her, captured by her, taken by her. Like a chain reaction, she ignited him and Jamie McCoy vanished. All that was left of him was energy, ecstasy and the soul-shaking knowledge that Allison Winslow had changed his world.

Oh, yes. He was lost.

CHAPTER THIRTEEN

SHE'D REALLY DONE IT this time. She'd won the Gold Medal in the Stupidity Olympics. All that was missing was the playing of the national anthem.

She was too honest to blame what had happened on sleepiness or sympathy or Jamie's eyes—or on the hours she'd spent comforting and bonding with his fretful little daughter last night. No, Allison had managed to fall in love with Jamie all by herself. And, like a world-class athlete, she'd discovered, in the physical expression of that love, that she was capable of giving more, feeling more and wanting more than she'd believed possible.

He propped himself up above her. He'd shaved since she'd last seen him, but his hair was mussed—no doubt her questing fingers were responsible for that. His lips were damp from her kisses. His lean, hard chest hovered above hers, and she gave serious thought to flinging her arms around him and pulling him back down on top of her.

His body was still locked deep inside her. She fluctuated around him in ebbing pulses—and each pulse was so sweet, so utterly lovely. She'd never known sex could be this wonderful. If she had, she probably would have thrown herself at Jamie a whole lot sooner.

How could she love him? He was the sort of man

who slept with strangers, who spilled his seed indiscriminately, who knew how to get a woman to do what needed doing. He'd figured out a way to lure Allison to his house, to have her care for his sick child all night long and to carry her, literally, off to his bed the following morning.

Yet gazing up into his face, seeing the sublime pleasure radiating in his eyes and curving his mouth in a faint, astonished smile, she couldn't ascribe such base motives to him. In any case, he hadn't taken anything she hadn't given willingly, blissfully...stupidly.

"I'm sorry," he murmured, bowing to brush a kiss against her lips.

"Are you?"

"I rushed. I got carried away. I wanted you so much, for so long.... Can we do it again, slower?"

If they did it again, it just might kill her. If she didn't die, she would surely fall even more deeply in love with him—not a particularly good idea.

As if that mattered at this point. What was the old saying about shutting the barn doors after the horse had run away? She was already in love with Jamie, foolishly, recklessly in love with him. Even though he himself had won the men's gold in stupidity thanks to his mistake ten months ago, even though his life was still a disastrous mess and she was afraid to get saddled with the chore of sorting it out for him, she loved him.

"Yes," she said. Gold medalists ought to revel in their prizes, at least until the thrill wore off and the repercussions set in. "Yes, we can do it again. As slowly as you want."

A sound passed through his parted lips, almost a

groan, almost a sigh of pleasure. He flicked his tongue against her teeth, moved his hips in a leisurely circle and grinned when she gasped at the way his body revived inside her. "Did I mention that you're beautiful?" he asked, framing her face with his hands, pushing her hair back from her cheeks and peering down at her as if he intended to memorize every freckle, every pore.

"You don't have to say things like that." She skimmed her hands along the knotted ridges of his shoulders. "I don't need sweet talk."

"I said it because it's true. Sweet talk is not one of my many talents."

"What was that, then? Sour talk?"

"True talk." He moved his hips again, and she felt a sharp tug in her womb, her own arousal blossoming once more.

"Tell me about your many talents," she challenged him, her voice oddly breathless.

"Why tell you? I'll show you," he promised.

He withdrew from her, and she wanted to protest. But she couldn't, because he was kissing her, and kissing him back seemed like a better idea than arguing with him. He rolled off her to lie beside her, bringing her with him so they could face each other, their heads sharing a pillow. Running his hand down her side, he followed the slope of her waist, the rise of her hip. "Did I say you were skinny?" he murmured, ending the kiss just when she was beginning to contemplate whether passing out from a lack of oxygen was worth losing contact with his lips. "You aren't."

"I'm fat?" she countered, pretending to be hurt.

"You're slimly feminine."

"And you're a writer. Clever with words."

"You asked about my talents. That's one of them," he joked, stroking the outer edge of her thigh before gliding back to up to her hip and clamping his fingers over the curve. He rolled again, onto his back, and lifted her onto him. "There," he said. "I'm giving you the upper hand. This is your chance."

She straddled him, sandwiching his hips with her knees and settling herself provocatively against his groin. "My chance for what?"

"Your chance to seduce me."

"I thought I already did that."

"You were half asleep."

"And I thought this was about *your* talents, not mine."

"One of my talents," he teased, playing his hands deftly over her belly and up to her breasts until her breath caught in her throat, "is that I can persuade you to seduce me."

She wasn't a seductress. She wouldn't know how to go about seducing anyone, let alone an experienced man like Jamie. But when she moved against him again, he moaned and reciprocated, twisting below her, using his body to stroke her.

"Jamie." She closed her eyes, felt her elbows become too wobbly to hold her up and sank onto him. "Tell me what to do."

"You know what to do," he encouraged her, bringing his hands up under her arms and pulling her higher on him.

"No, I don't." Losing her balance, she grabbed hold of the headboard above him.

"Sure you do," he said, and she realized that

grabbing hold of the headboard was exactly what he'd wanted her to do. He slid her higher and rose to kiss first one breast, then the other, then the hollow between them.

He was the seducer, she the seduced—but it didn't really matter. Not when her reflexive response was to tighten her thighs around him, to curl her toes against the sides of his hips. Her reactions only seemed to arouse him more.

"Come higher," he whispered. She didn't know what he meant until he showed her, guiding her up against his chest and then cupping his hands around her bottom. "Let me love you this way."

What way? she wondered, panicked but unable to resist as he urged her higher yet, up to his mouth. He slid his tongue between her legs and she let out a cry of shock.

"Stay with me, Allison." He kissed her again, and again, deeper. Her hands gripped the headboard so hard they hurt. Her hips wanted to move, but he held them too tightly. His lips did wicked things to her, his tongue... She shook, trying to withstand the pressure, trying not to explode into a million pieces, trying to remain in control of herself.

Trying but failing. She felt herself convulsing, tumbling down into a vortex of hot, throbbing sensation. Jamie had caused this conflagration, this eruption, this indescribable pleasure. He'd seduced her. All she'd done was given him her heart and soul, and now look at her. She was nothing but love, nothing but trembling emotion.

Sighing brokenly, she collapsed on top of him. She barely felt him nudging her shoulders, rearranging her down over him, easing her legs apart around him—but she felt his entry, deep and possessive. And then she was burning again, exploding, succumbing to ecstasy. This time he was with her all the way.

"IF WE DO THIS AGAIN, I really will die," she said a long time later.

"It wouldn't be the worst way in the world to die," he said, sounding as weak and happy as she felt.

The sheets lay tangled around their bodies. Jamie occupied a surprisingly large portion of the bed, his long legs and arms everywhere around her, his chest cushioning her, his chin resting against the crown of her head.

"I still don't know how this happened," she muttered. "I swore to myself that it wouldn't."

"Well, now that it did, what are you going to do about it?" The question was not accusing but curious.

Allison knew damned well what she was going to do: love him and love his little daughter, hope that somehow he would be able to work out his situation—and that whatever solution he came up with would have room for her in it.

But she couldn't tell him that. "I'm not sure," she hedged. "I think we should check Samantha. And then I'd like to wash up a bit."

"Good idea." He shoved himself off the bed, moving a bit less vigorously than usual. No doubt their activities of the last few hours had left him, like her, aching in muscles and joints he'd forgotten he had. He strolled over to the dresser, tugged open a door and pulled out the gray T-shirt he'd lent her the last time she was in this room. "You can borrow this," he offered, tossing the shirt to her. "It looks better on you than me." He returned to the dresser and pulled out a pair of sweatpants, which he donned.

Allison ordered herself not to grieve over losing her spectacular view of his anatomy. As a nurse, she saw bodies in various states of undress quite often—mostly female bodies, but she'd had enough training to be able to work the emergency room and the general wards when the need arose. At Arlington Memorial, bodies were a clinical concept. They were the homes of human beings who had come to be healed, and Allison helped to repair the bodies while caring for the humans living inside them.

Bodies at the hospital were not sexual. They were not gorgeous enough to make a woman's mind turn to mush. They were not a magnificent assemblage of parts, each one chanting "I'm male and I want you," the way Jamie's did.

She put on his shirt and swung her legs over the side of the mattress. Jamie walked back to the bed and grasped her hands, hauling her to her feet. He released one hand and clasped the other more tightly. As if he couldn't resist, he leaned over and kissed her brow. "Let's go."

They left the bedroom. The silence in the hall could mean that Samantha was still asleep—or it could mean trouble. Allison unconsciously moved a little faster, hurrying Jamie along.

In the crib, Samantha was sound asleep, snoring serenely. "She looks good," Allison said in a muted tone after a quick visual inspection. The baby's complexion was a healthy pink and her hair was no longer stringy with sweat. No dried mucus crusted her nose or eyes. A few fingers were jammed into her mouth.

"I love it when she's asleep," Jamie admitted, also keeping his voice down. At Allison's reproachful scowl, he grinned. "Just being honest. When she's asleep, it's like the whole world's at peace. When she's awake—" his grin widened "—it can seem like I've taken a detour and wound up in the middle of a revolution."

"I think you and she are on the same side of the war," Allison returned. "You're supposed to be allies."

"Tell her that," he protested. "I'm ready to sign a truce. She's not. Every time I think we've achieved détente, she stirs things up."

"Learn to practice peace," Allison advised. She studied the baby for a moment longer, then turned. "I think she'll be all right for the time it'll take us to shower."

"We could save time by showering together," he suggested, his eyes twinkling mischievously.

If they showered together, she doubted they would save time. Quite the contrary. But she wasn't about to reject his offer. "Only if you wash my back," she said.

He led her out of the nursery and back down the hall to his bedroom. "I'll wash your back and your front. You'll feel cleaner than you've ever felt before."

She laughed. "That would depend on your definition of *clean*."

He wiggled his eyebrows lecherously, which told her all she needed to know about his definition of *clean*. Still holding her hand, he ushered her through

the master bedroom and into the bathroom. Seeing
the glass wall, she hesitated.

She felt as if the entire world could see them.
Well, of course that wasn't true—but the trees could.
So could birds and squirrels. That huge monarch butterfly gliding above a cluster of flowering clover
could peek through the glass and see Jamie loosening
the drawstring of his sweatpants and letting them
drop to the floor. Fluttering its wings, it could aim
its antenna at Allison as Jamie lifted the T-shirt over
her head. Through the glass, the butterfly could feast
on the sight of two naked lovers approaching the
shower.

"This isn't exactly private," she murmured.

He misunderstood her. "If you want me to leave,
I will."

"No—I mean, the glass wall. Anyone outside
could look in and see us."

"Well…yeah. But I wouldn't worry about it.
There's nobody outside."

"What will you do when Samantha is old enough
to play out there?" she asked. "You won't be able
to shower if she's sitting and making a clover chain
on that log over there." Allison pointed to a pine
tree knocked horizontal at the edge of the woods.

Jamie paused before reaching for the faucets and
turning on the water. "Hmm," he grunted.

Allison wondered whether the idea of Samantha's
growing old enough to go outside had ever crossed
his mind. Did he actually think she was going to
remain an infant forever? Had he considered that
once she reached a certain age, her father's nude
body should not be on display through a glass wall?

What would he do when she reached that age?

Replace the wall? Hang an opaque curtain over the glass? Refuse to take showers?

There was one other possibility, of course—but it was a possibility Allison couldn't bear to consider. She stepped into the tub, leaning on his steadying hand, and then moved beneath the rush of warm water. He stepped in behind her, and after a minute she felt him rubbing a spice-scented bar of soap between her shoulder blades in such a soothing swirl of lather that she decided she wouldn't permit herself to consider the other possibility at all.

She was in love with this man. She simply refused to consider that he might give his daughter up.

"I'VE FOUND the mother," Detective John Russo said.

It was Monday morning, but Jamie's thoughts were still firmly lodged in the recent past, a weekend so sublime he felt the heavens—and his perfectly proportioned Botticelli angel—must have decided to forgive him for his sins, after all. Otherwise he would have been suffering right now, not walking around humming and grinning like a dope and feeling like the luckiest man in the world.

Samantha wasn't suffering, either. The antibiotic seemed to have triumphed over whatever bug had caused her ear infection. She was back to ingesting formula in one end and expelling it out the other without missing a beat. She was back to grabbing his nose and whining and belching like a longshoreman and threatening his keyboard with her rambunctious limbs. Perhaps Jamie was imposing his own feelings on her, but she seemed truly glad that Allison was once again back in the McCoy world.

The three of them had gone out for lunch on Saturday. From the gourmet sandwich shop where they'd eaten, they'd driven to Allison's house to see how Allison's grandmother was faring. The elderly woman had instantly taken to Samantha. "Sammy, I'm Grammy," she repeated over and over, as if she were reciting a Dr. Seuss poem. "Your dad is a bum, but he's a very nice bum."

While Allison's grandmother was simultaneously complimenting and insulting him, Allison was fussing over her grandmother. She fetched her grandmother's cane and escorted her into the backyard, where the elderly woman and the young child could sit in the shade of a crab apple tree beside the flower garden, which Grammy told him Allison had planted and tended herself.

Saturday evening, for want of a baby-sitter, Jamie brought Allison, Samantha and a shopping bag packed with containers of take-out Chinese food back to his house, where he and Allison dined on the porch. Then they retired to the den to watch a rented video of *It Happened One Night*, which Allison insisted was a romance but Jamie knew was really about superguy Clark Gable getting the better of Claudette Colbert.

And then they went to bed, where they made love as if it were the first time and they had to discover each other all over again.

Now Monday morning had arrived. He'd spent the past few hours guzzling coffee, engaging in a surprisingly fruitful telephone conversation with his old boss at the *Arlington Gazette* and getting started on a new column. He didn't want to think about Luanne Pierson—or Luanne Hackett or Luanne Eldridge or whatever name the woman was going by these days. He didn't want to think about all the crapola currently jamming up his life. He didn't want to think about child abandonment, police investigations and custody battles. He wanted only to think about Allison Winslow and sex and the way she and he and Sammy all got along so well.

"You've found Luanne?" he asked into the phone, trying to force some enthusiasm into his voice.

At the other end of the line, Russo didn't bother to sound enthusiastic. "You could say she found me, actually."

"You mean she contacted you?"

"Her husband did. Hugh Pierson."

Oh, God. Her husband was after Jamie. "Do you happen to know if he has a permit to carry a concealed weapon?" he asked Russo, figuring there was no harm in expecting the worst. In all ignorance, he'd slept with Hugh Pierson's wife last September. Hugh Pierson was rich. Hell, Hugh Pierson didn't have to carry a weapon. He could probably afford the best hit man in New England.

"Concealed weapons aren't your problem," Russo returned.

"Oh." Jamie was hardly reassured. "What's my problem, then?"

"According to Hugh Pierson, Luanne wants the baby back," Russo informed him.

Jamie's stomach lurched. He gripped the phone in one bloodless fist; his other hand clung to the arm of his desk chair. Five feet from his desk, Samantha was strapped into her state-of-the-art stroller, which Jamie had found could also serve as a baby seat. Its versatility wasn't surprising, given how much he had paid for it.

Would Hugh Pierson's wife have paid so much for a stroller? Jamie wondered irritably. Did it matter? What mattered was whether she was going to fight to get Samantha back—and what Jamie would do if she did.

Silence crackled along the wire. Jamie realized that Russo wasn't going to say anything more, not unless Jamie jump-started the conversation. "Not that I'm committing, one way or the other," he ventured, "but can she do that?"

"She's the birth mother. And then there's another thing," Russo added. "Hugh Pierson says he's the father."

This time it was Jamie's heart that lurched, slamming into his rib cage so hard he could almost feel the bones bruise from the impact. He took a deep breath, and another, not at all sure why this news was getting him so worked up. He was confused, certainly. He was confused to the point of mild dizziness. But much to his surprise, he was also angry.

Shouldn't he be relieved? If he wasn't Samantha's father, no one could fault him for turning the baby over to the Piersons. He could deliver Samantha back to her true parents and resume his bachelor life of fun and frolic, all the while being viewed as a hero for taking such good care of Samantha. He'd fed her, mopped up after her, stayed awake nights with her, rushed her to the hospital and nursed her through an ear infection, with Allison's help.

Another silver lining: Allison couldn't condemn him for returning Samantha to the Piersons if they were Samantha's blood parents. She couldn't accuse

him of being immoral or irresponsible. What could
be more responsible than reuniting a child with her
parents?

On the other hand, what could be more *ir*responsible than abandoning a baby on a stranger's back
porch? "Given that Luanne dumped the baby and ran
away, can she take the baby back? I mean, legally,
does she have a shot?" Jamie asked, amazed at how
tense he was about Russo's answer.

"I'd have to run that by Youth Services and the
D.A.'s office," Russo told him. "I don't know if
she's a fit mother. The husband told me she's hired
a hotshot lawyer to represent her. I can imagine this
is going to be one of those lawyers you don't want
to tangle with, what with the family connections and
all. All of which may be academic."

"Why?"

"As I said, Pierson claims the baby's his. He
didn't abandon it. He says ever since he found out
what his wife did, he's been trying to locate the
child."

"He couldn't have been trying too hard," Jamie
muttered.

Russo ignored the jibe. "No court is going to de-
prive a loving father of his baby."

"A loving father?" Jamie erupted. Later he would
figure out why he was so irritated by the notion of
handing Samantha over to the Piersons. "What kind
of loving father lets his wife ditch her baby and take
off?"

"The kind of father who was estranged from his
wife and didn't know she was pregnant. I'm just telling you what's going on, Mr. McCoy. Pierson wants
the baby."

"Okay." Jamie glanced at the stroller. Samantha stared at him from her semireclining position, her eyes as round as silvery gray marbles. Meeting her luminous gaze caused his heart to slam into his ribs again. "Just theoretically," he said, "and I'm only asking out of curiosity, but what if I refused to give the baby back?"

Russo didn't reply immediately. "Well, if you wanted to keep custody of the baby, the first thing you'd have to do is get yourself an attorney as good as the one they've got. The next thing you'd have to do is take a blood test to establish paternity."

"You mean if I don't take a blood test, the court might simply assume that Pierson is the father?"

"They might. Especially given that nobody's arguing that Pierson's wife is the mother."

Jamie took another deep breath. It didn't clear the rubble from his brain, which felt as if it had been carpet bombed. "What's Pierson planning to do in the meantime?"

"I don't know. He said he had to confer with his lawyer and then he'd discuss terms."

"Terms? He wants to discuss terms with us? His wife committed a crime! He's harboring a fugitive!"

"She isn't a fugitive unless she's running from the police. Which she isn't. Yet."

"She left her kid on my back porch. What kind of a mother is that?"

Again Russo paused before responding. He seemed to like to consider his words from every angle before he voiced them. "There are two possible answers to that," he said. "First answer, she was distraught. Postpartum depression. She wasn't thinking. She regretted it the instant she did it. I have the feeling this is the tack Pierson intends to take.''

Great. A postpartum mother. If Jamie was a judge, he'd be sympathetic. ''What's the other answer?'' he asked with trepidation.

''The other answer is, it has nothing to do with her. Pierson is the one who wants the baby. If that's the way they decide to play it, you can fight them by taking a blood test and establishing your paternity. If, in fact, the baby *is* yours. If she isn't, you lose big.''

''And if I don't take the blood test?''

''The court will probably assume in favor of Pierson. They like intact families.''

Jamie swiveled in his chair to look at Sam again. She was stretching her cheeks to accommodate as many fingers as she could cram into her mouth, and she was making moist little grunts. She was probably fouling her diaper. As soon as he got off the phone with Russo, he'd be hauling her off to the bathroom to hose down her butt.

He wasn't cut out for this. Washing soiled infant butts had never been his life's goal. If he didn't fight Pierson, didn't take the blood test, didn't hire a lawyer, this whole thing would be over. No more sleepless nights, no more panic about baby-sitters, no more walking around with splatters of baby barf on his shirts.

And as for Samantha... Well, she'd have the intact family she deserved. A rich father, a rich grandfather, a flaky mother, and if none of them was up to the task of raising her, their money would buy a nanny to do it.

Jamie could hire a nanny, too, of course—but

damn, he'd only just turned thirty. He was a guy. What did he know about nannies?

What did he know about babies?

"Let me think about this," he told Russo, rotating his chair so he didn't have to look at Samantha anymore. His heart had stopped pounding and was now plummeting, dropping so fast it seemed to be pressing down against the soles of his feet.

"All right," Russo said. "I've got Hugh Pierson's address and I've got his lawyer's number. If he really wants the baby, he's not going to disappear on us. We'll sit on it until you decide what you want or until Pierson or his lawyer pushes. If we've got to bring charges against the mother, we will. But for now... We could wait a day or two. The baby isn't in any danger."

"Right."

"Meanwhile, you'd better take good care of her," Russo said.

"I will."

"Take care of yourself, too." With that, Russo ended the call.

Jamie lowered the phone. His heart was still in a free fall, below his feet, below the floor, below the surface of the earth, down where hell was alleged to be.

He forced himself to rotate back to Samantha. She had stopped grunting, which he knew meant she'd probably finished filling her diaper with digestive waste. But she looked so serene in her stroller, he could almost forget about her diaper and think she was perfect.

For a whole lot of reasons it would be better for her to go to the Piersons. If she did, she would soon forget all about Jamie. She might have a strange blur of memory covering a few weeks of her life when things took an odd turn, but other than that, he would be nothing to her. She would be back with her mother and her birth certificate. She would live a nice, normal life as a daughter of privilege and power.

Really, he told himself, giving her back to the Piersons was the wisest thing to do.

Turning away from her, he slammed his fist against his desk so hard the pain brought tears to his eyes.

CHAPTER FOURTEEN

MARGARET, THE NEONATAL unit's nursing supervisor, swept into a hectic birthing room and tapped Allison's shoulder. "They want to see you downstairs in Human Resources," she announced.

Allison almost didn't hear her. She was assisting an understandably foul-tempered woman through the final stages of labor. The small room was crowded with a hospital bed, an isolette, a row of warming lamps, a fetal heart monitor, an obstetrician, a practical nurse whose job it was to run and fetch bowls and towels, and the pregnant woman's husband, who fancied himself the next Francis Ford Coppola. While the wife grunted and panted and vented language more colorful than the rainbow, the husband swooped and circled, aiming his video camera every which way and offering directorial advice.

"Could you look this way, honey?" he asked, aiming the camera at his wife's face.

"Stick it in your ear," she roared, and then, "Aaargh! Another contraction!"

"You look gorgeous, sweetheart," the husband cooed. "Do that breathing thing, okay? I'd like to get you in profile doing that breathing thing."

Allison held the woman's hand and counted breaths for her while she got through the contraction. "You're doing just fine," she assured the woman.

"It hurts!"

"I know."

The woman groaned. "That lady who taught the birthing classes? She said we weren't supposed to think of it as pain. Well, I've got news for her. It's pain. Have you ever been through this?"

"Not yet." But she hoped to go through it someday in the not-too-distant future. She hoped to go through it with a man she loved, creating a child they would both love.

A picture of Jamie floated through her mind, causing her to smile.

The woman yanked on her arm as if to pull her back down to earth. "You don't want to go through this, ever," the woman told her. "It stinks. If God were a woman, we'd be designed with zippers. You'd just unzip the pouch and pull the baby out. None of this pain. I want a drug."

"No, you don't," her husband scolded, darting to the other side of the bed and photographing her sweat-streaked face in close-up. "Drugs might damage the baby."

"I'm going to damage you if you don't—aaargh! Another one!"

"Keep breathing," the auteur reminded her. "We're doing this scene in one take."

"Allison?" Margaret repeated. "They want you downstairs in Human Resources."

Allison managed a smile for Margaret. "Can it wait a few minutes? We've got a baby to deliver here." Before Margaret could answer, Allison turned back to the woman, who was reciting expletives in an assortment of foreign languages. The woman's face was flushed, her skin beaded with perspiration.

Allison pulled the blood pressure cuff from the its wall bracket and strapped it around the woman's upper arm.

"HR said it was important," Margaret nagged, clearly peeved about being ignored.

Allison held up a hand to silence her, then put on her stethoscope and squeezed the pump.

She didn't know what the bureaucrats in the Human Resources department could want with her, unless it was to fire her. She'd done nothing to deserve termination, but the bean counters were always looking for ways to save the hospital money. One of their favorite ways was to lay people off. They'd save less money laying off four nurses than one unproductive executive earning a six-figure salary, but it always seemed to be the nurses and orderlies they went after with the budget ax, the folks earning the least and working the hardest.

The possibility that Allison might be downsized out of a job ought to have upset her. But she was too busy helping a baby into the world to worry about it right now. And she was too happy.

She was in love.

Ever since she'd said goodbye to Jamie Sunday evening and gone home, he had been a part of her, a permanent resident in her mind, a constant presence in her heart. Jamie, a fiercely passionate lover and a doting, devoted father. A family man. A man who had proven his willingness to rise to any challenge, to accept his responsibilities, to try his hardest to do what was required and all the while to keep his sense of humor. A man who had managed to make her feel things—more than just physical things—that no man had ever made her feel before.

Oh, yes, she was in love—so blissfully in love, she couldn't imagine anything upsetting her. Not even getting laid off.

Losing her job would be a calamity, of course. She couldn't live off Grammy's meager pension. She would have to find another job, and Arlington General was the only hospital in town. She might be able to get a job with a doctor in private practice, but that would mean less variety in her work, less patient contact and fewer opportunities for advancement.

All right, then. Having to see the folks in Human Resources was not a good thing. But she'd worry about it later. Right now, she was going to bring a baby into the world, and she was going to let the exhilaration of loving Jamie energize her.

"This is killing me!" the laboring woman announced, although her vital signs indicated otherwise. "This is ridiculous! Why don't you just give me a C-section and get it over with?"

"You've been in labor all of four hours," the obstetrician noted. "I think you can stick it out a little longer."

"You're beautiful when you're in labor," the father purred, zooming in for a close-up of his anguished, impatient wife.

"Trust me," she confided to Allison. "You *really* don't ever want to go through this. Kids aren't worth it—aaargh! I'm having another one!"

Allison rubbed the nape of the woman's neck and counted breaths with her. She did her best to move out of the way when the father-to-be complained that she was blocking his shot. She checked the fetal heart monitor, conferred with the obstetrician and allowed herself to believe that for this moment, at least, everything that mattered in the world was located right in that birthing room.

A half hour later, the father was filming his son's very first moments of life. The mother, her eyes awash with tears of relief and happiness, was cooing and babbling as if no curse had ever crossed her tongue. The pains of labor and delivery had mysteriously been forgotten in a deluge of joy.

After congratulating the exultant parents, Allison left the room. In the time it took her to remove her scrubs and wash up, she realigned her brain to the real world. A strong, healthy baby had been born, his parents were thrilled and Allison was as much in love with Jamie as she'd been an hour ago, two hours, two days. Whatever the Human Resources department wanted to do to her, she could handle it.

On her way to the elevator, she glanced at Margaret, who had resumed her usual post behind the desk at the nurses' station. Allison searched her supervisor's face for a clue about what to expect. Could the hospital fire her without Margaret's input? Could Margaret have recommended her for dismissal? She and Allison weren't the best of friends, but they got along well enough, and Allison was a good nurse. She'd never even come close to harming a patient, let alone losing one. She'd never mixed up a med, never misidentified a baby, never let a problem go undetected. If the hospital planned to fire her, they'd better have a good reason—and a damned good separation package.

As usual, Margaret's expression implied that she'd been sucking lemons for the past two years. Sighing, Allison told her she was heading downstairs to the business offices and then summoned the elevator.

Don't worry, she ordered herself as the car descended to the first floor. *You're going to be fine. Jamie loves you and you love him. Everything's going to work out.*

She entered the HR department and gave her name to the secretary. "Allison Winslow. Right. Please follow me," the woman said ominously. Why had she recognized Allison's name so quickly? Why was she ushering her into the office of the director of Human Resources without even announcing her? How bad could this thing be, anyway?

Allison glanced at the name on the plaque beside the door the secretary opened: Ronald Katsakis. If it was as bad as she was beginning to fear, she wanted to enter his name in her memory bank so that when she raced in hysterics to the only attorney she knew—Molly's sister Gail—she would be able to identify the villain. Of course, Mr. Katsakis was probably only following orders, firing her because someone truly villainous—Margaret? The hospital's chief of nursing?—had offered Allison up as Sacrifice of the Month.

"Ron?" The secretary stepped across the threshold and motioned for Allison to follow her. "This is Allison Winslow. You know, the nurse from neonatal."

Allison entered the office. It wasn't particularly large or luxurious. The narrow window overlooked the parking lot, and the furniture—a broad desk with two tweed-upholstered chairs set across from Mr. Katsakis's matching tweed chair—might have come from an office furniture discount store. She took some satisfaction in the understanding that personnel directors weren't living high on the hog while she was about to get laid off.

Expecting the worst wasn't like her, though. Why was she assuming that a trip to Human Resources was a trip to the professional gallows? Maybe Ronald Katsakis was about to give her a raise, or a promotion, or both. Maybe he'd summoned her to his office because the hospital's board of directors had decided to rename the place Arlington-Winslow Hospital. Or maybe he wanted to give her an award for her after-hours work on—

"Ah, yes, the Daddy School," said the man behind the desk as he rose from his chair. He looked to be on the far side of middle age, his black hair and mustache streaked with silver, his eyes framed with crinkly skin. They were benign eyes, Allison told herself. Smiling eyes. Not the eyes of a hatchet man.

The secretary left and Ronald Katsakis gestured toward one of the chairs across the desk from him. Allison sat, trying to quell her nerves as he shuffled some papers. "How are you doing?" he asked familiarly.

"Okay," she said. "We just delivered a boy upstairs."

"Really?" Katsakis shuffled some more papers. "Everything go all right?"

"Everything was perfect. The baby was eight pounds, two ounces, and the parents named him Peter."

"Peter. Nice name." Apparently he found what he was looking for, because he stopped rooting around the clutter on his desk and smiled at her. "It's been brought to my attention that you run an off-site program for young fathers.''

Off-site did not bode well. He was probably going to chastise her for devoting so much of her professional energy to a program not directly affiliated with the hospital, or at least one from which the hospital couldn't profit. "Not all the fathers are young," she explained, thinking of the oldest student in her class. If Jamie were here, he would put her at ease. He would whisper in her ear that Katsakis had nothing on her, that he was just a paper pusher, that nobody needed him the way the Daddy School students needed her.

"I guess I should have said *new* fathers," Katsakis clarified.

Allison nodded, holding her breath and waiting for the guillotine blade to fall across her neck.

He skimmed a sheet of paper in his hand as if to refresh his memory. "I understand you've been informed that your program has lost hospital funding."

She nodded again.

"Well, it seems someone somewhere doesn't like that. A private benefactor would like to pay to keep the program going. We've received a phone call and a fax to confirm that if Arlington Memorial will endorse the program and provide auxiliary supplies and so on, this benefactor will donate the funding to keep the school going."

She breathed deeply, as if she were in labor. Unlike Peter's mother, Allison wasn't in pain. But she was definitely uncomfortable. This couldn't be happening—not unless someone somewhere had done something.

Jamie McCoy.

Allison had told him she didn't want him bailing her out. She didn't want him flinging his money around to keep her program alive. It was a worthwhile program, an exceptionally good program, and it deserved to be funded legitimately. She didn't want it to turn into a gift from an affluent man to his current sweetheart.

"May I ask who this benefactor is?" she asked.

"Actually, it's not a 'who.' It's a 'what.' The *Arlington Gazette*."

"The newspaper?" The spasm of discomfort passed but left behind a waning ache. Jamie used to work for the *Arlington Gazette,* didn't he? He must have pulled strings, twisted arms, called up friends and said, "Do this for my girlfriend."

"The newspaper maintains a special benevolent fund. They underwrite the city's annual road race for cancer, you know, and they sponsor local athletes for the Special Olympics every year. They have a college scholarship program and so on. I'm sure you know about these things if you read the paper. They're always tooting their own horn about their good deeds."

"And they want to pay for the Daddy School out of this special fund?"

"They do indeed. We received word this morning that they're willing to make up the hospital's shortfall. They feel this is an essential program for young fathers."

They aren't all young, she almost blurted out again. She tried to shove aside her uneasiness. What Ronald Katsakis was telling her made sense. The *Arlington Gazette* was involved in many community programs. The newspaper's charitable works bought goodwill; they provided the paper with a public relations bonanza. Arlington's citizens benefited from the *Gazette's* generosity and they showed their appreciation by buying the newspaper.

Ronald Katsakis was rambling on about the financial support the newspaper would give, and the support in kind the hospital would contribute to the program. If the city's premier newspaper believed this was a valid program, by golly, the hospital wasn't going to pull the rug out from under it. Details needed to be ironed out, paperwork attended to. The hospital would like to explore other venues for the next class—perhaps the high school instead of the YMCA. Perhaps several classes at once, in different locations, on different nights. Call it outreach, a way to introduce youngsters not only to the pleasures and challenges of becoming fathers but also to the fine facilities at Arlington Memorial.

It occurred to Allison that this would be a good time to negotiate for more. If the hospital was prepared to support her, perhaps they would also support the toddler class Molly wanted to teach. Allison ought to request the additional support now, while Katsakis was talking about money and paperwork.

But she was having difficulty concentrating. Below the placid surface of the discussion, a tide whirled and tugged, dragging at her, trying to suck her under.

Jamie had done it. She couldn't escape that certainty—and she couldn't escape her uneasiness about it.

Maybe Molly was right. Maybe there was something wrong with her that she was constitutionally unable to accept help from others. Except that she could accept help. She'd been very happy to accept the hospital's support for the first Daddy School class. It was *Jamie* whose help she didn't want to accept.

Why?

Because she was already too vulnerable to him. Because she gave her love freely and she didn't want to feel as if he were trying to buy it. Because she didn't want him doing favors, making things easy for her, flaunting his clout.

She had the presence of mind to stop Katsakis before he got too caught up in his monologue on the paperwork she would need to do. "I'm very grateful to the newspaper—and the hospital," she remembered to add. "I think the Daddy School is important, and I'm glad it isn't going to fold. But as far as the details... Well, I've just helped deliver a baby and I've got a lot of other things on my mind—not least that I'm teaching a Daddy School class tonight. So maybe we could discuss the paperwork another time. That won't jeopardize the program, will it?"

"No, of course not. I hope we can get this put together sometime this week, though. I'd hate to give the *Gazette* the opportunity to change its mind."

"Tomorrow," Allison promised. "If we don't have any crises upstairs in neonatal, I could come back around lunchtime."

"Anytime between noon and one should be fine," Katsakis told her. "Let my secretary know on your way out."

"Okay. And thank you. I'm very glad the hospital is backing the program."

"The hospital is very glad you're running this program for the city in our name," he said, rising from his chair when she did and reaching across the desk to shake her hand. Allison gave him her most winning smile as she backed out of his office. Not until she'd shut the door behind her did she drop the cheerful facade.

She felt disoriented, out of sorts, troubled by Jamie's power play. She ought to give him the benefit of the doubt and find out if he was behind the newspaper's largess before she condemned him for meddling. But she trusted her suspicions more than she trusted him.

She was going to have to decide what to do. The Daddy School was more important than her pride. It might even be more important than her relationship with Jamie. She was going to have to explain to him that he wasn't going to win any points by pulling strings for her after she'd explicitly asked him not to.

She confirmed the following day's appointment with the secretary, then left the suite of offices that housed Human Resources. Out in the hallway, she eyed first the bank of elevators that would transport her back upstairs to the neonatal unit, and then, just beyond the elevators, a public telephone alcove.

If she had Jamie's phone number handy, she could call him.

But she didn't have the number with her and she didn't have time to phone Directory Assistance and get it. The maternity ward was hopping today. Allison was needed upstairs.

She would see Jamie tonight at the Daddy School. After class, they could go to what Allison had come to think of as "their" place, the coffee shop across the street from the YMCA, and Allison would give him a piece of her mind. Unlike him, she didn't sneak around. If she wanted to help someone, she did it openly. And if someone asked her not to help, she respected that person's wishes.

Jamie wanted her respect? Well, he could earn it by showing a little respect for *her*.

HE GOT AS FAR as the YMCA...and then kept driving.

The evening was clear, the sky a fading, cloudless blue. The postworkday city was muted, almost restful. The YMCA building loomed ahead, a solid mass of dark red brick. Inside that building, in the room at the end of the hall, Allison was waiting for him.

He couldn't go.

The Range Rover gulped the city streets, strained at the red lights and zoomed at the green ones. Next to him, Samantha sat calmly in her seat. Hot summer air gusted through the open window and fluffed her hair. She didn't seem to notice. She was too busy experimenting with her hands, shoving one finger and then another into her mouth. The pink polish had almost vanished from her nails. Jamie didn't want to think about where it had gone. Was he going to discover pink stuff in her diaper the next time he changed her?

How many more times would he change her before she was no longer his?

He turned left, heading out of the downtown area. After a few blocks the tall office buildings were replaced by strip malls, gas stations and supermarkets. A few more blocks, and commercial buildings gave way to garden apartments, condominium complexes and modest private homes.

He paid little attention to his surroundings. He had too much to think about.

All he had to do was fill a test tube with his blood, and forensic scientists would take it from there. They would run their tests and determine once and for all whether or not he was Samantha's father.

If he wasn't, he would lose her. Which was as it should be. After all, why should he, a happy, foot-loose bachelor, be raising a child who wasn't even his?

But if he *was* her father...he still might lose her. If he was one parent and Luanne was the other, they had equal claims on Samantha. His claim might be a bit stronger, because he had never abandoned the baby. But then, Luanne's might be stronger because she was the mother, and mothers were traditionally the number-one parent.

He continued cruising away from the heart of the city, past houses on larger lots, spread farther apart. Past a golf course. Past a pond and a small orchard. Samantha closed her eyes and he felt no compunction to rouse her and point out the beauty of the western Connecticut countryside.

What kind of father was he, really? So far, in the couple of weeks he'd had Sammy, it had been a lark. Granted, she'd been sick, she'd screwed up his hot date with Allison, she'd spit up on him and awakened him with her screams. But he'd gamely kept going, washing when she barfed on him, adapting his social life to her demands. Yet had he ever truly felt that this was the life he was meant to live? Had he ever seriously contemplated that he could be enduring screwed-up dates and vomit and screaming fits for the next decade?

He didn't know.

Maybe he should have attended his class at the YMCA. If he'd seen Allison, been in the same room with her and listened to her explain how to be a father, making it sound plausible, he would believe himself capable of it. Allison seemed to consider fatherhood a role anyone—even Jamie McCoy—could master. Everything Allison said was reasonable. Everything was possible.

Which was exactly why he hadn't gone. Whenever he was near her, he *did* believe that he could do it. She enhanced the possibilities, embodied them, encouraged them. Her conviction, her morality, her beauty and her incredible stability were enough to give him more faith in his abilities than he deserved. She imbued her students with the confidence they would need to get through the next eighteen years as daddies.

He couldn't let her influence his decision about Samantha. He couldn't let himself be distracted by his lover's green eyes, by her voluptuous hair, by the way he'd felt sleeping with her, and waking up to her, and joining his body to hers.

The Piersons could give Samantha a two-parent family. Jamie could never do that—unless he married quickly. Unless he married someone like Allison who could do everything for Sam that Jamie hadn't yet figured out how to do.

They were miles out of town, now, in the bucolic region surrounding Arlington. A dairy farm spread to the west, several cows with blotchy black-and-white hides munching lazily on grass in a fenced-in meadow. Jamie kept driving, following the sinuous road up a hill. At its peak, he was treated to a panorama of gentle rolling mountains, lush greenery, woods, small farms and scattered houses. His windshield framed a breathtaking vista, but Samantha couldn't care less. She had started to snore, a sure sign that she'd fallen asleep with three fingers in her mouth.

Why should he fight to keep her? Had she ever really been his? Not by plan. Not by hope. It was purely a fluke that he'd found her on his porch.

Sighing, he reached for the cellular phone in the glove compartment. He dug his wallet from his hip pocket and searched for Russo's card. Russo wouldn't be at his desk at this hour, but Jamie didn't care. All he wanted was to leave a message, something he wouldn't be able to retrieve, something permanent, something he couldn't deny.

He punched in the button, waited, and got a nightshift desk sergeant. "John Russo isn't in, is he?"

"No," the sergeant reported. "You want his voice mail?"

"Sure." Jamie waited while the call was connected to the computerized message system. His gaze remained on Samantha. She moved her legs as she sucked on her fingers, but she was definitely asleep. She was so small, so pretty. So oblivious to the route her life was about to take.

"Hi," he said into John's voice mail. "This is Jamie McCoy, " he said. "I'm calling to ask you to set up a meeting with the Piersons. I believe we've got some business to discuss."

CHAPTER FIFTEEN

"YOU LOOK LIKE HELL," Samantha's grandmother said, peering out through the screen door at him. "I remembered you as being a handsome man. I must be mistaken."

"You're not mistaken," Jamie muttered. "I feel like hell and I've been through hell, so I probably look like it, too. Is Allison home?"

Samantha's grandmother lifted her hand to squint at her wristwatch. She had a TV remote control in her hand. "Do you know what time it is?"

"Yes," he said, tugging at the tie knotted around his neck like a noose. It was too warm for a necktie, but he'd felt obliged to dress for the occasion. "It's six-thirty Thursday night. I stopped by the hospital, but she had already left. I really need to see her. It's important." The understatement of the century.

The elder Ms. Winslow shook her head and pursed her lips in disapproval. "You're not her favorite person in the world, you know," she chided.

"Yes, I do know. But I *really* need to see her."

"You've gotten yourself in trouble, haven't you. Don't tell me you've knocked someone else up."

"No, I haven't." He struggled not to lose his composure. His problems were not Allison's grandmother's problems. For that matter, they weren't Allison's problems, either. They were all his, and he intended to do whatever he could to fix them. But without Allison by his side assuring him that he was on the right track, that he wasn't digging himself even deeper into a hole, that he could accomplish what he had to and accomplishing it wouldn't destroy him...

He needed her, damn it!

"I'm sure she's angry that I haven't called her, but—"

"Haven't called her? You played hooky from class. She's going to flunk you."

Cripes. He'd managed to wheedle a 7:00 p.m. appointment with his attorney, Dennis Murphy, but Dennis wasn't going to wait past 7:05. He had told Jamie he was expecting his kids for the weekend and he wanted to spend the evening stocking up on junk food for them.

But Jamie had pleaded, he'd begged, he'd groveled—his pride was beyond salvaging, and he didn't care. And Dennis had succumbed. "Seven," he'd said. "Don't make me wait."

Jamie didn't think he could survive his appointment with Dennis, let alone the actuality of what he was attempting, unless he had Allison holding his hand, cheering him on, assuring him he was going to make it. So, after pleading, begging and groveling for Dennis Murphy, he was now at Allison's house. Pleading, begging and groveling.

"Well," her grandmother reported, "she isn't here."

"Where is she?"

"She went out for dinner."

Oh, swell. As if his life wasn't horrible enough. Allison was on a date with someone else. Probably someone who didn't drag a puking baby along to the restaurant for the sole purpose of ruining her dress. Someone who knew what he was doing. Someone who didn't try to do the right thing, realize too late that he'd done the most absolutely wrong thing and then try to backtrack and undo everything he'd done.

"With her best friend, Molly Saunders," her grandmother added belatedly.

Jamie inhaled and attempted to exert mind control over his rising blood pressure. "Can you tell me where they went? I've got to find Allison."

"What will happen if you don't?"

Forget about his blood pressure. He was running out of time. "Life as we know it will end," he said.

"Oh. Well, you should have said so. They went to Dominic's. It's an Italian place—"

"I know it," he said, already hurtling down the front walk. "Thanks!" he shouted over his shoulder.

He dove into the top-down Miata without bothering to open the door. He was revving the engine before he had his seat belt on. He tore away from the curb, heedlessly breaking speed limits throughout the quiet residential neighborhood until he reached the modest Italian café across the street from the four-plex cinema which always seemed to be showing at least one movie that featured buildings blowing up or aliens invading the earth—or, if Jamie got lucky and Hollywood heard his prayers, both.

He screeched to a halt in a handicapped parking space, vaulted out of the car and sprinted into the restaurant. Like a magnet, he was drawn to Allison's table, knowing intuitively where she was before he spotted her.

She had her back to him. He saw the cascade of

red-tinged curls down her back, the slight hunch of her shoulders, the white of her slacks and blouse. She must have met her friend straight after work, he thought, his heart beating faster because he was in the same room with her, and stronger because now that he'd found her he could almost allow himself to believe things might somehow work out.

The woman across the table from her, facing him as he stood in the doorway, was a pixieish woman with a heart-shaped face and straight dark hair. She must have seen him staring at their table, because she frowned, leaned toward Allison and said something. By the time Allison turned in her chair, Jamie was half the distance to the table.

Allison's jaw dropped. Her eyes flashed with fury, and she opened her mouth to speak. He could guess from her expression that he didn't want to hear what she had to say, so he didn't give her a chance to say it.

"Allison, I need you. It's awful. I can't believe how awful it is. Please—you can hate me later, but I need you right now." Sheesh. He'd used the word *need* more in the past ten minutes than he had in his entire life. The pathetic part was, he'd meant it every time.

"You look like hell," she said. "That's a nice tie, though."

"I've lost Samantha," he said.

Her jaw dropped. So did her friend's. Allison rose to her feet, gripping the edge of the table as if afraid she would teeter and fall. "You *lost* her? Oh, my God! How could you lose her?"

He sighed. "The Piersons—Luanne and her husband—requested custody, and I..." God help him, he was going to cry, right in the middle of an Italian restaurant where—he slowly realized—every single diner was gawking at him. He was going to break down and cry. Jamie McCoy, the ultimate guy, was going to weep in front of all these strangers with red sauce on their chins.

The hell with them. The only person who mattered right now was Allison. He didn't give a damn if she saw him crying. "I thought it would be better for her to go where she could have two parents," he concluded lamely.

Allison struggled to close her mouth. The color had drained from her face. "What do you mean, two parents?"

"Luanne's husband claimed he was the father. They made their case before a social worker here in town. They brought a lawyer with them. The lawyer had an affidavit stating that Luanne had been under treatment for depression."

"What are you saying?" Allison gaped at him as if he were speaking Farsi.

"They made a case for custody. I thought it was a good one. Hugh Pierson said he was the father—he said Luanne had been pregnant when I met her. Without a blood test, I couldn't prove otherwise. But I thought— Hell, even with a blood test, Luanne was Sammy's mother, and maybe Sammy belonged with her mother. And maybe Sammy wasn't even mine. Allison—I don't *know* if she's mine. All I know is, I want her back." Another tear slid down his cheek. He ignored it.

Allison glanced at her friend. "Go," her friend said simply.

Without another word, Allison grabbed her purse

and hurried out of the restaurant ahead of Jamie. "You need a lawyer," she said as they headed for his car.

"I've got a lawyer. He's waiting for me at his office right now."

She nodded and yanked open the passenger door of his car, not bothering to wait for him to open it for her. "And you need a blood test."

"I'm scared about that, Allison. What if it turns out I'm really not Sammy's father? I'll lose her for good."

"You've already lost her," Allison reminded him. Not a comforting thought, but she was only speaking the truth. "On the chance that the blood test will strengthen your case—"

"I know." He cranked the engine until it roared, then skidded out of the parking lot and pointed the sports car toward downtown. "I'm not sure how to go about getting this blood test. Can you help me with that? I know I haven't got the right to ask anything of you, but—"

"Jamie." He saw her hands fisting against her white cotton trousers. "This isn't about who has the right to ask anyone for anything."

"That's exactly what it's about." He took a corner so sharply the inner tires practically left the asphalt. "It's about what's right, who has rights—and it's about asking you for something. I know you probably hate me, but I'm on my knees here. I'm begging."

She sighed and held her hair out of her face as the wind lashed it. "I don't know what to think."

"Do you hate me?" He braced himself for her

reply. If he knew anything about Allison, it was that she would answer honestly.

What he heard was another sigh, shattered by the wind blasting past the windshield and into their faces. "No," she said so quietly he almost didn't hear her over the roar of the engine. "I don't hate you."

"Okay. We can work out the rest later." They'd reached the office building that housed Dennis's office, just a block away from the *Gazette* building—a block away from the YMCA where he'd skipped class on Monday. "I'm sorry I didn't go to the Daddy School this week," he remembered to say. "That was the evening I was doing the most idiotic thing of my life—deciding that Samantha would be better off with the Piersons."

"It wasn't idiotic," Allison told him.

"Of course it was!" He punctuated his self-loathing by leaving rubber as he veered into the first space he found in the underground parking lot beneath the office building. "It's because of that idiotic decision that I lost her."

"You made that decision because you thought it would be best for her," Allison consoled him. "That's not idiotic. It might have been the wrong choice, but you made it for the most loving reason in the world. You wanted what was best for your daughter."

"Yeah," he grumbled. "That's me, the wisdom of Solomon. We'd better run. Dennis is probably ready to bite my head off for keeping him after hours."

Neither of them spoke until they were safely enclosed in the elevator leading up from the garage into the building. "Is this lawyer good?" Allison asked.

"He was great when some clown brought a slander suit against me last year. The jerk was positive that a column I wrote was about him, even though I'd never met him. I had no idea who he was, and suddenly he brought a suit claiming that his wife recognized him in my column and walked out on him. Dennis not only got the suit thrown out, but he got the court to make the plaintiff pay my court costs. When you reach a level of renown, you become a target. The chump thought I'd settle quietly and he could take me for a few grand. Thanks to Dennis, that didn't happen."

"Can a lawyer who handles nuisance suits also handle custody battles?"

"We'll find out, won't we." The elevator door opened on the third floor, and they stepped out into the foyer. Across from the elevator, a glass-enclosed entry welcomed them to Schenker, Murphy, Lopes and Associates, Attorneys-at-Law. On the other side of the glass stood an unoccupied reception area. The place looked empty, but the lights were on.

Jamie took a deep breath. He'd never had to fight for anything in his life. Either he'd gotten what he wanted without much struggle or he'd concluded that what he'd wanted wasn't worth the effort. All of a sudden, though, he'd discovered that some things were worth fighting for. He had learned that there were things—people, relationships—he wanted so much that he would fight with all his strength, fight until he fell, fight until there was no life left in him. He would willingly die fighting for them.

One of those people was Samantha.

The other was Allison.

She started toward the doors, but he clasped her

hands and pulled her back, turning her to face him. "Allison," he whispered, gazing into her eyes. So earnest. So resolute. So unspeakably beautiful.

He yearned to kiss her, but even more, he yearned to make her understand, to find out where he stood with her, to prove to her that even though she might flunk him for missing her class, even though he looked like hell, even though he hadn't talked to her since that spectacular weekend when they'd made love, he was worth her attention. He was a good man, and he was doing everything in his power to become a better one.

"I wanted to call you," he said.

She lowered her eyes, waiting for him to explain.

"I kept thinking, this is my problem, not yours. I've got to work it out myself. I had no business dragging you into it. And I was so unsure of myself, I thought I'd better steer clear of you until I knew what I was doing."

She lifted her gaze to his again. He studied her face, looking for a sign that she comprehended why he'd kept his distance from her.

"I thought if I went running to you for guidance, you would either tell me to grow up and take care of my problems myself or you'd give me your opinion. And then, if you were right, I'd always think it was you who'd solved this problem for me. And if you were wrong, I'd blame you. I had to deal with it myself. Can you see that?"

"Oh, yes," she said fervently. "Yes, Jamie."

"Unfortunately, I came up with the wrong solution. All by myself."

"Are you sure it's wrong?" she asked.

If he weren't so upset, he would have laughed.

"Am I sure? The minute I turned Sammy over to them, I went home, walked into her room and fell apart. It wasn't a pretty sight, Allison. I just stared at that mobile—you know the one I got her, with the helicopters? I stared at it, and a breeze came in through the window. All the little rotors started spinning, and I went berserk. If I could have just kept reminding myself about how she kept me up all night, how she was always puking on my shirts and how she was constantly pooping in her diapers..." He was about to fall apart again, just thinking of it. "The thing is...she liked professional wrestling."

Allison's eyes grew round and her eyebrows arched like two horizontal parentheses. "Professional wrestling?"

"I explained it to her, and she was getting into it. Those people, the Piersons...they aren't going to explain Pit-Bull Howland's technique to her. She learned to count to three watching professional wrestling."

"She can count to three?" Allison appeared stunned.

"I want her back. If there's any way, if I've got any chance, I want her back."

Allison raised her eyes to his, and their glow was like sunlight streaming into him, warming him. She cupped one hand against his cheek and rose on tiptoe. She pressed a light kiss on his other cheek. "Let's go get her back," she murmured.

DENNIS MURPHY WAS a lanky fellow nearing his fortieth birthday, with dark blond hair and surprisingly kind gray eyes. He was wearing a summer-weight suit of beige linen, and his tie hung loose around his neck. He didn't look like a cutthroat lawyer, and that troubled Allison. Right now, Jamie needed the sharpest, smartest lawyer in New England.

But the way Murphy smiled, all white teeth and dimples, reassured her. "What can I say, Jamie?" he began. "You really put your foot in it this time. But I think I can save your shoe."

Step by step, he reviewed Jamie's predicament. Allison alternated between listening to him and watching Jamie. If he'd looked exhausted during the weeks he was taking care of Samantha, he looked harried now, drained and grim, with dark circles ringing his eyes and a permanent crease etched into his brow. He looked like a man who had been deprived not only of sleep but of laughter. He looked like a man who had tried to go it alone and considered himself a failure—even though, in Allison's view, he had done the most fatherly thing he could do. He'd proven his love for Samantha by yielding her to a nuclear family, and without even realizing it, he'd earned Allison's love by tackling his problems alone instead of pressuring her to make things right for him.

She'd been bewildered and hurt when he'd failed to show up at her Monday-night class. She shouldn't have taken it personally, but of course she did, because she and Jamie were no longer just teacher and student. A part of her wondered whether his behind-the-scenes arrangement of money for the Daddy School was a payback for the fun weekend they'd had.

She had fallen in love with him, and he'd raised some money for her. It had made her feel cheap and used and...what was his word? Idiotic.

But now she felt only sorrow for him, and sympathy, and support. He was in the battle of his life. That he wanted her to stand by him was an honor.

He had obviously filled Dennis Murphy in on the hearing he and the Piersons had participated in at the Department of Youth Services. A social worker had mediated, and Detective John Russo of the Arlington Police Department had sat in as well. Jamie's lawyer seemed to be in possession of every note and document from that meeting. He thumbed through the folder before him, skimming and speaking simultaneously.

Yes, he conceded, the Piersons' attorney had made a strong case to the Social Services department about Luanne's mental state upon having given birth to the child. Yes, she and her husband had legally separated just before she'd fled to Eleuthera and met Jamie. Yes, they'd been separated throughout her pregnancy and hadn't reconciled until after she'd given birth to the baby and left it with Jamie. Yes, a compassionate judge might choose to award permanent custody to this poor, confused woman under the influence of raging postpartum hormones.

"Sexist tripe if you ask me," Murphy remarked. "Women want equality until they think that acting hysterical can give them an edge. Then suddenly they're the victim of their hormones."

Allison bristled at his accusation. Jamie squeezed her hand gently, and she subsided without telling Murphy what she thought of his comment.

"All that notwithstanding," Murphy went on, "the woman did abandon her child. The criminal charges are there if Detective Russo decides to file them. We could push for that if you'd like."

"I don't want Luanne in jail," Jamie explained. "I just want Samantha back."

Murphy shrugged. "Actually, if Luanne went to jail, it might put you at a terrible disadvantage. Hugh Pierson could take the kid and disappear, and then where would you be?"

A muscle ticked in Jamie's jaw. Obviously he didn't want to think about where he'd be if Pierson spirited Samantha away.

"You're going to have to donate some DNA," Murphy told him. "I don't see how you can fight Pierson unless you first establish paternity."

"I'll donate whatever I have to," Jamie vowed.

Murphy smiled, another impish, dimpled grin. "Wait till you see my bill," he warned. "You'll learn how much you've got to donate. Get the test done. You can go to the police lab. Or maybe the hospital can do the test. Permanent custody hasn't been awarded yet, and it won't be until Luanne Pierson proves she's up to snuff, which maybe she won't be able to do. So far, her performance as a mother is less than stellar."

Allison bristled but once again held her tongue. If she pointed out that perhaps everything Luanne Pierson had said was true, that she'd actually suffered from a severe postpartum psychosis and that Hugh Pierson had in fact fathered the child, Jamie was going to lose his case.

Jamie looked less than confident when he and Allison left Murphy's office a few minutes later, escorted down to the garage by the lawyer himself. "I wouldn't work this late for just anyone," Murphy remarked to Allison. "But Jamie gives me my best laugh of the week, every week. His column is a hoot."

"I haven't had a laugh this week," Jamie muttered. "This week's column sucks eggs."

"Cheer the boy up, would you?" Murphy instructed, shooting Allison a smile before he veered off to his own car in the garage.

"You do need cheering," she said as they settled into Jamie's car.

"I need a blood test" was all he said. He started the engine, tapped the gas pedal and eased out of the parking space. No wild driving now, no race against the clock, no race against fate. Fate would be determined by the DNA profile his blood produced. If Samantha was a Pierson, science would determine it. If she was a McCoy, Jamie's blood would prove it.

And then he'd still have to fight to get her back.

"Let's go get you that test, then," she said.

SEVERAL HOURS LATER, Allison settled into one of the chairs on Jamie's screened porch, a glass of wine in her hand, the song of the night's crickets filling the darkness. Jamie sat on the opposite side of the porch, drinking Scotch. He had removed his tie and rolled up his sleeves. An inch of beige adhesive tape showed from the inside of his left elbow where his blood had been taken.

"So," he said, "do you hate me? Or do you just think I'm crazy?"

"Are those my only two choices?" she asked.

Even in the gloom, she could see a hint of his smile. "Go ahead, fill in your own answer."

"I don't hate you. I don't think you're crazy. I

want you happy, and if getting Samantha back will make you happy, then that's what I want for you.''

''She's my daughter,'' he said. ''I took her in. I took care of her. I fed her, I rocked her, I supported her head when I held her. I carried her around, I washed her clothes. I sat up at night with her. What does it mean to be a parent, Allison? It isn't about contributing a sperm or an egg.''

''I know.''

''I'm her father,'' he said with such conviction, she couldn't help but believe the blood test would bear out his certainty. He sipped his Scotch, and she felt his gaze boring into her through the darkness. ''So you don't hate me. You're just immeasurably ticked off.''

She took a deep breath. ''Yes, I am. After last weekend, Jamie, I thought— Well, I thought we had reached a certain level of candor. I thought that after that—that weekend...'' She couldn't begin to talk about the astonishing intimacy they'd shared, the wild passion. ''I was pretty upset to find out you'd been doing things behind my back.''

''I explained why I didn't involve you in the situation with Sam,'' he said defensively.

''That's not what I'm talking about.'' She sipped her wine and studied his silhouette against the textured gray of the porch screen. ''I know it seems kind of petty after what you've been through, but, Jamie, I asked you not to raise money for the Daddy School, and you did. You badgered your friends at the *Gazette*, didn't you?''

He hesitated before responding. ''I didn't badger anyone,'' he said.

"You hit them up for money, though. Didn't you?"

"I asked someone I knew there if they thought this was something they might want to contribute to. That was all."

"I asked you not to do that."

"And I thought you were being stubborn. I thought the Daddy School is so useful you ought to put your ego aside and take whatever money you can get."

"Oh, my ego," she snapped. It was late, they'd endured an intense few hours and this wasn't a good time to fight about her project. But she'd had a lousy, miserable, heartbreaking week, too, and Jamie was the reason. "Do you think I have a problem with my ego?"

"In this case, yeah, I do. You're too damned proud, and you're hung up about accepting help. The money's there and you can do good things with it. And if it bothers you to think you owe me for this, well, you don't. All right? I don't want anything from you in return."

"Yes, you do," she argued. "You want me to get you through this trauma with Samantha."

His voice rose to a bellow of rage. "I don't want your help because I asked an old buddy at the paper to get you funding! I want your help because I love you, and I need you, and I don't think I can survive this without you!"

The crickets chose that moment to fall silent. Allison could hear herself breathe. She could hear the air vibrating in the wake of his angry confession. Her eyes filled up, spilled over, and she had to put down

her glass before it slipped from her trembling fingers.
"Oh, Jamie," she whispered.

"What?" He still sounded tense and bitter.

"You're right. I do have a hang-up about accepting help."

"So take the damned money and run your damned
school."

"I will."

"And learn that sometimes people get as much
pleasure from helping you as you get from helping
them."

"Okay." Her cheeks were wet. Her lip was quiv-
ering. The crickets began to chirp again, and she snif-
fled and wiped her eyes with her hands. "Jamie?"
She sounded weak and watery.

"What?"

"I love you, too."

Only the crickets responded to her announcement,
shrill and persistent. And then she saw him rise, saw
his silhouetted form approach her chair, saw his arms
reach for her. In an instant she was in them; in an
instant she and Jamie were kissing, holding each
other, clinging to each other. Her tears dampened his
face, which in turn dampened her cheeks. Or maybe
it was his tears she felt against her skin as he kissed
her.

"We'll get Samantha back," she whispered. "I
know we will."

"I've already got more than I dared hope for," he
said, closing his arms so tightly around her, she knew
he would never let her go.

THE DAY JAMIE'S LAWYER sent word of the blood-
test results to the Piersons was the day the hotshot

Boston lawyer informed Dennis Murphy that the
Piersons had changed their minds about custody.
Their marriage was falling apart once more. Hugh
couldn't trust Luanne after she'd had an affair and
gone through a pregnancy without informing him.
They were going to get divorced, she didn't want the
baby, and now that he knew for a scientific fact that
Samantha wasn't his, Hugh didn't want the baby,
either.

Jamie couldn't have been happier.

Allison drove with him to Boston to pick up Samantha. They drove home together. Home, to Arlington, to Jamie's house, to the place where they
could be a family.

There was still a great deal to work out. Allison
worried about her grandmother living all alone in the
house across town, and Jamie, to his sheer amazement, heard himself say that if she wanted to move
her grandmother into his house, she could. The very
idea was shocking: him and three women coexisting
in one house. Jamie, the Ultimate Guy, forming a
household with three generations of females, each
one more opinionated and mouthy than the next.

Allison's grandmother said no. She wasn't going
to live with that bum even if he was cute and successful and really quite handsome when he didn't
look like hell. If Allison insisted, her grandmother
would tolerate having a paid companion in the house
during the evenings, but honestly, she wasn't an in-
valid. She just had a funky knee.

So Allison agreed to move in with Jamie. And she
agreed, after very little discussion and a great deal
of hot and steamy sex, to marry him. She asked how
he would feel about her adopting Samantha. He

showed her how he would feel by kissing her ec-
statically and then progressing to more hot and
steamy sex.

He only had one real problem—other than the minor challenges of trying to sleep when Sammy was
throwing a hissy fit at 2:00 a.m. or maintaining an
adequate supply of diapers in the house at all times
or buying Sammy a new wardrobe every week or so
because she was eating constantly and spitting up
less and growing like a weed.

His problem was that he earned his living writing
a column about being a guy. And suddenly he wasn't
the guy he used to be. He had turned into a man—a
man who happened to be madly in love with two
women.

The morning after Allison agreed to marry him,
he sat down at his computer and started to type.

GUY STUFF by James McCoy—

This is a tough column for me to write. Here I
am, just barely thirty years old, and suddenly I
seem to have moved on to a whole other stage
of guyhood. My lady says what this means is,
I've grown up. Which, I've got to tell you, is
pretty darned scary.

Yes, there's a lady in my life now. Also a
baby daughter, so I guess you could say there
are two ladies in my life. One of the secrets of
being a guy is, you can't really indulge in guy
stuff when there are ladies around.

Ladies are odd. My daughter—well, she's
about two months old now, and she's got potential. For instance, she thinks belching is fun.

Toilet humor is exactly her speed. And her idea of high-class entertainment is professional wrestling.

But the other lady, the woman I'm going to marry, expects me to be civilized. She says there's already one messy baby in the house, and one is quite enough, especially given that the other messy baby celebrated his thirtieth birthday a few months ago.

So the kid gets to do all the neat stuff—not just burping but throwing food, having a whiz whenever she wants, making obscene noises at inappropriate times. And meanwhile, I'm supposed to behave myself.

It's been tough, but I'm working on it. One thing I've learned: it helps if you keep your sense of humor. That's one thing my woman has done for me: she's taught me that you can grow up and fall in love and still keep your sense of humor.

Like I said, it's a whole new style of guy stuff. Watch this column: I'll let you know how it goes. So far, I like it. I like it a lot.

HARLEQUIN SUPERROMANCE®

COMING NEXT MONTH

#766 WHO'S AFRAID OF THE MISTLETOE? • Margot Early

Sarah needs help, and she can get it from only one person—her ex-lover, Tage. But Tage's life and responsibilities have changed since she last saw him. He's recently become guardian to two young children—his orphaned niece and nephew from Sweden. Add Sarah and her impossible dog to this household and you have a Christmas unlike any other! A strikingly original book from an author who's become known for the drama and emotional depth of her writing.

#767 FATHER CHRISTMAS • Judith Arnold
The Daddy School

Hardbitten cop John Russo is hot on the trail of ATM thieves—who turn out to be the precocious children of a powerful lawyer. But neglecting his own motherless son for his job isn't part of the plan. It takes the ebullient Molly Saunders and her Daddy School classes to bring the two back together and teach John the true meaning of Christmas. *Don't miss lesson number three in January!*

#768 UPON A MIDNIGHT CLEAR • Lynn Erickson

The reintroduction of a wolf pack into Colorado is Brigitte Hartman's dream. A dream that has almost become a reality until ranchers like Steve Slater rebel. Is it the wolves—or is one of the ranchers killing local cattle? Brigitte is determined to find out...until it begins to look as if Steve may be more involved than she thought. Suspense and excitement...and Christmas.

#769 A CHILD'S CHRISTMAS • Eva Rutland

Ten-year-old Eric Archer is the child at the center of this inspiring Christmas story. Eric's benignly neglectful father, Lyndon, has left him in the care of his brother, Dave—Eric's uncle. Which is how Dave comes to meet—and fall in love with—one of Eric's teachers, Monica Powell. Then Lyndon meets *her* friend Lisa...and the circle of love continues to expand, drawing other people into its sphere. It all culminates at Christmas....

Born in the USA

Every month there's another title from one
of your favorite authors!

October 1997
Romeo in the Rain by Kasey Michaels
When Courtney Blackmun's daughter brought home Mr. Tall,
Dark and Handsome, Courtney wanted to send the young
matchmaker to her room! Of course, that meant the single
New Jersey mom would be left alone with the irresistibly
attractive Adam Richardson....

November 1997
Intrusive Man by Lass Small
Indiana's Hannah Calhoun had enough on her hands taking
care of her young son, and the last thing she needed was a
man complicating things—especially Max Simmons, the
gorgeous cop who had eased himself right into her little boy's
heart...and was making his way into hers.

December 1997
Crazy Like a Fox by Anne Stuart
Moving in with her deceased husband's—*eccentric*—family
in Louisiana meant a whole new life for Margaret Jaffrey and
her nine-year-old daughter. But the beautiful young widow
soon finds herself seduced by the slower pace and the much-
too-attractive cousin-in-law, Peter Andrew Jaffrey....

**BORN IN THE USA: Love, marriage—
and the pursuit of family!**

Available at your favorite retail outlet!

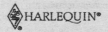

Look what Santa brought!

CHRISTMAS DELIVERY

Capture the holiday spirit with these three
heartwarming stories of moms, dads,
babies and mistletoe. *Christmas Delivery*
is the perfect stocking stuffer featuring three
of your favorite authors:

A CHRISTMAS MARRIAGE by Dallas Schulze
DEAR SANTA by Margaret St. George
THREE WAIFS AND A DADDY by Margot Dalton

**There's always room for one more—
especially at Christmas!**

Available wherever Harlequin and Silhouette
books are sold.

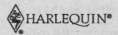 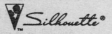

FREE BOOK OFFER!

**With every Harlequin Ultimate Guides™ order,
receive a FREE bonus book!**

#80507	HOW TO TALK TO A NAKED MAN	$4.99 U.S. ☐ $5.50 CAN. ☐
#80508	I CAN FIX THAT	$5.99 U.S. ☐ $6.99 CAN. ☐
#80510	WHAT YOUR TRAVEL AGENT KNOWS THAT YOU DON'T	$5.99 U.S. ☐ $6.99 CAN. ☐
#80511	RISING TO THE OCCASION More Than Manners: Real Life Etiquette for Today's Woman	$5.99 U.S. ☐ $6.99 CAN. ☐
#80513	WHAT GREAT CHEFS KNOW THAT YOU DON'T	$5.99 U.S. ☐ $6.99 CAN. ☐
#80514	WHAT SAVVY INVESTORS KNOW THAT YOU DON'T	$5.99 U.S. ☐ $6.99 CAN. ☐

(quantities may be limited on some titles)

TOTAL AMOUNT	$
POSTAGE & HANDLING	$
($1.00 for one book, 50¢ for each additional)	
APPLICABLE TAXES*	$ _____
TOTAL PAYABLE	$ _____
(check or money order—please do not send cash)	

*New York residents remit applicable sales taxes.
Canadian residents remit applicable GST and provincial taxes.

To order, complete this form and send it, along with a check or money order for the total above, payable to Harlequin Ultimate Guides, to: **In the U.S.:** 3010 Walden Avenue, P.O. Box 9047, Buffalo, NY 14269-9047; **In Canada:** P.O. Box 613, Fort Erie, Ontario, L2A 5X3.

HARLEQUIN ULTIMATE GUIDES™
What women really want to know!

Official Proof of Purchase

Please send me my FREE bonus book with this order.

Name: _____

Address: _____

City: _____

State/Prov:. _____ Zip/Postal Code: _____

Reader Service Acct.#: _____ **KFZ**

Look us up on-line at: http://www.romance.net   NFPOP